THE HIGHLANDER

BY ZOE SAADIA

THE HIGHLANDER

The Rise of the Aztecs, Book 1

ZOE SAADIA

For more information about this book, the author and her work, please visit www.zoesaadia.com

ISBN: 1536884200
ISBN-13: 978-1536884203

AUTHOR'S NOTE

"The Highlander" is historical fiction and some of the characters and adventures in this book are imaginary, while some are historical and well documented in many accounts concerning this time period and place.

The history of the region is presented as accurately and as reliably as possible, to the best of the author's ability, and although no work of this scope can be free of error, an earnest effort was made to reflect the history and the traditional way of life of the peoples residing in those areas.

I would also like to apologize before the descendants of the mentioned nations for giving various traits and behaviors to the well known historical characters (such as *Nezahualcoyotl, Huitzilihuitl, Acamapichtli,* and many others), sometimes putting them into fictional situations for the sake of the story. The main events of this book and the followings sequels are very well documented and could be verified by simple research.

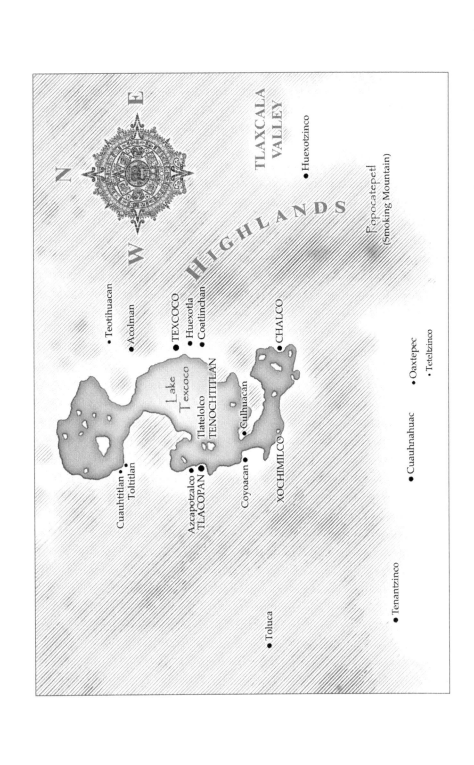

PROLOGUE

A loud, desperate howl tore the silence. Followed by a jumble of ranting, screaming, and sobbing, it rolled between the plastered walls, shaking the Palace out of its usual afternoon rest, prematurely so.

Coyotl jumped to his feet, his heart pounding. Blinking in the strong light, he tried to concentrate, to understand what had happened. Both of his half brothers made an admirable effort to stay asleep, burying their heads into their mats and pulling their blankets over their heads. He watched them, contemplating doing the same.

The screaming began dying away, as though the upset woman had been hushed behind the closed screen. He could hear her muffled voice, still screeching, her harangue interrupted by an occasional sob. The Chief Wife of the Emperor, his father. Oh, the vile woman could be easily upset, but not like that. He could almost feel her anger rumbling down the passageways.

Grabbing his loincloth, he slipped out of the room, making his way along still-deserted corridors, abandoned for the duration of the midday. Yet this time, maids and servants rushed about, their faces excited, eyes gleaming.

He brushed past the cool plastered walls, not bothering to conceal his presence. He was just a boy of ten summers, someone of no consequence, with his mother being only one of the minor wives. She was the sister of Huitzilihuitl, the current ruler of the Aztec Tenochtitlan; not a complete nonentity, but not a rival to the Emperor's Chief Wife, the daughter of the mighty Tepanec Ruler, Tezozomoc. Yet, now the impeccably noble Empress was shrieking at the top of her voice, and Coyotl could not keep his curiosity at bay.

His sandaled feet made no sound upon the polished tiles of the floor as he sneaked toward the imperial quarters, located on the other side of the Palace.

"Oh, he will regret it. He will regret it dearly." The muffled voice of the Empress shook. "He thinks himself a great Emperor, the one who can oppose my father. With this pitiful town of his and the few surrounding provinces. How ridiculous!" Her voice rose. "The Lord of the Chichimecs, mind you! He wants the title of the first ruler of Texcoco. Imagine that! The Acolhua nobleman, the Emperor of Texcoco, suddenly wants to be the lord of the barbarians." Another sob cut the harangue. "Oh, but my father will put him in his place, you just wait and see."

The sobs grew quieter, overcame by the murmuring of the nervous female voices. Coyotl frowned, then slipped behind the carved wooden column when a group of maids swept by, unwilling to be noticed.

What was that all about? he asked himself, puzzled. So the Emperor assumed another title. So what? Why would it make his Chief Wife so upset? And why did the annoying woman think it would make the powerful ruler of the mighty Tepanecs angry; or even interested?

The woman began yelling anew, evidently done with the previous bout of sobbing.

"How dare he to treat me like that? How dare he? Me, the daughter of the mighty Tezozomoc, put aside like a woman of no significance? Oh no, he cannot get away with this! Never! My father will see through him, and he will come down and tear this pitiful province of Texcoco apart. This *altepetl* and all surrounding towns will be just ruins when my father finishes with it!" A convulsive breath seeped through the cracks in the screen. "And then he will ruin Tenochtitlan as well. These cheeky Mexica-

Aztecs should have been put down a long time ago." The hollow sound of pottery being thrown against the wooden screen interrupted the screaming fit, making Coyotl jump. "How could he? To make this silly, good-for-nothing Mexica woman his Chief Wife. This ugly, little, stupid mouse. His Chief Wife? The Empress? I ask you! That dirty lump of—"

Coyotl's heart was thumping so loudly, he could not listen anymore. Clutching onto the polished column, he blinked, his palms sweaty, slipping against the carvings. *Had he heard it right?* Had the Emperor actually advanced his, Coyotl's, mother to be the Chief Wife? It could not be true. The hysterical woman must have gotten it all wrong.

He tried to listen, but more maids rushed past him. Then came the small army of the Emperor's servants. Coyotl pressed against the opposite wall, then sneaked further down the hall, knowing that he would be punished severely if caught eavesdropping outside the Empress's quarters. Being held over the fire filled with *chili* peppers, inhaling its stinging smoke, was not his idea of having a good time.

His feet took him toward the great hall and the marble columns guarding the entrance. The brilliant light outside beckoned. At this time of the day, the patio and the gardens would be utterly deserted, he knew, and he needed the solitude it offered.

Paces light, he ran down the polished stairs, diving into the unmerciful heat of midday, his thoughts a jumble. No, it could not be true. Would the Emperor truly dare to put the daughter of the powerful Tepanec ruler aside to favor the sister of the small city-state's ruler, another tributary of the mighty Tepanecs?

Coyotl's mother was a princess, oh yes; the daughter of Acamapichtli himself, the first Aztec emperor and, in Coyotl's private opinion, the most successful ruler that had ever lived. He adored his grandfather, who was reported to be wise and vigorous—a great ruler, great warrior, great engineer. He had never been to Tenochtitlan, but he had heard all about the canals and the causeway that connected the city to the mainland. Acamapichtli was reported to have been personally involved in the planning of all those; and the temples and the Great Pyramid, too. Oh, how he wished he could see it for himself, could meet this remarkable man.

The gardens swept by, and he hadn't realized his feet had carried him past the gate until he noticed the royal guard warriors who eyed him indifferently, more concerned with the identity of those trying to enter the Palace's grounds than with those trying to leave it. He was of no significance; just one of the Emperor's many offspring, and not even by the noble Empress. It was not their duty to keep an eye on him. There were personal slaves to do that.

However, now all that might change, he reflected as the dusty alleys swept by. His glance swept past the neat rows of stone houses adjacent to the Palace's grounds, not caring for their colorful beauty. The possibilities of being the First Son of the Emperor's Chief Wife were dazzling. No more slapping from the bad-tempered Tepanec Empress, no more being sent away whenever he wanted to play with Iztac-Ayotl, his half sister, the first daughter of that same Tepanec woman, now only one of the minor wives. Iztac was the best girl in the whole World of the Fifth Sun, funny and swift, running around, climbing fences and trees like a boy. Maybe he should go back and find her.

When the outskirts of the city swept by, he knew where his feet were taking him. He measured the sun. There might be enough time to climb his favorite hill, the one dedicated to Tlaloc, the revered earth and rain deity, and still be back for the evening meal.

He stood on the slope, breathing heavily. Sweat ran down his back and his face, threatening to penetrate his eyes. Craving a gulp of water, he licked his lips, but it didn't help. How stupid he was, going out climbing hills in this afternoon heat with no flask attached to his girdle.

Actually, he had no girdle at all. And no cloak. Forsaking the customary midday rest, while slipping out of the boys' set of rooms on an impulse, he had planned neither leaving the Palace, nor climbing hills, and now his skin burned, and he was dead thirsty.

He narrowed his eyes, trying to enjoy the view in spite of his discomfort, this vantage point rewarding him, offering his *altepetl* Texcoco like a wooden, highly elaborate toy, like a drawing on a bark sheet, or maybe this special expensive paper they were making in the Highlands. His father should have built a palace here, he thought, welcoming the slight breeze. It was so much more pleasant up here.

Suddenly, he shivered. The trees up the slope rustled, yet there was no breeze. His heart thumping, he peered into the bushes above his head. Nothing. He might have just imagined it. Yet, his heartbeat refused to calm down. What if someone was out there, watching him? Having no girdle, meant he had no dagger attached to it. He had been a *calmecac* pupil for more than two summers by now, attending the warriors' school, allowed, and even required, to carry this simple weaponry.

Oh, gods. What if there was some beast up there? A jaguar maybe. Or something worse than that. A warrior from the Highlands!

Frowning, he peered into the bushes. Someone was watching him. Now he was sure of it.

"Come out, whoever you are," he called, pleased to hear his voice steady and imperious.

There was a silence. Then the bushes parted as a boy jumped down the trail, landing gracefully despite the disadvantage of the slope's incline. Tall and lean in frame, the intruder looked strikingly outlandish, wearing a loincloth and a strange cloak, his broad jaw adorned by a line of tattoos, his lower lip pierced, sporting a glittering turquoise stone, his eyes large, widely spaced and wary.

"Who are you?" asked Coyotl uneasily, eyeing the obsidian dagger attached to the foreigner's loincloth. This boy was no resident of Texcoco or the surrounding towns, that much was obvious.

The large eyes narrowed, studying Coyotl's face with a certain amount of curiosity. "And who are you?" The foreigner's Nahuatl was accented but good.

Coyotl gasped, unprepared for such an obvious contempt. "I'm Nezahualcoyotl, the Emperor's First Son by his Second Wife," he said, trying to control his temper.

The wide lips quivered. "You are a liar!" His unasked-for companion laughed, displaying a wide row of large teeth, with the gap of one missing.

"I'm not! How dare you? You are obviously nothing but a savage from the Highlands. How dare you laugh into my face?"

The boy frowned, thrown off balance for a heartbeat, his narrowing eyes measuring Coyotl from head to toe. "You can't be the Emperor's son, running all over the countryside sweating, sunburned, half naked and alone." The pointy eyebrows lifted. "Or, if you are telling me the truth, if that's how the Emperor's sons are, then you filthy Lowlanders are real savages. Not us!"

Coyotl gasped, at a loss for words. Staring at the broad, now smirking face, he longed to punch it until it lost any trace of contempt. Trained to use his fists as well as his weapons, he could fight well enough, yet the boy was armed with a knife, carrying it with an easy confidence of someone who knew how to use it.

His adversary laughed. "Don't turn all red on me. You might faint. Here, have some water."

The flask offered to Coyotl was dusty and made of skin. He eyed it with disbelief. "I don't want your water!"

The boy shrugged, eyes flickering with more mischievous derisiveness.

"You know what?" cried Coyotl. "I'll take your water, but not before I beat you so hard, you will never be able to take it back!"

The smile widened. "You will never manage as much as to make me sway! Not even with my hands tied behind my back."

The boy took out his dagger, and Coyotl tensed, watching his opponent's movements alertly, ready to evade the blow, or maybe to run.

"You, *calmecac* cubs, are soft," said the boy, placing his dagger carefully behind the rock, not in an easy reach. "They are supposed to train you to be great warriors, but all they do is pamper you and make you feel good about yourselves. My brother says that and he would know." He came back to the trail and stood there, legs wide apart. "We, on the other hand, are fighting and hunting as soon as we can walk straight. So who do you think will win this?"

With no dagger in sight, Coyotl felt his heartbeat calming. Watching his adversary closely, he calculated his movements. Although tall, the boy was lean and not that well-muscled. He could take him, especially by surprise. *Make this one fall, then go for his throat and don't let it go.*

"Your savage fathers may take you out to war as soon as you stop wetting yourself, but this is what makes you into savages. Your people can fight, but they never stop to think, and when you're at war you have to think as well as fight. That's why you are stuck in your Highlands. That's why my Acolhua people took Texcoco and all the surrounding areas from your Chichimecs." He saw the boy's eyes darkening with rage, losing their confident amusement. It made him feel vindicated. "But why would you know any of it? We are taught history in *calmecac*, while you are busy making strange noises upon some petty battlefield with another group of other savages."

As the boy threw himself forward, moving with the same grace he had displayed while jumping the slope, Coyotl leaped aside, avoiding the blow. However, either he was not fast enough, or his rival was good, his clenched fist brushing past Coyotl's ear, making it ring. He reeled a little, but managed to keep his balance.

His fingers claws, he grabbed the boy's cloak, pulling so suddenly that they both lost their balance and fell into the dusty road. All learned techniques forgotten, Coyotl punched and kicked, trying to push off the weight of his opponent's body. The foreigner was the one to grab for his throat, and he did it expertly, yet when Coyotl's knee sank into the softness of his belly, his hands slipped off.

More punches and kicks were exchanged, before the voices of the nearing people penetrated his mind, making him spring to his feet. Breathing heavily, he eyed the boy's dusty face and the bleeding lip with satisfaction. The large eyes met his, reflecting the same sentiment. Then, in one leap, the boy was off the trail, diving behind the rock, grabbing his knife, swift and purposeful.

"Wait!"

His adversary turned around, tense and ready to flee.

"They are not coming this way." Surprised with himself, Coyotl held out his hand. "They are going down the slope. Can't you hear that?"

The boy listened alertly, eyes narrowing into slits.

"There is another trail. It leads to the villages and the fields."

The large eyes watched Coyotl, still slits in the broadness of the handsome face. "You know this hill well, don't you?"

"Of course, I do. I was born here in Texcoco half of twenty summers ago. Enough time to know the place." He pushed his dusty hair out of his face, the beautiful woven string that held it in place gone.

"But you are not the son of the Emperor."

"Yes, I am!"

The boy picked the skin flask up off the wet ground and eyed it dubiously. Taking a swig, he shrugged, then offered it to Coyotl. "That was stupid of me not to take it off. But I think there is a little of the water left."

Coyotl hesitated, then took the flask. The water was tepid, but he emptied it in one gulp. It tasted good.

"Thank you," he said, returning the flask.

His companion shrugged again. "So, what was your name?"

"Nezahualcoyotl."

"The fasting coyote, eh?" The wide lips twisted in a crooked sort of a grin.

"And your name is?"

"Kuini."

"Just that?"

"No. But that would be enough for you."

"What does it mean?"

"Jaguar."

"Jaguar, eh?" He watched the boy wiping his face with the back of his palm, smearing more dust. "You are not from around here, are you?"

"No. But I've been here before."

"Where are you from?"

"The Highlands. Where else?"

"How did you get so far down here?"

The boy shrugged, raising his eyebrows. "Too many questions, Emperor," he said, grinning. "I don't need your father's warriors combing the area in an attempt to lay their hands on me and my brothers. Although, by the time you reach the Palace, we'd be well away, of course."

Coyotl's heart missed a beat. "Are there more of you around here?"

"Yes, of course. Why would I make my way here all alone?" The boy frowned. "It's more than two dawns of walking and most of the way the roads are not as well kept as this one." He pointed toward the trail, eyes twinkling. "I'm telling you, your people are soft."

"Not as soft as you thought we would be!" exclaimed Coyotl, but the challenging amusement in his converser's eyes did not make him angry this time. "So, where are your people? The ones who came here with you."

The boy's grin widened. "I won't tell you, so just leave it alone. They are yet to teach you how to ask the right questions, those *calmecac* teachers of yours." Still grinning, he busied himself with tying the dagger to his loincloth. "They are nowhere around though, so you don't have to worry. I came that near to your *altepetl* on my own." He shrugged. "I like to watch it. It looks pretty from up here."

For a while they said nothing, watching the city sprawling at their feet. Letting the breeze cool off his scratched, burning face, Coyotl narrowed his eyes, seeking the sight of the Palace, finding it easy to make it out, with its walls clinging to the Great Pyramid. He wondered if the displaced Tepanec Chief Wife was still screaming. Or had she calmed down enough to think of the way to inform her father, the Tepanec Emperor?

His eyes brushed down the broad strip of the road, sliding over the cluster of temples. "If I were going to be an emperor one day, I would build the best palace here that they could ever imagine.

With beautiful gardens, and terraces, and pools. I'd cut the stairs in those rocks, and I'd bring all sorts of rare animals and plants. We'd hold magnificent festivals up here, and not only to honor the mighty Tlaloc. No! I'd build here all sorts of temples." Sinking into his vision, he forgot all about his foreign audience.

"You can't do all this. The stupid hill is so dry. No spring, no brook, nothing. And I did look for some, trust me on that."

"So what? We can bring the water here."

"By hand?" Kuini's broad face crinkled with laughter. "It'll take you an army of people to water your plants every day."

"No, no." Still immersed in his vision, Coyotl forgot to get angry. "The water can be channeled, don't you know that? I studied the way they divert water. I saw the drawings. They do that in some *altepetls*, I'm telling you! My grandfather wanted to bring water to Tenochtitlan. The Tepanecs didn't let him, but he planned to do this. I saw his drawings, I swear!"

The boy's eyes widened. "Your grandfather was an Aztec?"

"Yes. He was the First Emperor of Tenochtitlan. He was incredible and so wise! You would never believe there were such people in the whole world of the Fifth Sun."

"Acamapichtli was your grandfather?"

This time Coyotl turned to watch his companion, startled. "You Highlanders know the names of the Mexica emperors?"

Kuini wrinkled his nose. "No, we don't, and we could not care less about your Lowlander rulers." He shrugged. "But my father has some interest for Tenochtitlan. He sometimes talks about this *altepetl*, and he always wants to know what's happening there." The boy's face twisted. "When that First Emperor of theirs died, my brothers say he was so upset that he almost ventured into that island-city. Disguised, of course. They say Mother talked him out of it with great difficulty."

"Why would he want to go there? What has he with the First Emperor of Tenochtitlan?"

"I don't know. I think it's strange, too."

"Did you ask him?"

The boy's laughter was even louder this time. "No, of course not. He is busy. He is the War Leader of the United Clans. You don't bother such a man with silly questions."

"Then it's good he didn't venture to Tenochtitlan. They would be only too happy to sacrifice such a leader to Huitzilopochtli, that strange Mexica god of theirs."

"They would never lay their filthy hands on my father, you can be sure of that," called Kuini hotly. "But of course, it would not have been wise to take an unnecessary risk." He made a face. "Still, I would love to find out what interest he has in Tenochtitlan."

Their shadows stretched across the trail, long and unnaturally slender.

"I have to go back," said Coyotl. "Before they start looking for me." He glanced at his companion. "Will you still be here tomorrow?"

The boy flashed an unguarded, surprisingly charming smile. "I don't think so. My brothers would be in a hurry to go back." He shrugged. "But I'll come here again, and next time you'll take me to see this *altepetl* of yours. I really have to see it. And the drawings of the channels to carry the water. I won't believe it until I see it."

"Do this. Find a way to let me know. I would love to take you around the city. I promise not to tell anyone who you are." Coyotl looked around, frowning. "You know what? We can leave notes, behind this rock, see?" He peeked into the niche where the boy had previously hidden the knife. "It's perfect!"

"Notes?"

"Yes. When you are around, you leave me a note. On a paper, or a bark sheet. I guess you won't have any paper." He smiled broadly, watching Kuini's puzzled look. "I'll come here often from now on. Or I'll send a slave. You leave your bark and come here again in a day or two. When I find the bark I will know to come the next day." He warmed to this idea. "It'd work!"

"Just a piece of bark?"

"Carve something on it. Or draw a glyph. Whatever you like."

The boy grinned, oddly unsure of himself now. "That would be a strange sort of letting you know."

"They didn't teach you to read the drawings, did they?"

Kuini's eyes flashed. "A warrior spending his time drawing? He might go and start cooking food next. A waste of time!"

"Maybe for a warrior. But not for a leader." Coyotl smiled. "When your reading improves, I promise to bring you one of those bark-sheets with channels I told you about. But only when I know you'll take it seriously. When you'll be able to read and understand them." He began walking down the path. "I'll be checking this rock often."

"Don't you dare to patronize me," called the boy after him, but his smile was wide. "Maybe I'll come, maybe I won't. I'll have to decide whether your company is worth the trouble."

CHAPTER 1

The Highlands,
1415

Kuini stretched, enjoying the meager shade of the wide tree. It was well into the afternoon, and the breeze strengthened, bringing along the much-longed-for coolness.

He fought off the sleepiness, forcing his mind to concentrate on the thin, wrinkled sheet of paper, the drawings carved upon it faded and unclear, difficult to follow. Smoothing the rolling edges of the precious scroll, he studied it once again.

Those were not the channels Coyotl had promised, but Kuini didn't mind. He was not as obsessed with the water supplies as his friend was. He loved anything related to buildings and great things, and this particular drawing depicted slabs of stone and a plentitude of poles and sticks, referring to the construction of Tenochtitlan's Great Pyramid. Or so Coyotl had maintained, and the Lowlander would know.

The piece of paper was old, thirty and more summers or so, coming straight from the Palace of Tenochtitlan, where its most revered First Emperor had drawn it allegedly all by himself. Kuini inhaled loudly. Just to think of it! When the mighty Emperor had held onto this same *amate*-paper, the Great Pyramid had not existed.

"Oh, there is the studious warrior!"

A group of girls swept by, shouting and laughing. He tried to pay them no attention, but it was difficult to tear his eyes off their shins glimmering with water, their long skirts tucked high, their hips swaying as they carried their heavy baskets.

"He'll be fighting with his bark sheets if attacked," said one of the girls to the loud merriment of the others.

He eyed her shiny, sparkling, wet face. "Come up here and attack me. I don't mind."

Her friends burst into another fit of laughing, but the girl blushed, and her eyes lingered upon him, making his stomach twist.

"Careful with your drawings."

He winced as the drops of water reached him, sprinkling around, wetting his paper. Another girl eyed him challengingly.

He tucked the precious paper behind his back. "Go away, you lot," he said, now angry. "This paper is worth more than all of you put together."

"You go away!" The girl who had splashed him frowned, put a hand on her hip, and advanced forward, ready to fight. She was pretty, but not as pretty as the first one.

Springing to his feet, he retreated hastily, deeper into the grove. Some of the girls looked familiar, coming from the same town as him. A silly lot. But beddable. He thought about the first girl, remembering the way her skirts were tucked high, exposing the golden smoothness of her thighs, as if inviting one to explore further up. And she had nice eyes too.

He checked the scroll. Stupid *cihuas*. This thing could not be damaged for any reason. He had promised Coyotl to guard it with his life, and he knew he would do just that.

Grinning, he remembered their first meeting, more than five summers ago. Just two hotheaded boys, eager to beat each other. Yet, somehow, they had stopped fighting and started to talk, and then began to meet occasionally, against all odds. Texcoco was a long way from the Highlands and the town of Huexotzinco. Too long of a way. Yet, he kept going there, drawn toward the Great Capital of the Acolhua people – his enemies! – almost against his will. He had gone there before meeting Coyotl, but this palace boy's company had made the mighty *altepetl* more attractive.

So every few moons, they would meet, sitting on the hill,

talking, laughing, planning what could be done to improve this place, what they would build there and how. Coyotl had taught Kuini to read the drawings upon the bark-sheets or the expensive and rare *amate*-paper. It was a thrill to pore over those ancient, or not-so-ancient, scrolls, deciphering their meaning. It made him feel powerful, like a person who could see beyond the obvious. His mother must be feeling like that, with her being the priestess of the Obsidian Butterfly Goddess, having the ability to summon visions, to connect to the mighty deity.

The rustling of the bushes startled him and his right arm sneaked toward his dagger as he tensed, listening. The footsteps were careful, but unconcealed, their owner light and surefooted. His heart leaped.

"Still reading?" The girl towered above him, eyes challenging, back straight, hands free of any burden now.

"No." Disappointed, he eyed her long skirt that now covered her legs, leaving no glimpse of the golden smoothness underneath.

"No? Then what do you do?"

"Nothing." He searched for something to say.

The girl hesitated. "I want to see this bark-sheet of yours," she said finally.

He was taken aback. "What for?"

"I don't know. What are you looking for there, peering into this thing all the time?"

"I'm not peering into it all the time." He wanted to curse his clumsiness, embarrassed by the disdainful glimmer in her sparkling eyes. "You won't understand any of it, anyway."

"Oh, so I'm too silly to show this bark to. Never mind, then!" She whirled around.

"Wait. I'll show you."

There was a victorious spark in her eyes as she turned back, pondering, poised on one leg.

"Well, I don't know." She wrinkled her nose. "Maybe you aren't worth the trouble."

His stomach twisted again as he watched her, his palms sweaty upon the scroll. When she knelt beside him, he moved a little, making a place for her.

"So, what are those things?"

He took a deep breath, his thoughts – a jumble. "That's how they were planning to build their Great Pyramid."

"What pyramid? Where?"

"In Tenochtitlan."

"Tenoch-what?"

He laughed, but his tension kept welling. It was difficult to concentrate.

"Tenochtitlan. The Capital of the Mexica Aztecs."

"Oh, the Aztecs," she called bitterly. "Those dirty pieces of rotten meat!"

"Yes, them," he agreed, sharing her sentiment. "They have this city upon an island. And they built many things, pyramids and causeways."

"They are heartless lowlifes!"

"Yes, they are that, too."

She peered at him. "Why would you try to read their bark-sheets?"

"Because I'm curious. We can build those things, too."

"We have beautiful things of our own. The temples in the Sacred Grove."

"The temples are not really large. We can do better things. We can build pyramids like in Texcoco?"

"What's Texcoco?"

"The Capital of the Lowlands, down by the Great Lake. You know, Acolhua people."

"Oh, more of the dirty rats!" She shook her head. "Why are you fascinated with them?"

"I don't know." He could feel the warmth of her body, and it made him dizzy. He tried to remember what he had wanted to say.

"You should concentrate on being a great warrior. You should kill or capture and sacrifice as many of those lowlifes as you can." She still peered into the scroll, so close he could feel her breath brushing against his bare shoulder.

"I know. I'll do it, anyway." He leaned closer, the temptation unbearable.

As she turned to face him, he saw her eyes twinkling. Still tense and on guard, he reached for her shoulders, pulling her closer. She did not resist, and it gave him courage.

Her body was soft and pliant against his limbs. He brushed his lips over her shoulder. It smelled of river. The scent of her skin intoxicated him, made his hands tremble as his palms sought their way under her blouse.

"Better than your bark-sheets, eh?" she whispered.

He was too busy to answer, fighting his loincloth, his fingers clumsy. The forest, the river, the afternoon breeze, they all disappeared, taken away by the warm wave of elation, of carelessness, the vital surge of life gushing inside them.

As they lay upon the soft grass, their limbs still entwined, their breath coming in gasps, he felt his elation welling. The glimpses of the cloudless sky came and went as the branches above their heads moved.

"What's your name?" he asked.

"Iso." She moved, placing her head more comfortably upon his shoulder.

"Iso…what?"

"Just Iso. I don't like my full name."

"This one doesn't suit you either. You should be called after a deer or some other graceful creature. You are beautiful." He could feel her smiling, snug in his embrace. "I'm Kuini."

"I know that."

"How?"

"You are the War Leader's son, everyone knows it."

"Oh." He fought off a sudden wave of irritation.

Why should he feel irritated? he asked himself. Even if she'd lain with him because of that, why should he care?

"Will you make me your woman?"

He shrugged. "Maybe."

"You should," she said, an urgency creeping into her voice. "We lay together. I may have a child."

He frowned, not having thought of that. "If you have a child then we'll talk about it again."

Curse it, he thought. That would be an unnecessary complication.

She sat up abruptly. "You were very eager to lay with me, but now you are all cagey and indifferent. It's not right!"

He got up and busied himself tying his loincloth. "Let's not ruin it," he muttered.

Pulling down her skirt, she jumped to her feet, looking at him searchingly. "Will you come and take me to the river tomorrow?"

Oh gods! He forced a smile. "Yes, why not?"

"Then meet me on the plaza, when the sun is at its highest."

"Yes, I will."

He made his way cheerfully along the town's alleys, his elation welling. He had lain with a girl, at long last, and he had seemingly not disappointed her. Even her demand of an escort on the next day did not irritate him, not anymore. He was sure to get more of this pleasant pastime if he did this.

He smiled to himself. Now he was truly a man, a warrior and a man. He contemplated going to his father's house, then changed his direction. Neither Mother, nor Father would be there now. Father had left on the previous morning, heading for the main town of Tlaxcala Valley, because of the reported group of Acolhua messengers that had arrived there. He wouldn't be back for dawns upon dawns. Mother, on the other hand, would still be busy with the upcoming festival, preparing her goddess for the festivities. She wouldn't be home either, and anyway, she seldom cooked and did not excel in that.

Having many brothers scattered around the town, he just drifted along the dust-covered alleys and one-story wooden or stone houses until spotting the wide-shouldered frame of Nihi, his eldest sibling, crouching above the half-severed carcass of a deer.

"I see the great hunter has been busy again," called Kuini, crossing the muddy patio.

His brother did not bother to glance up. "Unlike this lazy piece of meat that calls himself my youngest of brothers," he said, cutting the dripping meat, separating it from the covering hide.

"When I have as many wives as you have, I'll get busy." Crouching beside the sweating man, Kuini took out his knife.

"You will never have as many wives. That would be too much trouble for a troublemaker like you," muttered Nihi, but his smile was wide. "And don't you think that those few cuts that you are about to make in this meat will earn your lazy carcass a decent meal tonight. You'll have to work harder than that."

"I'm not lazy," protested Kuini. "I'm a warrior, and there have been no decent raids for, oh, moons. One could die of boredom."

Nihi's laughter was infectious. "I can just imagine you dying with those bark-sheets clutched in your hands. Your spirit will drift, still trying to decipher their meanings." The massive palm rose, wiping the sweat off the broad face, smearing the juices of the fresh meat upon it instead. "What's with those scrolls, little brother? Be careful, or you'll turn into one of those dung-eating, good-for-nothing Acolhua warriors from the Lowlands."

"I'm careful," muttered Kuini, not amused. There was something wrong with him, oh yes. His fascination with the Lowlands, especially Texcoco *altepetl*, was unhealthy, unworthy of the proud Chichimec warrior. He shifted uneasily. "So, what's happening? Did you hear something from Tlaxcala? Father went there in quite a hurry on the previous morning."

"The same Acolhua dung-eaters. Have the gall of sending here a delegation, imagine that!" Nihi looked up, frowning. "There are rumors about a trouble with the Tepanecs. No more, no less. They may be coming to our side of the Great Lake."

Kuini's heart missed a beat. "The Tepanecs are coming?"

"So it seems. To put those Texcoco dung-eaters in their place. Their emperor did some things to make them angry, apparently."

"I know, but I think he hoped to get away with it. A few summers ago he shoved aside his Tepanec Chief Wife, the daughter of the mighty Tepanec Emperor himself, to favor his Aztec wife. And he calls himself The Lord of the Chichimecs, or something of the sort now. But the Tepanecs only made him pay more tribute, that's all. So he paid. Why would they war on Texcoco now? Although, when you think of it, he has been busy seeking sympathy with other Acolhua towns of the Lowlands."

The widening eyes of his brother stared at him, astonished. "How would you know all that?"

Kuini busied himself with separating the soft meat around the deer's ribs. "I just heard those things." He lifted his gaze. "What? I listen to what people say!"

"No people say such things around here. They wouldn't know any of this Texcoco gossip. I didn't know the half of it, and I talk to Father. If it's true what you say, then the Tepanecs are sure to land on their shores and squash those stupid Acolhua lowlifes. It's farewell Texcoco, little brother." The deeply set eyes narrowed. "But why would you care?"

Kuini shrugged. "I don't."

The penetrating gaze bore at him. "Oh yes, you do. You are so tense and angry now, you would jump half of twenty palms high should someone come up behind you." The older man laughed. "You are a strange one, little brother. I always wondered where you have been spending your time on those frequent disappearances of yours. But now I think I know. Although, I don't understand why you would go all the way to the Lowlands, to learn those Texcocan dung-eaters' gossip." The large knife got back to work. "And it would explain the scrolls you've been running around with."

Kuini cursed as his own knife sliced his finger. "What I do is no one's interest!" he called out, throwing the knife away angrily. "I do fight those filthy Texcocans when they come here and that's enough. If I want to sniff around their *altepetl*, I'll do just that, and no one could tell me not to!"

"Not even Father?"

The open amusement in his brother's eyes made Kuini wish to strangle the man. "You would do just that, wouldn't you? Go and tell him?"

"Maybe. Maybe not. You think yourself a man, little brother, but you are nothing but a hothead that has hardly seen fifteen summers. You've been taken to a raid or two, but you haven't fought properly yet, haven't captured your first enemy." The broad face grew sterner. "I've seen over thirty summers. I captured my share of the enemies. Mostly your Texcoco-Acolhua Lowlanders. I don't want to hear that those dung-eaters have cut my brother's heart out, to dump it on this or that altar. Even if this young hothead is stupid enough to go out there all alone." The dark eyes narrowed once again. "Our warriors are the most prized sacrificial offerings among the scum of the Lowlands. Did you know that? Even the Mexica Aztecs would go to great lengths in order to capture any of our people. And what do you do? Run around Texcoco *altepetl* to get a scroll to read? Alone, exposed, unprotected." The wide mouth moved into a scornful grin. "You'll make a good warrior, Kuini. Even a leader, maybe. But you will have to get rid of this strange passion for reading bark-sheets. You are fascinated with our enemies too much. And it'll do you nothing but harm, mark my words, little brother."

They went on, working on the carcass in silence, their mood spoiled. His brother was right, thought Kuini painfully. This fascination with Texcoco and its people was an abomination. He should not wander around the Lowlands, should not cherish friendship with its people. Coyotl was now an official heir. He would be an emperor one day. He'd rule the enemies of his, Kuini's, people. He'd send expeditions into their Highlands, trying to capture many warriors to cut their hearts out and as many women to sell on the slave markets. Why, he would probably be leading those expeditions himself.

He ground his teeth. No, he should not be friends with the future Texcoco emperor. They would meet on the battlefield soon enough. He felt the scroll in its skin bag, attached to his girdle, safe and sound. He would return the drawing and then never go to Texcoco again, unless he was a part of a war party.

A group of warriors came up the alley, as the delicious aroma of the roasted meat began spreading, tickling one's senses. Both brothers, washed and at peace, squatted on the mats, watching Nihi's wives arranging the place for the evening meal with children running everywhere.

"It's Father! I can't believe it," cried out Nihi, leaping to his feet.

Kuini narrowed his eyes. Even in the spreading darkness it was easy to make out Father in the crowd. Short in stature and not as broadly build as the rest of his country-folk, his father was, nevertheless, the War Leader of their nation, the united clans and tribes of the Highlands.

Not all of the peoples around the high ridges were united, mind you, reflected Kuini, amused, watching the nearing warriors. However, they all had to hold on against the common enemy – the Lowlanders of the Great Lake, with their great *altepetls*, empires, and their hunger for more lands and tributes. Still, the Highlanders would fight against each other on occasion.

The warriors poured in, bringing along much excitement and anxiety, mostly among the womenfolk of the house. Additional mats and pottery were brought, and more meat was thrown into the large pots of stew.

"What a reception!" laughed Father, squatting comfortably, acknowledging their greetings. "I swear, from now on, every time I'm away I'll be coming here first."

The other leaders either chuckled, or smiled politely.

"That's the price for keeping a priestess as your Chief Wife," someone ventured.

"Is Mother still busy in the temple?" asked Nihi.

"Oh, yes. The festivities are about to begin. In two dawns, I think." The man laughed. "I say, life is tough for some warriors."

Kuini watched them, safe in doing so. No one paid him any attention. At fifteen, he was not old enough to participate in such conversations, yet he was allowed to stay, to eat with them, to hear and not to be heard. A situation that suited him well. He liked watching and listening, although the conversation did not, yet, reach any important topics. *What happened at Tlaxcala Valley? What did the cheeky Texcoco Lowlanders want?*

He watched his father's narrow, outlandish face as the man talked, eating heartily, elbowing his companions, sharing jokes. The man did not fit the image of the stern Chichimec leader, with his foreign-looking face, his tendency to laugh, his steady refusal to take an additional wife or two. Yet, he had been the War Leader of the United Clans for more than ten summers, leading the

Highlanders against the surrounding empires with much success. He may have been short and lean, but he was strong, and his inner power was immense, his grasp on warfare and politics unmatchable.

Kuini hid his grin. His father must have been *sent* here, to lead the Chichimec people against their powerful neighbors. Some divine power must have been involved. Otherwise, how could one explain the man's lack of history? Father had no family, no relatives, and he looked like no nation around the Great Lake, neither the Highlanders nor the Lowlanders. A man with no origins; a mysterious man, with his independent manner and thinking, and this slightly accented speech of his.

"Well, those Acolhua bastards surprised us once again," Father was saying. "Not enough that they asked us to stop the hostilities. An outrageous demand, considering the raids they had launched against Tlaxcala Valley towns last summer." The narrow face darkened. "Suddenly, they want peace, now that their Tepanec overlords are busy preparing to invade their shores."

"I gather they had asked for a trouble, with their emperor's activities - switching wives, taking new titles, enlisting the support of the Acolhua provinces," said Nihi, tearing the juicy meat with his large protruding teeth.

Father looked up, surprised. "You are well informed. Where would you hear something like that?"

"Oh, here and there. The rumors were circulating." Nihi shrugged guiltily, and Kuini breathed with relief, grateful that his brother was not about to turn him in.

"Next time you share those rumors with me," said Father, returning to his meal. "I might be less surprised with the cheeky demands of their messengers."

"I'm sorry, Father."

"So what did they want?" Kuini almost shut his mouth with his palm, wishing to push the words back. All eyes were on him, some startled, some amused, many reproachful.

To his relief, Father chose to see the funny side of it. "Oh, I apologize for trying your patience, oh Honorable Warrior," he said, amidst outbursts of hearty laughter.

Kuini wished to disappear from the face of the earth. "I'm sorry," he whispered, staring into his plate.

"I'll tell you what the filthy dung-eaters wanted. They asked us to take a part in their upcoming war against the Tepanecs."

A stunned silence prevailed, interrupted only by buzzing mosquitoes.

"What did you tell them?" breathed one of the elderly warriors in the end.

The War Leader shrugged. "I told them to come back in half a moon," he said, resuming his eating.

"Why? Our warriors would never fight for those heartless lowlifes. After all they have done to us? Never!"

"We won't necessarily discuss this," said Father unperturbed, and Kuini applauded the man's self control. The tempers on such council would fly most certainly. They could start flying right about now. "We'll have to call the council of all clans and nations. The situation is serious, and all the leaders would have to participate in taking the decisions. *Any decisions*. The Tepanecs are ruthless and dangerous. They may make our Acolhua enemy look like a meek coyote. I'm not sure we would benefit from switching our neighbors."

"We know nothing about those Tepanecs," said another warrior. "They may turn out to be easier to deal with."

The narrow face closed. "I know those people. We don't want their warriors or slavers on our side of the Great Lake."

Kuini watched his father, his heart beating fast. The man sounded like he did actually know those people, those terrifying Tepanecs. But how? How could he possibly know them?

CHAPTER 2

Coyotl shifted uneasily, eyeing the people of Xicotepec, bored. His eyes counted and recounted the representatives of the neighboring province, studying their colorful cloaks, their monotonous speeches brushing past his ears, not entering his mind. He knew everything they would wish to say to the Emperor and everything the mighty ruler, his father, would answer back. These meetings repeated themselves on a daily basis these days.

He stifled a yawn and glanced at the opening in the wall, measuring the sun. It was nearing midmorning. Still plenty of time left to reach his favorite Tlaloc's hill by the height of the day.

Carefully, he unfolded the small piece of bark paper and glanced at it once again, smiling. The painting was beautiful, depicting two human figures facing each other, clearly warriors, with their locks drawn elaborately. Both figures looked vivid and alive, holding onto spears, stern and foreboding, the rich colors applied to them with much care.

Oh, but Kuini was turning into a great painter, he thought, remembering the young hotheaded boy he had met almost five summers ago, on that remarkable day when his life had changed forever; on the day he had been made the heir to the throne, the future Emperor of five provinces and countless villages and towns. Oh yes, the gods had favored him that day!

And they had kept favoring him ever since, he knew, forcing himself to concentrate. The future ruler should not be bored with the delegations of his subjects. Father seemed to handle these meeting quite easily, and he was held to be an impatient person, warlike and determined, not a man who would prefer spending his time making speeches.

He folded the paper carefully, tucking it into his girdle. The day before, he had found it behind the rock, in their usual hiding place, and it meant only one thing. Kuini was around.

Why warriors? he asked himself absently. Was his friend referring to the impending war with the Tepanecs? The beautiful painting aside, the picture had an ominous tone to it. Were the Highlanders worried about the Tepanecs?

Coyotl grinned. The Acolhua people from all over the fertile Lowlands would take care of the pushy invaders from across the Great Lake, and Kuini's Highlanders would help. He was thrilled to hear about the delegation that had been sent into their towns.

He made an effort to concentrate once again, but this time his eyes were distracted by a maid who had just slipped into the vast hall, a bowl and a cotton cloth in her hand.

A cotton cloth for cleaning?

He watched the girl crouching beside the wide base of the great serpent's statue, her back toward them, carefully so. She knelt gracefully, but her movements, when she began rubbing the polished marble, were clumsy.

No, he thought, recognizing the slim, delicate, well groomed palms as they moved along the glittering, perfectly clean surface. *She would never do this. This would be just too much.*

"Oh, elders of Xicotepec," the Emperor was saying. "You have seen how Azcapotzalco have not only demanded the tribute, thinking our proud, independent Acolhua *altepetl* to be just another tributary. Now, they want our lands to themselves. What would be your advice? We have pretended to ignore this problem, but would it be wise to continue ignoring the growing demands of the greedy Tepanecs? Would their presumptuous *altepetl* be satisfied with the heavy tribute? Are they not preparing to invade our lands as we speak?"

Coyotl listened, impressed with the way the Emperor had paused, encircling his subjects with a sincere, imploring gaze. As though he hadn't given this same performance with the representatives of another province only a day before. And another one the day before that.

His gaze drifted to the kneeling girl who was also listening, forgetting the cloth and the statue. *A cotton cloth*, he thought, hiding a grin. *She was so silly.* He stared at the crouching figure, willing her to start moving. It would be embarrassing should she get caught eavesdropping at the Emperor's audience.

"With the Acolhua provinces united, could we not repulse the Tepanec invasion? Perhaps, with our people helping each other at last, with the stern leadership and the benevolence of the gods, we will carry the war into their side of the Great Lake."

As the representatives of Xicotepec murmured in consent, Coyotl hid his impatience. The sun was climbing higher and higher, and he needed to start moving out.

He saw a tall warrior making his way toward the bulky figure of the Chief Warlord. A quiet exchange and the leader of the warriors nodded, shifting uneasily as if pondering his possibilities, finally making it toward the Emperor, waiting for permission to whisper into the revered ear.

The cold eyes of the Emperor rested on Coyotl, startling him.

"Nezahualcoyotl, go with the Chief Warlord, and listen to our people who had just returned from the Highlands. Report to me afterward."

His interest piquing, Coyotl sprang to his feet. "Thank you, Revered Emperor," he said, lowering his head.

"Come to see me after my midday meal," said the Emperor, turning back to his Xicotepec subjects.

She was still kneeling beside the statue, all ears. He brushed past her.

"Come and eavesdrop at the other hall," he whispered. "It would be more interesting, and the statues there could use some cleaning."

She tensed, but managed not to look up. He could see her shoulders trembling as if trying to hold back laughter. She was impossible, he thought, grinning. But invading the Emperor's hall was just too much. He'd have to talk to her before he went out.

The Chief Warlord was already in the other, simpler and less presentable hall reserved for the Palace's unofficial meetings. Coyotl neared, forcing himself to walk slowly, importantly, the way a future emperor would walk.

"Well?" He eyed the group of tired-looking men. They were clean but clearly exhausted from a long journey, their faces gray with fatigue. Kuini was making this journey on and off with not much of a visible effort, he thought, amused. Some people of the Lowlands *were* soft.

"We were just telling the Chief Warlord—" began the head of the delegation, a stocky, middle-aged man who looked like a trader.

"Why didn't you wait for me?" demanded Coyotl, interrupting his speech. "The Emperor sent me, his heir and the future emperor of Texcoco, to accompany our Honorable Leader of the Warriors. You should have waited with your message!"

It came out well. The trader looked terrified, while the Chief Warlord nodded reservedly, approving. Relieved, Coyotl gestured for the man to continue.

The head of the delegation swallowed. "We crossed the mountains safely, entering the second main town of Tlaxcala Valley at noon, about a market interval ago," he began, still unsure of himself. "The Highlanders received us cordially, with all the hospitality our Revered Emperor's delegation deserves."

"How do their towns look?"

The man took a deep breath, once again thrown out of balance, this time most likely by the digression. "It's just a town, sprawling upon the lowest ridge of the Blue-Skirt Mountain."

"What sorts of buildings? Do they have a pyramid, temples?"

"No, no, Revered First Son. We saw no pyramids and only a few temples. Just plenty of wooden and stone houses. Their other main town is reported to have a Great Serpent Pyramid of the ancestors."

"Well, go on." Coyotl stood the glare of the Chief Warlord, cursing his own impatience. He should have waited for the audience to end before trying to satisfy his private curiosity.

No pyramids? No wonder Kuini was so fascinated with the view of Texcoco from their favorite hill. He should find a way to bring his friend into the city.

"Their war leader took his time to arrive, but after a few dawns we were granted an audience with the man." The trader paused. "At first we were not impressed with this infamous leader. He is short and lean, just a man of two times twenty of summers or more." A covert glance at the trader's companions was brief but unmistakable. "We had expected to meet one of their impressive, fierce warriors – tall and wide-shouldered, with scars and tattoos."

"The ones you occasionally see sacrificed at the Great Temple," muttered the Chief Warlord, his grin lacking in mirth.

The trader blushed. "Yes, I suppose so."

"So what was your impression of this man?" pressed the stern warrior, his own curiosity now aroused.

"He is an impressive man, regardless of his appearance. Clearly a dangerous warrior with great willpower. Surprisingly, he speaks perfect Nahuatl, accented like this of the Tepanecs, and his grasp on the activity occurring around the Great Lake is more than impressive. Apparently, he knows the history of the Lowlands and the other side of our Great Lake surprisingly well. He asked the right questions and made many apt comments as though seeing through our intentions."

The Chief Warlord frowned. "What was his answer?"

"He told us to come back in half a moon."

The warrior gasped. "That's an insult!"

The head of the delegation shivered. "He was careful to explain that the delay is not intended to be an insult. He told us they have to call the council of the clans to decide on such matters. His manner was cold and arrogant, but polite."

"As soon as we are through with the Tepanecs, we will launch so many raids against those savages, they will rue the day they refused to come to our aid!" hissed the Chief Warlord through his clenched teeth.

Not if I am the Emperor by then, thought Coyotl, controlling his facial expression. But what were the chances of that?

He glanced at the climbing sun, remembering that the Emperor had requested his presence after the midday meal. *Oh Mighty Tonatiuh, please slow your progress, just a little bit,* he thought. He needed to go out and find Kuini.

"Is that all?" he asked, trying to sound matter of fact.

"Yes, Revered Master. Our journey back was uneventful. The Highlanders had clearly taken to heart our peaceful intentions and did not try to bother us on our way back."

"Then go and take a rest. Be ready to be summoned back to the Palace."

Once out, he almost ran toward the stairs and the blazing sun outside the small side entrance, bursting into the unmerciful heat, hardly managing to halt before bumping into a girl. Catching her shoulders, he stopped her from falling, but her bowl went flying off, clattering as it rolled down the stairs, splashing its unappealing contents.

"Careful!" she cried out, her imperious tone not sitting well with the plainness of her muddied blouse and skirt. Then she looked up. "Oh, it's you!" she added, eyes dancing.

"Yes! And you are just the person I needed to see." He pulled her toward the stairs. "I'm on my way out, but we will have a little talk down there on the patio."

"Later," she said, resisting his pull. "I need to visit the baths and rest. My maid will tell on me if I don't get back in time for the midday rest."

"I will be the one to tell on you, if you don't stop acting irresponsibly." He pulled at her elbow firmly. "Come."

As they ran down the stairs, he released his grip, her wet, mud-and-sweat covered sleeve unpleasant to touch.

"So you were afraid I'd get caught," she said, breathing heavily, her paces light upon the polished stone. "But I didn't. So you can save your lecturing for another time, oh Future Emperor."

"When you would get caught, it would be too late, oh wild princess. The Emperor will lock you up, and then give you away to the most insignificant ruler of the smallest of his subjected provinces."

"He didn't promise to give me away to any of his most important subjects either. And in the meanwhile, you are having a good time, participating in all those councils, allowed to go where you please, while I'm supposed to spin, and read, and paint glyphs all day long." Her glare had an angry glint to it. "It's not right!"

"That's how it works," he said. "You are a girl."

"No, it's not. Chief wives have plenty of freedom to go wherever they like and to order everyone about. If I was the first daughter of the Chief Wife, I would have more freedom, I'm sure." She shrugged, then looked at him teasingly. "But the Emperor preferred your mother to mine, so here I am, spending my time doing nothing."

He shifted uneasily. "I don't think it would have been any different had he still preferred his Tepanec wife. Well, we would not have all this war on our hands, granted. But for you, it would not change a thing. Girls don't get to go to councils or run around the city."

"The commoners run around aplenty."

"Oh, so now you want to be a commoner!"

She pulled a face. "Maybe." Balancing on her toes to reach his ear, she whispered. "I sneaked into the city two dawns ago. In those clothes and all. It was amazing. I didn't make it as far as the marketplace, but I will next time."

He grabbed her shoulders, appalled. "Iztac-Ayotl, tell me you are just teasing!"

Her eyes sparked, large and dark, two precious jewels made from polished obsidian. "I did, I swear I did."

"I can't believe it. You could get hurt, killed. Or worse!"

"But I didn't." She broke free from his grip. "Stop grabbing me. I'm your sister, not your lover." Her shoulders lifted in a shrug. "You are always afraid I'll get caught, but I never do, so there is no need to worry so much. When I get caught, I'll deal with it." She laughed. "And in the meanwhile, I know what the delegation from Xicotepec wanted, or what our father wanted from them. I like to know those things."

"You should be doing your time in one of the temples, you know. You are fifteen. It's about time. And maybe it would keep you busy."

"I should have been there a summer ago, but they never got around to doing it. Mother is always busy being angry at everyone and other Emperor's wives don't care." She beamed at him, her smile innocent. "I told you, I'm not important enough. I'm not the first daughter of the first wife. So no one would mind me sneaking around."

"I mind," he said, off balance again. The Emperor's switching wives worked out well for him, but not for her. "I'll talk to my mother tonight. She'll make sure you get sent to the best temple in the city. The mighty Tlaloc or Quetzalcoatl?"

She pondered for a heartbeat. "Which one would you choose?"

"Tlaloc."

"Then Revered Tlaloc it is."

It twisted his heart, the way she looked at him, so trusting, so innocent. He shook his head. "Listen, I have to hurry now. I'll see you this evening. So just go get that bath and act like a princess for one single afternoon."

She pulled a face. "Very prince-like of you to run out in this heat. I suspect your destination is quite dubious."

Laughing, he pushed her toward the stairs. "Go away, you wild thing." He measured the sun, exasperated. "I'm to wait for the Emperor to finish his midday meal, if you wish to know. Some dubious activity, eh?"

It was already well into the afternoon when he reached the top of the hill, diving into the merciful shadow the small grove provided.

Halting, he listened carefully, then smiled. The swish of a knife brushing against the wood interrupted the silence, with his friend sitting on the stump of an old tree, working on a small figurine, his knife moving methodically, dreamlike, monotonous.

"It took you summers to arrive," the Highlander said, not raising his head, but obviously grinning. "You truly should build a palace here. To accommodate the guests who might be forced to wait the entire day and night. Those pools and pretty animals. I could use all of them today."

Coyotl dropped onto another fallen trunk. "I tried to get away earlier." He peered at the wooden figurine. "Let me see."

The tiny image of a man-like creature with a large head, small limbs and protruding eyes felt pleasantly smooth in his palms.

"It's beautiful!" he exclaimed, turning the figurine in his hands. "What deity?"

"Camaxtli." Kuini shrugged. "It's not finished. It should be painted in red and white, with the black mask of a warrior." He took the figurine back. "It should also hold a bow and many arrows, but it's too much of a pain to carve all these. I was just bored."

"A war deity?"

"Oh, yes. And a mighty one at that. But he also watches over the hunters."

"It's beautifully made. Can I have this one?"

"Of course." Kuini grinned, but there were still shadows in his dark, widely-spaced eyes. "It should be painted, though."

Coyotl took out the paper. "The colors you used on your drawing. Could those be applied to wood?"

"Yes, of course. They are used for the wooden figurines mostly. I tried them on this strange paper of yours. Wasn't sure it'd work."

"It's a good painting. I'll keep this one as well."

"What do you do with those things? Why keep them?"

"I store them for now, but when I'm an emperor, I'll put them on display, so people could see how beautiful they are. I'll bring to Texcoco all the best painters. And poets and engineers, of course. And the ones who do the music. And I'll store all the scrolls and bark-sheets, so everyone can use them if needed. Or just read them for pleasure."

"I like that vision of yours."

Coyotl glanced at his friend's troubled face. "What's wrong?"

"I don't know." The broad palms lifted, running through the carelessly tied hair. "Everything is wrong. Didn't you notice?"

"No. Of course not. Everything is good, actually." He jumped onto his feet. "Just think about it. The Tepanecs will come, but we will squash them in no time. And thanks to them, our people are not at war at the moment. If your people decide to join, we'll be squashing them together, and so both of us would be able to fight side by side. Would it not be tremendous?" He smiled. "And when I'm the Emperor, my people won't war on yours, I promise you that."

Kuini's grin lacked its usual twinkle. "Sounds good, but I don't think it'll work." He shrugged, dropping his gaze. "I don't think my people will join this war."

Coyotl tensed. "Why? What do you know?"

"Me? I don't know anything. It's not like I'm invited to the leaders' councils. I just think so. The insults of the past are too fresh to brush them aside."

Frowning, Coyotl remembered the Chief Warlord flaring the moment he heard about the Highlanders' leader asking their messengers to come back later. Oh, the stern warrior looked like he wanted to order another raid against those people in the same breath.

"Talk to your father," he said quietly. "Try to convince him."

Kuini's eyebrows flew so high, they almost met his unshaven hairline.

"Me? Talk to him? You must be joking!" The dark gaze met Coyotl's, sparkling with indignation. "Why would a leader like my father listen to a youth of fifteen summers? There could not be a single aspect that he didn't take into account long before I even began thinking about any of it. He is the Leader of the United Clans for a reason. He is the wisest man you could possibly meet! He doesn't need my advice." The eyes narrowed. "And neither does he need yours."

Coyotl suppressed his irritation. "You have something he hasn't. You've been in touch with my people. Through me, I mean. You can tell him what's been said in the Palace, by the Emperor himself. You can relate to him that we are sincere in our offer."

Kuini's face twisted as if he had eaten something bitter. Pressing his palms against his forehead, he looked up.

"You know? The funny thing is I don't think my father would actually oppose. He seems to hate those Tepanecs as well. He thinks we'll have a harder time if they take your towns and provinces. So he may consider an alliance with your people." He shrugged. "But he could not tell our people to join yours on his say-so. To do something so unusual, he would have to convince the other leaders, and then the rest of the Highlanders." He shook his head. "I don't think it'll happen anytime soon."

Coyotl studied the figurine, trying to hide his disappointment. It felt sleek in his sweaty palms.

"Well, then we will just have to squash those Tepanecs all by ourselves." He looked up. "And we'll do it, too. Never think we won't."

"Will you? My father seems to think that the Tepanecs are the invincible menace that crawled straight from the Underworld."

"They are not that bad." Coyotl laughed. "We have plenty of them in the city. Not to mention the Emperor's former Chief Wife. They are nothing but arrogant snobs."

"You have Tepanecs in the city?" Kuini stared at him, wide-eyed.

"Yes, of course. Plenty. There is a whole district full of them. It's called Tepanecapan." He hesitated. "Listen, how about this tour of Texcoco I promised you once, long ago?"

Kuini's eyes sparkled, then died away. "I can't go into your city. They'll dump me on the nearest altar before you can say 'Huexotzinco'."

Coyotl frowned. "Wait. Let me think. I believe it can be done now that I'm an official heir. I can entertain guests from all kinds of places. You don't look that outlandish and we can say you are..." He chewed his lower lip. "Maybe from the Aztec island? Your Nahuatl is almost perfect."

"The Aztec island? Go on. It can't get any better."

"Don't laugh. I'm serious. If not for those tattoos, you could be easily taken for an Aztec. Or better still – a Tepanec! Your height, your cheekbones, your face. I swear you look like a Tepanec."

"And you look like a piece of dung!"

When able to breathe again, Coyotl dropped back upon the trunk of a fallen tree. "We have to think if it's worth the risk," he said, voice still trembling. "Stop laughing. I'm serious."

"Of course it's not worth the risk. It's complete madness."

But it was easy to see the indecisiveness in the broad face of his friend, imprinted too clearly in the large, expectant eyes. Oh, but this Highlander did look like a Tepanec, he did! The eyes, the cheekbones, the height – it all was there, possessed by the people who were about to invade Texcoco.

Coyotl frowned. No, they could not pass Kuini for such, not with the tattoos and the outlandish piercing, and his complete lack of knowledge about the other side of the Great Lake.

"You can laugh all you like, but I swear I'm serious. It can be done, and what's the better time? Before the war is on, whether you join it or not. Think about it."

"I don't know if it's the heat or maybe you just drank some *pulque* on your way here," said Kuini slowly, but his eyes were still tense, still undecided.

"*Pulque*? That drink is disgusting!"

"But it makes you do all sorts of strange things. Sometimes it's nice."

"Oh, we drink *octli* for this. *Pulque* is for the commoners." He watched the raised eyebrows. "That's it. You have to come with me. If for nothing else, then to drink some *octli*. You'll never touch *pulque* again after that." He sobered. "Stay around for the night. I'll come here first thing in the morning, and we'll go into the city. A half a day's tour among the pyramids and the temples, a short raid on the marketplace, and you are back on your way. What do you say?"

Kuini took a deep breath. "I say, come in the morning, and we'll see."

CHAPTER 3

The shadow of the Great Pyramid fell upon the Plaza, covering a considerable part of the vast square. Bordered by two smaller pyramids and more temples, it seemed to enjoy the protection from the fierce midmorning sun.

Kuini tried not to gape, finding it difficult to conceal his awe. It was one thing to hear about the pyramids, to see them in the distance, to study the way they were built, detailed upon the bark-paper. However, it was an entirely different experience to stand next to the wide base, touching the cool, slightly damp slabs of stone, each higher than an average man, making one feel tiny and insignificant.

"Are you going to stand here all day, staring?" Coyotl laughed, but his eyes sparkled proudly, satisfied with the effect.

"Can we go up the stairs?" asked Kuini, not concerned if he sounded silly, or even provincial, anymore.

"No, of course not. It's a temple up there. Be sensible. Can you enter your temples whenever you want?"

"No. But I didn't mean to storm your temples. I just want to feel those stairs, that's all. Just go up for half twenty of those, eh?"

"Oh, you are a strange one. Well, let us mount a few of those, but no more than half twenty. After all, we don't want to draw too much attention."

"What is it made of?" asked Kuini, eyeing the Plaza from his newly gained height.

So many people, he thought, his stomach twisting uneasily. How many of those are living in this great city? And where did the others come from? Oh gods, what a powerful nation! To be able to build all those things, to concentrate the multitudes of people together, to make them go about their business, orderly, busy and purposeful. He bit his lips. His peoples' enemies were much more powerful than he had ever imagined.

"Those are made out of marble," he heard Coyotl explaining. "Because it's the Great Pyramid with the most important temple on top of it. But you'll see that the other pyramids' staircases are usually made of simple stone." He winked. "Less expensive than marble. Shall we go?"

They crossed the Plaza and headed up the wide avenue, lined with temples aplenty. Surrounded by a multitude of people, sometimes jostled and elbowed, Kuini could not relax, his hand resting on the handle of his dagger, its touch reassuring.

"It's a market day, you see," said Coyotl, pushing his way forcefully through the crowds. "Oh, but it's good to spend a morning outside the Palace! I feel like a boy again. So good to run around the city unattended. I can get away less and less since I've been made an official heir. I miss my *calmecac* days."

"What do you do now?"

"Well, Father usually wants me to attend his morning meetings. People are coming from all over the provinces now that the war is looming. So the Emperor has to listen politely, then make them do whatever he wants. To pledge their allegiance, in this case. To join the upcoming campaign."

Kuini leaped out of the way as a litter with curtains swept by, carried by sturdy, grim-looking men. "Can't he just order them to join? He is an emperor."

"No, he can't. Some provinces are more independent than the others. Some are paying more tribute, some less. Some are not paying at all. They have a status of allies." Coyotl smiled proudly. "A wise emperor would try to make people serve him voluntarily. This way they'll do more for him. If their hearts are with what they are doing, they'll excel beyond their regular effort. See?"

"Yes, I see. You'll be that kind of an emperor."

"Oh yes, be sure of that!"

Kuini eyed the high wall that separated the avenue from the surrounding buildings. "Can we enter any of the temples? Maybe the smallest one?"

Coyotl grinned. "Yes, and I have in mind just the place for you."

The temple was dim, its shutters closed against the brightness of the outside. He stood there, blinking, his eyes having difficulty adjusting to the semidarkness. Watching the curtained niches and the damp, stony tiles of the floor, he pricked his ears. The slight odor of stale blood, so typical for the temples, enveloped him.

Glancing at Coyotl, who conversed with a priest, he let his eyes brush past the bright entrance. Two, three leaps and he would be outside, he estimated. He trusted his friend wholeheartedly; still, it was better to calculate one's way out. One could never know, entering the temple of avowed enemies. His heart would be more than welcomed in this place. Not as much as the heart of a seasoned warrior, like one of his brothers, but still.

Coyotl came back. "He says we can peek into their collection, but only for a short time. So let's do it quickly."

He led the way toward one of the niches, and Kuini followed uneasily, reluctant to leave the safety of the near-entrance. Yet, when he saw his friend lifting the lid of a large chest, he forgot all about his misgivings. Piles of scrolls and folded papers, bark-sheets and wooden tablets, lay in the box in seeming disarray. Some painted, some carved, some drawn, colorful or grayish, they looked at him, begging to be picked up and explored.

He gasped. "Can we?"

"Help yourself."

He could hear a grin in his friend's voice, but he didn't care, picking a scroll, then another. In the semidarkness he had to bring them close to his eyes, to see what they held.

"See this?"

Coyotl reached for a long sheet. Unfolding it carefully, he placed it on the floor, with the ends of the scroll glued to a wooden plaque decorated with turquoise, in a convenient way. Kuini studied the multitude of pictures, separated by decisively drawn red lines.

"You read it from left to right, or downward, you see?"

Kuini just nodded, awestruck. So much knowledge in one

neatly folded sheet of paper!

"What's that?" he asked.

"A calendar. But this one," unfolding another shorter sheet, Coyotl smiled proudly, "this one is an account of a battle." His grin widened. "The war we are facing will be documented, too. I'll see to that."

It was already high noon when they emerged back into the brilliance of the outside. Delighted to breathe the fresh air once again, Kuini felt a twinge of disappointment. He would rather carry this whole chest out, to study it leisurely back upon the Tlaloc hill. Or better still, in the woods of his hometown. His head reeled. So much priceless knowledge!

"Does every temple have so many scrolls?" he asked as they made their way up the wide avenue, the amount of people rushing past them growing with every step.

"Well, yes, but some temples keep only the papers that are related to them and their deities. Calendars and such." Coyotl looked around. "Time to storm the marketplace, I say. Before they come looking for me, all angry and indignant."

"Were you supposed to be in the Palace?"

"Well, yes. But let us say, there was nothing particular this morning. So it's not like I ran away against their direct orders." He winked. "I can deal with them, and anyway, it was worth it. I never thought I'd see you so stunned, gaping like a woman at the jewelry stand. Quite a vision."

"Oh, shut up!" Kuini shoved his shoulder into his friend's side, but immediately felt uncomfortable in doing so. They might be friends, friends and equals, upon their Tlaloc hill, but here, in the mighty Capital, Coyotl was the Emperor's heir. The careful glances of the passersby confirmed this impression. His friend seemed oblivious of the stares, or the way the crowds moved to clear their path, but Kuini felt every pair of eyes. So far, they had not been approached, but he knew that it might change at any moment.

He frowned, trying to remember which nationality he was supposed to belong to. What was the name of the province they had agreed to mention?

"First we get that *octli* for you. And something to eat," announced Coyotl as the marketplace appeared in a colorful mess of alleys, stands, and people. So many people! If he thought the Plaza or the avenue with the temples was crowded, he knew now that it was nothing compared to the marketplace. Oh gods! Did that many people exist in the entire world? He clenched his fists tight and concentrated on his attempts to stay beside his friend in the turbulent flow of this human river.

"Here!"

Breathing with relief, Kuini dove into a side alley, also full of stands and people, but not to the extent of the main road. An oasis of peacefulness.

A plate of stuffed tortillas and a cup of *octli* – indeed a much more pleasant beverage than a *pulque* – helped him feel better. However, the good feeling did not last. As they ate, watching the market frequenters playing a bean game, a group of warriors appeared at the far end of the alley.

Kuini's heart picked a tempo. The warriors seemed to be heading their way. His hand found the dagger, his fingers slick against the string tying it to his girdle. As the warriors neared, even the bean players stopped their game, eyeing the symbols upon the newcomers' cloaks.

"Revered First Son," said the leading man, addressing Coyotl. "Your presence is required in the Palace."

Coyotl frowned. "Who sent you?"

"Your Revered Father," said the warrior, lowering his gaze.

"Is this to be an official audience?"

"Yes, Revered First Son. The Chief Warlord of the Mexica Aztecs has just arrived in the city."

"Oh," Coyotl gazed around as if pondering as to how to proceed. It was strange to see him losing some of his cheerful confidence. "Well," he said finally. "I'll be in the Palace shortly. You can go now."

The warrior shifted uneasily. "We have orders to escort you, Honorable First Son."

Coyotl's teeth sank into his lower lip. "I have a guest touring this city. I have to see him off first."

The leading warrior looked at Kuini for the first time, his gaze curious. "Why does your guest not accompany us?"

Coyotl's eyes lit up, and he grinned slightly, eyeing Kuini with a silent question, a challenging one.

Kuini shook his head.

"Listen," he said, fighting the urge to clear his throat. "It's all good. I can find my way out. I'll be all right."

Coyotl frowned. "Wait for me," he tossed toward the warriors quite imperiously, gesturing for them to step back. "Wait here, will you?" he added quietly, turning to Kuini. "I'll send two of my most trusted slaves to guide you out of the city. It won't take long, so just stay here and eat and drink some more." A small bag pressed into Kuini's hand.

"What's that?"

"Cocoa beans. To pay for things. Do you think they'll feed you because of your pretty tattoos?"

Kuini looked into the dancing eyes. "Take away your filthy beans!" He laughed, pushing the bag away. "I'll find my way out myself. Don't need your nursemaids around." Grinning, he lowered his voice to a whisper. "I'll sleep on the hill tonight. Come and see me tomorrow, if you can."

"Are you sure? I don't think it would be wise."

"I'm sure. Now, go before those manure-eaters grow restless and start wondering about these pretty tattoos of mine."

He returned the warriors' gazes, incensed with their study of him. The obsidian swords tied to their girdles sparkled against the strong sun. He wished he'd had enough sense to bring his club.

"See you on the hill," he muttered, taking a deep breath and diving into the hubbub of the main road.

This time it was somewhat easier to make his way among the crowd, he discovered, surprised. The stares that had followed him with Coyotl were no more. No one paid him any attention, no one bothered to look. He was just a youth of no significance. A foreigner with tattoos on his face, but still just one of many.

Feeling better by the moment, replete with food and a spicy drink, he strode along the main road, eyeing stalls with colorful materials and jewelry, mats with plenty of fruits and vegetables, the low tables of the food owners. This *altepetl* was something he could not comprehend.

Lingering beside a pile of vibrant material, he marveled at the rich coloring. If he dared, he would touch it to make sure it was real. A tall, slender girl in a plain maguey blouse and skirt brushed past him, halting next to the colorful pile. She picked a brim of the deepest turquoise and eyed it dubiously.

"It's nice," she said. "Nice touch. Are these Mayan cloths?"

"Yes, they are," answered the stall owner grimly. He looked the girl up and down, clearly taking in her dusty outfit. "And don't you touch any of it, unless you have enough cocoa beans to pay for them."

The girl tossed her head, throwing her thick, shiny braid behind her shoulder.

"Don't talk to me like that! You don't know how many of those beans I do have." She looked around, meeting Kuini's gaze. "And what are you staring at?" Her eyes were large and very dark, sparkling like a pair of polished obsidian earrings.

"Nothing," he said, unable to fight his grin.

"Then go about your business," she said imperiously, then turned back to the stall owner. "I don't have any just now, but the next time I'm here I will make a point not to buy any of your things."

"Go away," was the man's answer. "I know all about your type."

The crowds parted, and Kuini's attention leaped toward another group of warriors, his heartbeat accelerating. These wore shorter unadorned cloaks of a spotted pattern, and they moved through the pressing people aggressively, clearing the path. A large litter progressed at some distance, swaying lightly with the paces of its litter-bearers.

His instincts took him off the road, made him dive between the stalls and the packed gaping people. Calming down, he watched the warriors sweeping by, fascinated by their fierce looks.

"Who are they?" he asked the man beside him.

"Aztecs, who else? See their spotted cloaks? Arrogant bastards."

The Mexica Aztecs! Kuini took another step back, treading on someone's toes. He saw the palanquin nearing and felt the people pressing backwards. Contemplating diving yet deeper, he glanced back at the road, his eyes catching a glimpse of the girl who had argued with the trader earlier. She turned away from the pile of materials and watched the nearing entourage, seeming to be somewhat at a loss.

"Move away, you stupid *cihua*," barked one of the warriors.

She took a clumsy step back, but was not fast enough. Turning impatiently, the warrior shoved her aside with a swift thrust of his elbow, causing her lose her balance, crashing into the crowds behind her.

Kuini watched, unsettled. She looked so helpless and lost, sprawling there in the dust. Damn warriors, he thought, then gasped, seeing the girl springing to her feet with surprising agility considering her previous clumsiness.

"How dare you?" she screamed, leaping toward her assailant.

The armed man whirled around, his eyes wide with an obvious surprise. Her fists clenched, the girl grabbed the edge of his cloak and tried to punch the wideness of his chest. The rest of the warriors roared with laughter, and even the litter-bearers chuckled.

Displaying no difficulty, the warrior clutched her slender wrists in one hand. "What a wild ocelot!" he cried out, eyeing his companions. "What should I do with her?"

His attention still on his peers, he didn't notice the girl's arm slipping away. Only when the sharp, polished nails sank into his face did he pay heed. His gasp of surprise shook the air.

"You slimy, dirty, stupid market rat!" he roared, tearing her hand off his bleeding face, now clearly enraged. His palm rose again and again, and the girl lost her fighting spirit, whimpering and trying to cover her face, powerless to avoid the blows. "I'm going to kill you, you filthy rat!"

Kuini's legs carried him through the crowd of their own accord. Before he could give it any thought, his hands locked around the warrior's arms, pushing the man away with the strength he hadn't suspected himself capable of. His opponent staggered and fought to keep his balance, cursing, almost spitting with rage.

Another warrior stepped forward.

"Shove off, boy," he said, pushing Kuini violently. "Unless you are looking for a good beating."

Breathing heavily, Kuini tried to control his temper, knowing that to pick a fight on the marketplace, in the midst of his enemies' city, was the last thing he should have been doing.

Just as he began moving away, the first warrior regained his balance. In the corner of his eye he caught the man's pouncing and ducked as much out of an instinct as out of training, and the fist that was supposed to crush him senseless brushed against his shoulder, relatively harmless.

Unable to fight the temptation, the ribs of his opponent beckoning, he shoved his elbow into the tempting exposed belly, feeling the impact in his shoulder, knowing that it was a good hit. The gasp of the warrior told him that, while his sandaled foot crushed against the man's knee, sending him groaning into the dust.

Leaping aside, he felt more than saw another warrior moving toward him. This one had his sword already out.

"I swear I'll kill you, you filthy dung-eater!" Broadly built, he looked short, but only because of his wideness, reflected Kuini, leaping away and back toward the packed people. With the crowds pressing him from behind, it was difficult to avoid the first blow. He tried to dash toward the road behind the palanquin, but the other warriors blocked his way. They did not have their swords out, not yet.

His instincts urging him to try the other side, he ducked to avoid another blow, diving between the legs of the stunned litter-bearers, scratching his limbs against the rough wood of the palanquin's floor.

The freedom of the open road beckoned, but some of the warriors guessed his intention, and two of them already waited on the other side, their swords out.

He rolled away in time to avoid the touch of the sharp obsidian, the sword crashing the dusty ground. Springing to his feet, he leaped backwards, only to collide with another warrior. The blow in the side of his head sent him reeling, but he managed to keep his balance, leaping aside to avoid another one.

Dizzy, he tried to see where the warriors were not present, but the obsidian spikes sparkled everywhere, reflecting the fierce midday sun.

"Enough!" A powerful voice rang loudly in the dead silence.

Kuini's eyes darted toward the palanquin as the curtains moved aside and the man stepped out, his shoulders wide, bearing imposing. The broad, arrogant face looked at him briefly, then moved toward the warriors.

"What is this?" demanded the man, his voice dripping with disdain. There was a slight accent in his speech, different from the Nahuatl spoken in the Lowlands. "A hunt? My glorious warriors fighting with unarmed children? I'm impressed. Deeply impressed."

The warriors dropped their gazes, and the man with the damaged knee got to his feet, his face twisting with pain.

"So this is what we have come to? And the boy made you work! Alone and unarmed, while one of my warriors is hurt, and the rest can't breathe from the effort to hunt this cub down." The man's lips quivered. "What a show for the benefit of the market frequenters. Shall I enlist this boy to fight the Tepanecs instead of you lot?"

Fascinated, Kuini just watched, knowing that he'd been temporarily forgotten, and this would be the best time for him to slip away. Still, he could not tear his eyes off the imposing face. There was something familiar in the broad cheekbones, in the widely spaced eyes, in the way the man stood there, so straight and dignified. And there was this accent. Somewhere he had heard this accented Nahuatl before.

The Warlord measured him with his gaze, eyes distant and cold, but in their depths the amusement was flickering, too obvious to miss. "Come here, boy."

Kuini hesitated. *Maybe he could still dash up the empty road.*

The eyes measuring him sparkled. "Are you afraid? You fought well, and I thought you were braver than this."

The mocking tone made Kuini's stomach twist angrily. Concentrating on his steps, trying to walk as steadily as he could, although his head was still spinning, he came closer, seething. The man might have been handsome when young, he reflected, watching the strong, wrinkled, dignified face, but nevertheless he was an arrogant bastard.

The eyes crinkled with amusement as if reading his thoughts.

"Some warrior you are, boy." The generous lips quivered. "How old are you?"

Kuini swallowed. "Fifteen summers." He cleared his throat. "I've seen fifteen summers."

"Almost a warrior."

"I am a warrior."

The man winked. "Give it another summer or two in your local *telpochcalli*-school."

Kuini gulped, suddenly weak with relief. Afraid to say something that would give him away, he just nodded.

"So, what's your name?"

"Ku..." He was hardly able to stop himself from blurting his real name out. If his tattoos were not enough, his foreign sounding name would reveal his identity for certain. He licked his lips, trying to slam his mind into working.

"Well?" The amusement was spilling out of the large eyes. Like Father, this man was clearly prone to laughter, which seemed somehow inappropriate for his advanced age.

What name? Any word in Nahuatl would do, he thought, nauseated. His eyes leaped toward the stalls, desperate, taking in the ropes tying the wide beams of the construction. Rope, *mecatl*, could be a good shortened name.

"Mecatl," he said, voice breaking. He cleared his throat. "Mecatl."

"What?" The amusement fled from the dark eyes as the face of the man drained of blood. He frowned, then cleared his throat. "Is that your name?"

"Err, well, no," mumbled Kuini, heart thumping in his ears. The stupid word was clearly not one used to name people. Not with the frog-eaters of the Lowlands apparently, although what was wrong with the word 'rope'? Back at home, he had a friend called Twisted Rope. He swallowed. "It's not my name, but my family and friends call me that."

The man shook his head. "I haven't met anyone called that for many, many summers! Curious." He peered at Kuini as if searching for something in his face. "You do remind me of someone. Not the Mecatl I knew, but someone." The large eyes narrowed. "Let me guess. You live in the Tepanec district of Texcoco."

Kuini's heart made strange leaps inside his chest. "Yes," he said, his mouth dry.

"Thought so." The edge of the generous mouth lifted in a crooked sort of a grin. "What's with the piercings and the tattoos?"

His heart stopped leaping and now went completely still. One heartbeat, then another. *That's it. He was done for.*

"Well?" The grin of the man widened.

"I... my father is not a Tepanec. Only my mother is."

"Oh," The man nodded. "Any of her family still in Azcapotzalco?"

Kuini shook his head, afraid to venture a word. He tried to remember. Azcapotzalco? What's that?

"Well, it was an interesting encounter. Too many forgotten memories." The man grinned. "Run along, boy, and next time don't pick fights with warriors so readily. Not until you have finished your training and get a sword or a club attached to your girdle."

Kuini watched the wide back entering the litter with the easy grace of a younger man. This one was obviously older than Father even, he thought, and Father was almost fifty summers old.

The dark glares of the warriors tore him out of his reverie. Shivering, he retreated into the crowd that had watched the incident as though spellbound. The aftershock of the confrontation dawned and he clenched his teeth to stop his body from trembling.

As the litter took off, the crowd began breathing again. People moved, their quiet conversations picking back up, turning louder.

The marketplace gradually returned to its previous state. Yet, the space around him was still clear. He could feel their gazes piercing his skin. He was still not out of danger. Now he became aware of the pain pulsing above his nape, and his shoulder hurt. He brought his palm up to feel it, wincing at the familiar touch of the sticky dampness.

"Are you well, boy?" asked the stall owner, the one who had haggled with the girl about the colorful cloths. "You don't look that good."

He stared at the man.

"He put out quite a fight, this one," said another voice. "You are not from here, are you?"

"He is not from Tepanecapan. The stupid Aztec got it all wrong."

Kuini tried to push his way back toward the road when a hand grabbed his arm.

"Come, you need to drink something. And to clean the blood."

He pulled his arm away. "I have to go," he mumbled, near panic now. It all was happening too fast. One moment he was safe, anonymous in the crowd; the next he'd nearly gotten killed by the Aztecs, and now they were all staring at him, wondering, asking questions. *He needed to get away from this place.*

"You are not well, boy," insisted yet another person.

He pushed his way out more urgently, but people were everywhere, blocking his path, trying to talk to him, and he could not get enough air.

Another hand caught his wrist, but this one was small and gentle. "I know where he lives. I'll take him home," said the girl firmly.

He stared at her, recognizing the smoothness of her face, the unusually dark eyes, one cheek still red and swollen, her lower lip cut.

"Come," she repeated, frowning.

He followed her, still dazed, his mind refusing to work.

She peered into the alleys that crossed the main road. "I think I know how we get out of here, but I'm not sure," she mumbled. "It's supposed to look like an alley, but a broad one. Maybe this."

Clutching his arm once again, she pulled him into the relative quiet of a dusty pathway. "Come."

They went up the sloping road, making their way between low, one-story buildings. The clamor of the market began to fade.

"Do you know the way to the Palace?" she asked finally.

He stared at her. "Me? No."

"Oh, too bad. But you do live at Tepanecapan?"

"What?"

She wrinkled her nose. "Oh, you are a strange one. Is that from the blow on your head, or are you always this dense?"

"Who are you?" he asked, exasperated. "What do you want?"

She frowned, clearly offended. "I took you away from that crowd. You looked scared and about to faint." Her lips pursed in too obvious of a way. "You can thank me for that, you know."

He gasped at her impudence. "You can thank me too, for stopping that warrior from beating you up."

"Oh, yes." Her frown deepened. "Of course I'm grateful for that."

"Why did you attack him?"

Her eyes sparkled fiercely. "He was the one to attack me! He pushed me, made me fall."

"Well, you have to move away quicker than that. The rest of the marketplace managed to."

She looked as if about to burst. "I didn't have to move away. Who did they think they were this bunch of filthy warriors, with that filthy Chief Warlord of theirs? Some nobility!"

He could not fight his amusement. "You are the strange one, you know."

She glared at him, attractive in her righteous anger.

"So, where are you from?" he asked, mostly to keep her from storming away. She looked like she might do just that.

As she pondered her answer, he studied her face. Shaped in a sort of rectangle, her wide, sculpted cheekbones narrowed toward her gently pointed chin. A beautifully carved, perfectly polished, wooden mask, with a generously applied layer of copper, and two large obsidians for eyes.

"It doesn't matter where I come from. I can find my way

home," she said finally. "And I do thank you for saving me. You were very brave." Her face twisted. "They are such savages, those Aztecs."

"Are all of them like that?" he asked, curious yet not liking the word *savages*.

"Most of them, yes. Warriors, commoners, they are all the same. A wild, unpredictable lot."

"That warlord of theirs looked like a sensible man," commented Kuini thoughtfully, remembering the broad, noble-looking face.

"Oh, he is the worst of them all! He has had the reputation for ruthlessness and unpredictability for summers upon summers, since before any of us were even born."

"Did he come to join your upcoming war against the Tepanecs?"

The girl shrugged. "Maybe. Maybe not. With those Aztecs, one never knows." She peered at him, lifting one pointed eyebrow. "And what are you so excited about? Those are your Tepanecs we would be warring against."

"I'm no Tepanec!" he cried. "Why does everyone keep assuming that?"

"No Tepanec? But you do look like one. Except for the tattoos of the savages." She frowned. "And I heard you saying to the Aztec that you are from Tepanecapan."

"Where is this Tepanecapan?"

"Here in Texcoco. Where else?" She narrowed her eyes. "You are not from there, are you?"

He tensed. "It doesn't matter where I am from. I have to get out of the city. Can you show me the way to the Great Pyramid? I'll find my way from there."

She studied him carefully. "Why not? I lost my way too, but the Great Pyramid is a good landmark. We'll find it together. I'll know my way from there."

"Oh well." He pressed his palms against his forehead. The clubs pounding inside his skull grew worse by the moment. "Let's go."

"So you won't tell me where you come from?" she asked as

they made their way back toward the main road.

"No."

"Then I won't tell you where I'm from, either."

He glanced at her, amused once again. "There is nothing to tell. You are from Texcoco, it's obvious."

She lifted her eyebrows. "Texcoco is not a village. There are four large districts here. Tepanecapan is one of them. Where do you think I live? Guess!" He liked the way her eyes danced.

"In this same Tepanecapan," he said, laughing. "Or anyway, somewhere away from this marketplace. Aren't you supposed to know your way around here?"

"Oh, this is the first time I came here on foot, silly. I visit the marketplace from time to time, but in a litter. With servants."

He grinned. "Of course."

"You don't believe me?" She stopped abruptly, all sorts of expressions chasing each other across her face. He was hard put not to laugh at the way her eyes flickered, undecided, offended and amused all at once. There was something about this girl, something frolicsome and mischievous.

He laughed. "What do you want? I don't see this litter or that army of slaves anywhere around."

"Well, you would just have to believe me on that," she said, her imperious tone not sitting well with the bruised face and the dirtied maguey blouse.

The river of people gushed past them, circumventing her with angry glares and rude words.

"Come," he said, pointing at the crowds. "You are blocking the way." Frowning, he shielded his eyes against the glow of the afternoon sun. "If we follow this one, we will get to the pyramid, eventually."

"No, not necessarily," she offered, shielding her eyes in her turn. "See, the Great Pyramid is to our right, so if the road will go on like it does now, we'll have to leave at one point."

"Well, we'll try more alleys and turns when we see it exactly to our right."

"So, where did you learn to fight like a wild ocelot?" she asked, following him. "You gave quite a fight back there with the

Aztecs." She giggled. "I'm sure they don't teach you that in *telpochcalli*, the way you broke that warrior's knee."

"I didn't break it. He would scream like a coyote with twenty arrows in it, if his knee was really broken, and he would never be able to walk away."

"He limped badly as he went."

"I wish I had broken it. The filthy lowlife!"

"Yes, me too. I would like to watch you breaking his neck."

He glanced at her, amused. "Blood-thirsty, aren't you?"

"Me? No. Not really. I've never seen anyone get killed."

"You don't want to see it either. Not a pretty sight, in most cases."

"How do you know?"

He frowned, irritated. "I've been to raids."

"I don't believe you. You are a *telpochcalli* boy. Still in school." She peered at him. "Or maybe you were admitted to *calmecac*. Were you?"

He compressed his lips. "It doesn't matter."

"It does! Are you in *calmecac* or are you not?"

He hastened his step. "Forget it. Let us get to the Plaza."

"I'm dying of thirst," she said after a while. "And I'm hungry, too." Sniffing the air, she turned toward the aroma of cooked meat that lingered in the air, coming out of a small alley. "Let us stop to eat something."

He hesitated, recalling the stuffed tortillas he'd eaten earlier with Coyotl. And the *octli*. His stomach rumbled, but his thirst was the worst.

He remembered the bag with the large beans his friend tried to press on him. "Do you have any of those things they want you to give them for the food?"

She halted again. "The cocoa beans? Don't you have any?"

"No."

"Oh." Her open disappointment made him feel worthless.

"And you? You told that man with the cloths that you have plenty of beans."

"Well, I lied. I don't have any. The slaves bring some, every time they go to the marketplace. Even when allowed to go along,

I'm not allowed to get out of the litter." She frowned. "They just bring it to me and make me tell them what I like, and then they go back and pay for it."

"That doesn't sound so bad," he said, puzzled. Was she still making these things up? She sounded sincere, mostly in her open resentment of the procedure. "At least you get to choose what you like."

"It's bad. Believe me, it's bad." Her arms flopped in the air angrily. "I like it better running around like that, even if it means I have to move away when the filthy Aztecs want to pass."

He watched her smooth, gentle palms, her nails long and polished. "I'm almost tempted to believe you," he muttered.

"To believe me about what?"

"That you have this army of slaves and that you don't have to do any work by yourself."

"I told you so!" She looked up at him, eyes flickering. "And now your turn. Where do you really come from?"

"I won't tell you, so just leave it alone." He pondered. "Maybe I'll send you a note telling you who I am."

"A note?"

"Yes, a note. People do that, you know? People who can read and draw. Educated people."

"I can read and draw. They make us girls draw all the time. When we are not required to spin cotton. It's such a bore!" She slowed her step before another stand with tortillas. "What if we steal one?"

"What?"

"Can't you grab a tortilla and run? You can fight, so why can't you make a raid on one of those stands?"

Her eyes danced, and he felt the urge to grab her shoulders and pull her closer. *To do what? To shake her or to kiss her?* The thought made him uncomfortable.

"Come on," he said, frowning. "Let's go."

She still stood there, watching him expectantly and he knew her eyes would lose their spark should he insist on going away.

"You know what? Go and talk to that man. Make him look the other way."

The way her eyes lit made his stomach twist. He glanced at the warriors playing beans. Other people seemed to be watching the game. He drifted nearer to the roughly tied beams of the stall. *Now what?*

The tortillas piled on the dirty surface, thrown carelessly, gathering dust, cold and not rolled around anything. Just a pastry, and not freshly baked at that. Yet, on the other side, near the stand owner, he spotted a plate with hot rolls, their delicious aroma wafting on the breeze.

He drifted closer, noticing her trying to talk to the owner. As clumsy as with the seller of cloths, she didn't seem able to hold the man's attention. He watched the stall owner answering her rudely, ordering her to move along. But just as her nostrils widened with familiar indignation, a roar arose from the bean players. Several of the diners, as well as the owner of the tortillas, turned and looked at the warriors.

Kuini saw his chance. In one leap he neared the stall, grabbing a few pastries with one hand, and her arm with another. The hot tortillas scorched his palm, but he held onto them, pulling her along, away from the stand.

She got her clue, and together they dashed back toward the main road, the outraged cries of the stall owner following them, making them run faster. The crowds enveloped them again, but he still pushed on urgently, afraid of the warriors that might be tempted to take a challenge.

"We don't… have to run… all the way to the Palace," she gasped, panting beside him.

He slowed, then pulled her into a smaller alley. "It was your idea, remember?" he said, succumbing to an uncontrollable fit of laughter.

She dropped down on a fallen pole, breathing heavily, her face red and glittering. He busied himself with scanning their loot. The tortillas were squashed a little, their stuffing - avocado and other vegetables - smeared upon his burning palms.

"Here," he said. "Our reward."

She beamed at him, snatching one of the tortillas. "The avocado stuffing is my favorite one!" she cried out, eyes shining. "You are incredible."

Ridiculously pleased, he dropped down beside her, sinking his teeth into the pastry, enjoying it more than any food he had eaten in his entire life.

"But for a cup of *octli*, I'm well set."

"*Octli*? You can't drink that," she mumbled, her mouth full. "Only warriors are allowed to drink that beverage, and never in public. It plays with your mind."

"I am a warrior," he said. "I raided that food stall for you."

Her laughter trilled, making his heart beat faster. "It was more of a theft, but you are a warrior, and you deserve three cups of *octli* at the very least." She beamed at him, her eyes black and glittering, enormous in the gentle roundness of her face. Stomach hollow, he fought the urge to pull her closer.

"Do you think this way will bring us to the Plaza?" he asked instead, peering down the alley.

"It would be the right direction if this one is not a dead end." She sprang to her feet. "Let's go."

It was already deep into the afternoon when they reached the wide avenue lined with temples. Relieved, he hastened his steps. Maybe he'd leave this capital in one piece, after all.

"They are going to kill me back home," she said.

"Is this the first time you've run away?"

"No. But I never disappeared for so long, so my maid was able to keep it a secret. But now?" The girl inhaled loudly. "Now they'll know for certain, and they'll be mighty upset. My maid will be sold, and I'll be locked away." She sighed. "My brother always warned me against being caught."

"Maybe it'll be all right," he said, disturbed with her sudden sadness. "I did many stupid things today, but here I am. In one piece and about to get away with it."

"There was nothing stupid about what you did. You saved me."

"Not this. There were other things." He hesitated. "I shouldn't have come here, to your *altepetl*, in the first place."

"So you are not from here!" she called triumphantly.

He shrugged.

"You can tell me." She looked at him searchingly. "There have been so many foreigners in the city for moons now. Because of the war. Delegations upon delegations. Even if you are a Tepanec, it doesn't matter. There are plenty of Tepanecs around here, and I mean *plenty*! A whole district of them. They don't feel foreign. So, why should you?"

They stood on the Plaza, undecided, oblivious of the people rushing around them.

"I should take you to your home," he said hesitantly. "It is not safe for you to go all alone wherever you live."

She smiled broadly. "Yes, do that."

"Where to?"

"To the Palace, where else?"

"You don't live in the Palace!"

Her eyes were dancing again, making his stomach hollow. "So you didn't believe me after all. About the litter and the army of slaves."

He licked his lips. "I did. But the Palace? Why would you live in the Palace?"

"Because that's where I live. I told you. It may sound nice, but it's dreadfully boring. I wish I lived in the city. Or somewhere else around the countryside. Where do you live?"

"Far, far away."

"Will you be coming back to Texcoco?"

He shrugged, pleased with her asking that.

"Send me that note while you are here."

Her eyes sparkled in the descending dusk, the most polished obsidian he had ever seen. The breeze was stronger here on the Plaza, increasing with the rapidly disappearing sun. A silky tendril escaped her tight braid, fluttering across the soft curve of her cheek. Without thinking, he reached for it.

The touch of her skin made him shiver. His fingers lingered as she gazed at him, mesmerized. The sounds of the Plaza dimmed. The air stood still. He knew he had to pull her closer, whatever the consequences.

In another heartbeat, her gaze leaped aside and the magic broke. As she gasped, he heard the sounds returning with doubled strength. There was a lot of noise and some people were shouting, running in their direction. A large group holding torches, accompanied by warriors. His heart missed a beat. Unable to breathe, he stared at them as they neared, paralyzed.

A woman broke from the group, rushing toward them. "Iztac-Ayotl!" she shouted.

"Oh no!" breathed the girl. She clasped his hand. "I think you had better go. Quick!"

He did not wait for her to repeat her words. Darting aside, he turned around and charged for the deepening shadows behind the nearest temple.

He could hear their shouts, loud and threatening, could hear the pounding of their steps behind him. Doubling his efforts, he turned around the temple's corner.

A wall loomed ahead, blocking his way. Not very high, it was a solid, stony structure of many large slabs. Still, it presented cracks and small ledges. Enough for a highlander, skilled in climbing since before he could walk.

Leaping onto the lowest ledge, his fingers claws, he clutched at the cracks between the slabs, pulling with all his might. His legs slipped again and again, but he found his hold anew every time, working his way up. Someone managed to grab his sandal, but the hands slipped off, and then he was too high, out of their reach.

His palms reached the top, clung to it desperately as he relished the luxury of holding onto something wide and solid. A round stone smashed beside him, bouncing off the damp bricks. He doubled his efforts, his leg reaching for the top. His upper back absorbed a mighty blow, but still he held on, regaining his breath, readying himself for the last effort.

He could hear the girl's voice, and it distracted him for a moment.

"Don't do it!" she screamed, voice high-pitched and ugly, choking with tears. "Please! He didn't do anything wrong. Please, don't! You can't do it!"

When something pushed his head forward, he was about to throw his body over the edge. His face met the cold stones with such a force it stunned him. There was no pain, only a surprise.

He felt his fingers slipping, but the fall was strangely slow, like in a dream. He didn't feel any of it. Still, he was aware of the hands dragging him somewhere.

People were talking loudly, angrily. A woman was crying, repeating over and over. "Iztac-Ayotl, you are well. Thank all the gods, you are well. Thank all the gods!"

His eyes stung, awash with a warm sticky flow, but he still tried to open them. The girl sounded so very near now, still screaming. He could imagine those luminous black eyes of her sparkling with rage.

"You can't do it!" she screamed over and over. "Leave him alone. I hate you. I hate you all!"

Then darkness descended.

CHAPTER 4

The darkness dispersed slowly, painfully. As he climbed out of the black pit, he felt the pain enveloping him. His whole body hurt as if it had been dragged through a rocky ridge, and his face was on fire.

Lights flickered, nearing and swimming away, their movement nauseating in the swaying darkness. He blinked again and again, trying to make it stop moving. It didn't help, so he closed his eyes, gaining a measure of relief.

The voices floated nearby. Somewhere in the room, people were talking calmly, unhurriedly. His ears picked up the sound of clattering cups. Someone laughed, then drank, slurping loudly.

Kuini licked his lips. Water, he thought, nauseated by the salty taste on his tongue. He needed to get some water. And then to understand what had happened. *Where was he?*

He tried to turn around, but his hands refused to move, stuck awkwardly behind his back. It took him an effort to understand, then a wave of panic washed his whole being. He was tied. And wounded. And in the enemy's hands. Oh, gods!

He clasped his lips tight, suppressing any sound that might burst out unrestrained. *What had happened?* He tried to remember, but the clubs pounding inside his skull redoubled their efforts, making him dizzy with pain.

Blinking against the nearing light, he tried to see, but the figure above him blurred and swayed.

"Oh, the boy is back among the living," said a voice, sounding amused. The man knelt. "Can you hear me, eh wild boy?"

He stared at the man's face, trying to make it out in the

wavering fog.

"He doesn't look well," said the man. "I'll get you some water, you wild thing."

It took the man long to come back, or maybe just a heartbeat. He could not tell. A rough hand pushed his head up, releasing more pain in its back. He felt a flask being brought to his lips. The water tasted good, and he choked trying to drink all of it.

"Easy, boy, easy. There is enough water."

The hand pushed him farther up, but it made his nausea so much worse. He gagged, fighting it back, desperate not to vomit. Not in front of them! They would think he was afraid, scared, terrified. Well, he may be all of it, but he would not vomit because of the fear. It was just that the world was spinning too wildly.

He felt the flask reaching his lips once again. More water made him feel better.

"Where am I?" he croaked, then regretted the question. Why should they tell him? Why should he give them the power to refuse, to tell him to shut up?

"In the Palace's guards' quarters," said the man, taking the flask and wiping its spout carefully with the rim of his cloak. "Waiting for one of the leaders to take a look at you."

His stomach turned again. "Why?"

"Why?" The man laughed heartily. "The score of your crimes is higher than the Great Pyramid."

He took a deep breath, then another. It made the nausea lessen. "What did I do?"

"Oh well, let us see." Clearly amused, the man thrust his palm forward. "You made trouble on the Plaza, ran away from the guards and fought them, and of course, kidnapping a princess is quite a feat for a boy of your age."

"I did all that?" he asked, blinking. They must have been insane. But then, what would they be if not the insane Lowlanders? What could one expect from such a lot?

"Oh, yes. You'll be brought before the judge sometime during the morning, but in the meanwhile, one of the leaders might want to question you. Have to know who you are before bothering the courts."

The man turned around and left. Kuini shut his eyes, leaning heavily against the wall. Oh gods, let them get it over with fast. He could not hold out against this nausea for much longer, and he could not feel his hands anymore.

He shifted carefully, but the movement sent shafts of pain all over his body. He must have broken something, somewhere. His ribs or his arms, or maybe his head. The attempt to remember did not crown with success. He was on the marketplace, stealing tortillas for this pretty black-eyed girl.

The girl! The memories swept him, and he gasped. Oh, now he knew what the warrior was talking about. He had tried to run away from the warriors. He'd climbed the wall, but somehow he'd fallen off of it. How? He was an excellent climber.

The clubs pounding behind his forehead and above his neck answered the question. They must have shot him with a sling, accurately at that. Filthy lowlifes!

He watched the warriors as they slumbered near the entrance, throwing beans, drinking from large cups. Had he only managed to cut the ties...

He tried to rub his wrists against the rough wood of the wall, but the movement sent shafts of pain up his left shoulder, making him gasp. Clenching his teeth, he shifted into a better position, then resumed the rubbing.

They would fall asleep eventually. Or maybe go away. They were clearly not guarding anything special here, not even him. Their merry laughter reached him, confirming his observation. Were they drinking *pulque*? Or maybe *octli*? Their cups contained no water, of that he was certain.

A draft of night air burst into the room as the screen moved aside. The warriors sprang to their feet. Blocking the doorway, the bulky figure of a man stepped in, acknowledging the hurried murmuring of the warriors with an arrogant nod.

Kuini watched the newcomer, his stomach tightening as the man crossed the room with a long determined stride. For some time, he just stood there, arms folded, legs wide apart, studying the prisoner. Kuini returned his gaze with an effort.

"What's your name, boy?" asked the man finally, voice cold

and indifferent.

He remembered the marketplace. "Mecatl."

"Mecatl what?"

"Just Mecatl."

The man shook his head, his lips tightening. "Where are you from?"

Kuini took a deep breath. "I don't remember."

"You what?"

"I don't remember. They hit me on the head, more than once. I can't remember. They say I did things I don't remember, too." He stood the glare of his interrogator, feeling suddenly lightheaded. That's it. He would insist he did not remember anything. He has a bleeding head to present, if necessary. Let them keep assuming he was a Tepanec or whatever, just like they had back in the marketplace.

The unpleasant smile stretched the man's lips. "He doesn't remember, eh?" He turned to the surrounding warriors. "Shall we refresh his memory?"

"Honorable Leader," said the man Kuini recognized as the one who gave him the water. "He may be telling the truth. His head is cracked quite open, in several places. He may be just a boy from the city."

The leader lifted his eyebrows. "He may be. Or he may not be. He was the one to kidnap the First Daughter of the Second Wife." He turned back to Kuini. "So you don't remember, eh?"

Kuini just shook his head, his mouth too dry to form words. He saw the sandaled foot raising, and had he not been wounded and tied he would have been able to do something. As it was, the sandal crashed against his side, sending him flying back onto the floor amidst a wild outburst of pain.

He felt his teeth gritting against each other, stifling a groan. Another kick followed. He tried to pull his legs up, to curl into a ball, but his battered body just wouldn't react. The vicious kicks reached everywhere.

A hand grabbed his hair, yanked his head up off the bloodied floor. "Well, boy, do you still have difficulty remembering?"

He clasped his lips tight as his head pushed forward, met the rough wooden tiles. The pain exploded prettily, like a colorful ball. He gagged, the taste of the blood in his mouth nauseating.

A hand pulled his hair again. "Answer me!"

"Tepanecapan," he coughed.

"What?"

"Tepanecapan. I'm from Tepanecapan. Family there."

His hair was released at once, pushed back into the wooden floor.

"See," said the voice above, satisfied. "A little pressure and most people will remember things." A tip of a sandal brushed against his ribs. "Clean him some. Make him presentable for the court."

He heard the footsteps drawing away, his body limp with relief. Luckily, he had remembered the name of that Tepanec district, he thought randomly. A strange custom. To divide a city into different parts.

Coyotl watched the Aztec Warlord, consumed with curiosity. The torches blinked wearily, casting their shadows across the great hall and the people feasting around low tables. It was nearing midnight, but the visitors did not indicate an inclination to break the festivities, following their leader in his merry, careless mood of enjoyment.

Coyotl shifted impatiently, standing beside the Emperor's reed chair, bidden into the revered presence. Not to dine with the honored guests, not yet, but to listen and watch, which was more than enough for a youth of fifteen summers, even if an official heir.

He watched the Aztec squatting comfortably, amiable and at ease, eating heartily but hardly drinking any *octli*, clearly preferring to wash his food down with plenty of water. Such an imposing man. Tall and broad, the Aztec seemed to fill the room with his presence, the easy confidence spilling out of his large, well-spaced eyes, the air of arrogant self-assurance enveloping him, making one's nerves prickle. Where had he seen eyes like that before? wondered Coyotl, watching the broad face breaking into a polite smile.

"Revered Huitzilihuitl, the Emperor of Tenochtitlan, would be more than happy to do his best in settling the dispute between his most trusted friends and allies and the distant Tepanecs," the Aztec was saying. He picked another tamale stuffed with rabbit meat. "Oh, those are delicious!" he exclaimed. "Texcoco is unarguably the most luxurious *altepetl* of the Great Lake."

Coyotl could see his father's jaw tightening as the Emperor tried to hide his impatience. He didn't want to discuss the luxury of his capital, and he most certainly didn't want the Aztecs to try and settle his dispute with the Tepanecs. What he wanted was quite the opposite.

"I trust that our old friends and allies would not hesitate in supporting their most faithful neighbors should the Tepanecs choose the warpath," said the Emperor coldly. "In their gathering their forces, drawing more and more of the independent *altepetls* into this dispute, the Tepanecs demonstrated their warlike intentions."

"Oh, our Revered Emperor is certain to find the way to reach a peaceful solution," answered the Aztec, non-committal, picking another tamale. "The Tepanec Emperor, is a very old man. He is making a show of aggression, but he would not dare to invade your shores."

"I'm afraid Revered Huitzilihuitl is underestimating the greediness of the Tepanec ruler. He would not rest until putting all the lands around our Great Lake under his crushing yoke. Is my spiritual brother, Tenochtitlan's Emperor, not weary of the Tepanec oppression? Is he still content greeting their tribute collectors every full moon? The tribute Tenochtitlan pays is not as heavy as it was forced to pay during the Revered Acamapichtli's reign - Huitzilihuitl was brilliant in his ways of reducing the amount of goods required by Azcapotzalco – still, it must be an unnecessary burden. You were Revered Acamapichtli's first Chief Warlord and Adviser. How could you forget the insults of the arrogant Tepanecs?"

The Aztec's face froze as the perpetual amusement left the broad features.

"My personal history with the treacherous Tezozomoc goes deeper than the common knowledge would have. I remember the insults of the past, and my heart bleeds recalling the efforts of the most revered emperor in Tenochtitlan's history." The man sighed grimly. "However, Revered Huitzilihuitl is a prudent ruler. We cannot face the Tepanec Empire on the battlefield, not yet. We may win a victory or two, but we would not win this war. Tezozomoc is farsighted. Whether we like it or not, whether we are prepared to admit it, he is a brilliant leader, and his resources in supplies and manpower are enormous. Neither Tenochtitlan, nor Texcoco would be able to sustain this war in order to achieve a final victory." The man shrugged. "Maybe in twenty or so summers. Maybe when Tezozomoc is dead. Tenochtitlan is working its way toward the final independence, but it does so carefully, the way the Revered Acamapichtli has done." The penetrating gaze straightened, facing the Texcoco Emperor as an equal would. "I would advise your *altepetl* to do the same. Both our capitals need patience."

Appalled, Coyotl gasped at the effrontery of the guest. Did this Aztec Warlord presume to advise the Acolhua Emperor? Inconceivable! Even among the fierce Aztecs such arrogance would be surprising. Only the Tepanecs might presume patronizing Texcoco people. Why, the man even looked like a Tepanec, he thought, seething. With these broad features of his and those widely spaced eyes. Where had he seen such a face before?

He saw a maid hovering nearby, carrying no tray, her gaze seeking him, openly imploring. He frowned, but the maid kept stealing glances, clearly anxious to catch his attention.

Coyotl hesitated. He wanted to hear where this argument would lead, how his father would put the insolent Aztec in his place, yet now he recognized the maid as one of Iztac's personal slaves. Oh yes, he had forgotten to talk to his mother about his sister's temple training. It was too late to bother the Emperor's Chief Wife now, but the anxious face of the girl's maid made him uneasy. Something was wrong.

He slipped away silently, relieved to be outside, breathing the fresh air with enjoyment. The reception hall was choking with incense, spread everywhere to keep the mosquitoes out.

"Revered First Son." The woman's voice startled him. "Would you please be so kind as to visit your sister's rooms? She is most anxious to see you."

"In such a late part of the evening? She should be fast asleep. What happened?"

"Oh please, Revered First Son, please follow. Iztac-Ayotl is distraught and in need of your help. She would not talk to anyone, not even her Revered Mother. She was punished severely for what she has done, yet she is distressed over something none of us could understand."

He stared at the maid, startled. "Punished? What has she done?"

"Oh please, Revered Master, please come."

He followed the woman down the long corridors, his worry mounting. His sister had been caught, that was obvious. But caught doing what? Spying in the Emperor's hall? Not likely. Before the Aztecs arrived there were no official audiences, and after the formidable Warlord was received, he, Coyotl, was there, brought back from the city.

He thought about the first part of this day. Oh, how amazed Kuini had been, how awestruck. The effect the great *altepetl* had had on the Highlander was more than Coyotl could wish for. What a pleasant surprise. He should bring his friend here more often, now that they had discovered it was possible. There was so much more of Texcoco to show.

The cloud of incense pounced on him as he entered her set of rooms, making it difficult to see in the eye-stinging mist. Why wouldn't she open the shutters? His gaze brushed past the small woven podium with a bowl and other spinning facilities, scattered there in disarray.

"Iztac-Ayotl, are you here?"

There was a heartbeat of silence before she burst out of the second smaller room, pouncing on him, almost pushing him off his feet, clumsy as ever.

"Oh Coyotl," she sobbed into his chest, soaking his cloak with warm tears.

He stood there momentarily stunned, at a loss. Iztac crying? Impossible! She never cried. Not even as a young girl, the rebellious, wild little thing. She would take punishments with those clasped lips of hers and the challenging eyes, no matter how harsh the penalty was. Why, she didn't even cry that time, five or six summers ago, went they were playing in the gardens and she fell out of the tree and broke her hand. He remembered how proudly she had sported her sling to which her arm was fastened for quite a long time. Stifling a smile, he remembered the way she would climb a tree or a wall like a quick pretty lizard, light-footed and sure of herself.

"What happened? Are you hurt? What were you punished for?"

But she pressed closer, and her sobs became louder, threatening to go completely out of control.

He propelled her toward the nearest pile of mats. "Bring us some water," he ordered the maid. "Then leave." He looked at the woman sternly. "And don't listen by the doorway!"

When the slave returned, he made the girl take the cup. "Drink, Iztac. Drink the whole cup." He watched her throat convulsing as she drank. "Now here, take this cloth and clean your face."

She obeyed him without a word; another unusual sight. As she wiped her face, he noticed the bruised cheek and the swollen lip, his fists clenching on their own. If the Second Wife had beaten her for whatever crime the girl had committed, he would just go and kill the vile woman.

"Now tell me what happened?" he said, pleased to hear his voice still calm. "What were you punished for?"

"I went into the city this morning," she said, still sobbing.

"No!" He flung his arms in desperation. "Not again."

"I didn't get into any trouble! Well, I did, but I was all right and everything was under control." Her face twisted. "This was one of the most wonderful days—"

He cut her off impatiently. "What happened? How did you get

caught?"

Her shoulders sagged once again. "Well, you see, I lost my way, so it took me half a day to get back. That's how they knew."

"What punishment did you receive?"

She shrugged. "Nothing out of the ordinary. Like you said, locked in my rooms. A lot of yelling and lecturing on my unworthiness, of course. The usual things."

"But you've been hit. Your mother did it?"

She brought her palms to her face. "Oh, this? No. It's not her. And it's really nothing. Nothing to do with any of it, anyway."

"Who hit you?" he cried out, appalled, springing to his feet, unable to sit.

Her dark eyes shone with tears. "I'll tell you later, and it doesn't matter. It's not important now. But you must help me. You must!" She began sobbing again, difficult to control her convulsive breathing.

"Help you how? Do you want me to talk to the Emperor, to try to explain?" He frowned. "Yes, I'll do it first thing in the morning. Before he gets too busy with the Aztecs."

His last sentence brought a new bout of tears. She sprang to her feet and stood before him, her teeth white, making a mess out of her lower lip.

"Listen," she said when able to speak once again. "There was this boy on the marketplace. He saved me, and he helped me to find my way to the Plaza. He was there with me when the warriors came." She took another convulsive breath. "They attacked him. He tried to get away, but they shot him with their slings, and they dragged him away. They took him somewhere, and they didn't listen to me when I tried to tell them that he did nothing wrong." Swallowing, she clasped her lips tight, then went on, determined. "I think they are going to accuse him of all sorts of things that are related to me. But he did nothing wrong! You see, he saved me, and he helped me to find my way back. And he was amazing, nice, and interesting. We had a wonderful time together." Her voice broke. "I don't want him to get hurt. Please, find out what happened to him. Please, don't let them hurt him."

He tried to make sense of this jumble of words. She'd met a

boy, and he had helped her, but the warriors were angry with him anyway. Well, it did make certain sense. Why would they take kindly to the Emperor's daughter running around the city with this or that commoner? He frowned. But why would they shoot this boy, when all they had to do was to tell him to be off before taking her back to the Palace?

"Why did he try to run away?" he asked, finding the puzzling part. "Why would he do this?'

"Oh, he was jumpy all the time for some reason. He didn't want anything to do with the city officials, I think. Maybe he was someone they were looking for anyway." Her face twisted. "Still, you have to find him and help him to get away. He doesn't deserve this." The tears gathered anew. "He was covered with blood when they dragged him away. All over his face!"

Suddenly, he caught his breath. "What did he look like?" he asked urgently, heart beating fast. "What was his name? Did he tell you?"

"Mecatl," she said. "He didn't tell me, but I heard it on another occasion. He was a Tepanec, but he kept saying he was not. I suppose he doesn't like his origins so much now, with the war looming."

He barely listened, his relief welling. For a heartbeat he thought it might be his friend, but that would have been too much of a coincidence. Kuini must be safely away upon his hill, resting after the eventful day, dreaming of temple's scrolls or the Great Pyramid. He'd have to find him tomorrow, first thing in the morning. Well, not the first thing.

"Listen," he said, taking her hands in his. "I'll try to find out what happened to that savior of yours, and I'll talk to the Emperor about all this. I'll try to make him not go too harsh on you. But you have to promise to behave from now on. Promise?"

She peered at him with the same trusting innocence that always twisted his heart. "I can't promise you that. But I'll try. At least for the next moon or so." A smile dawned, one of her wonderful, innocently mischievous smiles. "If I plan another adventure, I'll tell you before. Good?"

He got to his feet. "Yes. And now try to get some sleep. You look exhausted and not at your best." He wanted to ask her about the bruises, but then decided against it. She had calmed down, at last. He should not disturb her anymore, not after such a difficult day.

"Will you remember to make sure this boy doesn't get killed?" she called after him, when he was already outside.

"Yes, of course," he muttered absently, forgetting all about it. The conversation with the Emperor about her was much more important than some Tepanec boy in trouble with the city officials.

"Wake up, boy."

Kuini blinked in the strong morning light. Dozing on and off, drifting between sleep and reality, he must have fallen asleep toward the dawn, as now he felt surprisingly refreshed. His body was stiff and in pain, but the nausea was gone, and it made him feel infinitely better.

"Come. There is no time for a refreshing nap. Get up." A hand grabbed his upper arm, pulling him onto his feet, steadying him as he swayed. "Don't collapse, boy. Not yet. You can do better than this. Want some water?"

"Yes." Kuini narrowed his eyes against the dizziness.

"Lean against the wall." The support of the hand disappeared, but the rough wooden planks were there, offering their firmness. He fought the urge to slide alongside them.

"Here, drink it all."

The water tasted good. It washed down his parched throat, bringing his insides back to life, clearing the light fog before his eyes.

"Now, let's go."

"Where to?" he asked, trying not to lean on his guard too heavily, every step sending shafts of pain through his body, making his head reel.

"To the Plaza, of course. The court will be assembled in a little while, and your case will bring the judges nice diversity in their usual boring city disputes." The warrior measured him with an appreciative glance. "It's not every day strange warrior-boys go around kidnapping princesses."

"I didn't kidnap anyone," said Kuini, sensing the man's curious affability. "Let alone a princess."

The man chuckled. "Well, it's too bad you've been caught with the First Daughter of the Emperor's Second Wife."

He blinked. "The First Daughter of the Second Wife?" *Then she had not lied about the litter and the army of slaves.*

The man nodded vigorously, chuckling.

"If she was kidnapped, then someone else did it. I just met her there. She asked me to bring her to the Palace, and I was about to do that." He turned his head, halting. "Have someone ask her!"

The man pulled him on firmly. "You talk to the judge. Not to me. I'm only one of the Palace's warriors. I do not talk to the royalty. And if you ask me, it keeps me from trouble. You should try it too, sometime." He chuckled. "Although, I'm not sure you'll have your chance."

"Will they execute me?"

"Oh, yes."

"Which way?"

The man pursed his lips. "I'd say the strangling. Or maybe a stoning."

Kuini's stomach turned. To take his mind off the prospect of stoning, he looked around, taking in the spotless pathways and the swaying trees of the gardens around them. The Palace loomed to their right, impressive like the Great Pyramid, bearing down upon its surroundings, casting the beauty of the groomed gardens and patios into insignificance.

A group of warriors appeared at the far end of their path and Kuini tensed, then forced his body to relax. He didn't care about any of them anymore. It was too late to be afraid of them.

He watched the man in the lead, broad and imposingly tall, talking cheerfully, gesturing, his paces wide and purposeful. There was something familiar about that one. Kuini narrowed his eyes, then tensed again. *The Aztec from the marketplace!*

He dropped his gaze as the group neared, somehow

uncomfortable with this man seeing him in such a condition. The slightly accented Nahuatl brought another forgotten memory. Whom had he heard speaking with this peculiar accent before?

The hand of his guard pulled him away hurriedly, making him sway. Involuntarily, he glanced up. The Aztec went up the path with a natural arrogance of a person accustomed for his way to be cleared. His eyes brushed past them indifferently, not even the slightest nod acknowledging Kuini's guard's polite gesture. Yet, something did attract the man's attention as, upon passing them, he turned his head, his gaze concentrating visibly.

"Is that not the market boy?" he exclaimed, the broad face registering a genuine surprise. He halted abruptly, and his followers did the same, puzzled.

Kuini dropped his gaze, his teeth clenched too tight to make them part. He could feel the wondering eyes measuring him from head to toe, taking in the dried blood and the tied wrists.

"Got yourself into another bunch of trouble, didn't you?" inquired the man, voice trembling with amusement. "And it did not take you long to do that."

Kuini stared at the ground stubbornly.

"Where are you taking him?" This time the question clearly addressed Kuini's guard.

"To the Plaza, Honorable Warlord," said the man humbly, uncomfortable and sweating. "He is to be judged by the court."

"What has he done?"

The warrior cleared his throat. "He tried to kidnap one of the Emperors daughters."

The Aztec gasped. "You did this, boy?"

"No!" Not caring about his appearance anymore, beaten and tied as he was, Kuini looked up. It was tiring, this particular accusation. He may be guilty of many things, but not this. He was not that stupid!

The eyes of the older man narrowed, losing their amusement, although the derisive grin was still in place, stretching the generous lips.

"You know what? This boy is too promising to execute him like that." The Aztec paused as if pondering his possibilities. "I'll take care of this matter from now," he declared finally, addressing Kuini's guard, his words phrased politely, but in the tone that invited no argument.

A brief silence prevailed.

"Take him to my quarters. Clean him and have the healer check on him." A curt gesture singled out two warriors, then one pointed eyebrow climbed up. "Keep an eye on him, until I'm back. Untie him, but make sure he is well guarded."

"But Honorable Warlord," protested Kuini's scandalized escort. "I have specific orders from the leader of the royal warriors. I'm to take this boy to the judge."

"Your orders are changed," said the Aztec sharply, obviously not pleased by a simple warrior offering him an argument. "Your leader is welcome to talk to my people. Or to his superior." Turning abruptly, the man headed up the road, not bothering to make sure his orders were followed.

Dazed, Kuini just watched. One must get used to so much authority, he thought randomly, following his new captors, unsettled. He kept switching hands, now falling into the hands of the people worse than the enemies of his countrymen. The fierce Aztecs, no more and no less. The arrogant, bloodthirsty, unpredictable lot, with their warlord being the worst of them all. The girl had said so. She said the man had the reputation for all of it and worse.

He shivered, suddenly cold in the soft morning sun. He should never have come to Texcoco, never! There had to be a way to let Coyotl know.

CHAPTER 5

He watched the warriors squatting outside the entrance. Leaning against the plastered wall of the corridor, they sat there motionless, at ease, conversing from time to time. Their spotted cloaks clung to their bodies, soaked with sweat. It was less hot in the spaciousness of the inner rooms, where the wide open shutters allowed a slight breeze to flow between the openings in the walls.

Shifting, Kuini made himself more comfortable. His tiredness welled, but he fought the urge to put his head down. He had to stay awake, to wait for the warriors to relax their guard. Those men looked more like the fighters they were, unlike the people who had guarded him at night, slumbering or drinking spicy beverages.

He leaned against the wall, hugging his knees. It was good not to be tied, to be able to move around as he pleased, clean of mud and dried blood. Shivering, he remembered the night, that horrible feeling of helplessness, to be tied and at the mercy of some damn filthy bastards. He should never have let it happen. When a warrior, truly a warrior, he would make sure to die if necessary, but never to get captured. Never that!

The warriors' voices reached him, too soft to try to understand. What were they talking about? Why wouldn't they leave for a short while, to get something to eat, or to drink, or to relieve themselves? He only needed a few moments to sneak away. When in the gardens, he would have no difficulty disappearing into the Palace's artificial groves, scaling the first wall he found to get out of that place, away from the accursed dangerous city, never to return.

He shifted his arm that the healer had fastened into a sling, with two firm planks enclosing it from both sides. It hurt to move it, but not overly so. The healer maintained it might have been broken, or maybe just cracked a little.

He sighed. He could not scale walls with this arm. Well, he thought, brushing this worry aside, then he'd just have to find a way out without scaling walls. There must be enough unguarded gates and entrances in such a vast structure as this magnificent Palace.

With his good unharmed arm he touched the bandages encircling his head. The healer was very thorough, washing his wounds until his eyes watered, then putting all sorts of hot and cold ointments on it. A good thing. There was no argument at his feeling much better now. If only they would have the sense to offer him something to eat. His stomach rumbled loudly, but he tried to pay it no attention. *Think of something else; think of how you can get out of here.*

His vision blurred, and he must have fallen asleep, as the vigorous footsteps of a newcomer startled him, his head dizzy, heart beating fast. The fierce midday sun flowed through the open shutters now, giving no relief of a breeze anymore.

Kuini blinked, staring at the Aztec as the man strolled in, the air of a dominant confidence enveloping him like a gown.

"Well, is it not our prisoner?" The man tore his imposing headdress off with an impatient gesture, rubbing his brow where the headpiece had actually left a mark. "You look better, boy. A few days of rest and a few more visits of that healer, and you will fight like a wild jaguar."

Kuini tried to collect his thoughts, but his mind refused to work. He watched the slaves removing the man's cloak, rushing to help him with his sandals.

"Get us some food," said the Aztec, addressing another slave. "Then leave us alone. All of you."

Without the feathered headdress and the cloak, the man looked even more impressive, reflected Kuini reluctantly, watching the strong broad face, the wide, muscled shoulders, the well-developed calves. This was the body of a man used to walking great distances, the body of a younger man. The Warlord's age showed in the wrinkled face, the thinning hair, in the calm, slightly amused wisdom the large eyes reflected. A dangerous bastard, reflected Kuini. But an interesting one.

Food arranged on the low table, the Aztec squatted comfortably.

"I'm famished," he said, snatching a tamale greedily. "Those crafty Acolhua have the tastiest tamales I've ever eaten." He nodded casually. "Help yourself."

Getting up with an effort, his head still reeling, Kuini neared the opposite mat, then hesitated, unsure how to proceed.

"Just drop over there and get to the food, boy. There is no need to make it as ceremonious as an imperial meal."

The tamales did, indeed, taste good. He devoured one, then another, having gone hungry for more than a day now, not counting the tortillas the girl had made him steal. He recalled her black glittering eyes as she beamed at him, happy and proud at his success at stealing the goods. She was here in the Palace too, he thought randomly. Somewhere around.

He forced his thoughts back to the Aztec, feeling the man's thoughtful gaze.

"Well, boy, now that you are not in a danger of dying of hunger, tell me your story."

The tamales suddenly heavy in his stomach, Kuini swallowed. "I... I don't know. What do you want me to tell you?" he hesitated. "Honorable Warlord."

The man's laughed. "No titles, boy. Not yet." He sobered. "Tell me who you are and where you come from. Also, how did they get to this ridiculous idea of your kidnapping a princess?"

"I don't know," said Kuini carefully, addressing the easiest of the questions. He had to think, to think hard, but the thoughts kept rushing around his head like a bunch of panicked squirrels. "I saw this girl and we talked. Then, the next thing I knew the warriors were running, waving their slings."

"Their slings? Why would a warrior attack someone with a sling, unless from a great distance?"

"I don't know." Kuini dropped his gaze, unsettled by the

openly amused doubt reflecting in the crinkling eyes. "But they did. They shot me with their slings."

"On the back of your head, eh?" The Aztec's eyes sparkled victoriously. "It looks to me that you were trying to run away as fast as you could. That would make a warrior grab his sling. But why? Why wouldn't you stay and try to explain?"

"They would never listen."

"Why?"

Forgetting his uneasiness, upset with the insistent questioning, Kuini glared at the older man. "Because they would never listen to a foreigner! You know that too."

The man's grin was wide and satisfied. "Indeed," he said. "You are right. They would never listen to a foreigner." The glimmer in the dark eyes deepened. "So what sort of a foreigner are you?"

Kuini felt the blood leaving his face at once. It made him dizzy, the air around him suddenly thick and difficult to breathe. He took a deep breath.

"I didn't... I didn't mean it that way," he mumbled, staring at the plate of tortillas, his appetite gone.

"Oh, but you did. You are not from Texcoco, in spite of that claim of yours being a boy from Tepanecapan."

"I do live there," he said in desperation, gathering the rest of his strength to meet the man's penetrating gaze. "I should be going there now. My family, they will be worried."

He stared at the smug derisiveness of the broad face, his anger rising. *I don't have to tell you anything,* he thought, hating the sense of helplessness, such an annoying feeling. *If you want to kill me, just do it already and get it over with.*

The gaze of his interrogator softened. "You have guts, boy, and I like that. I need it in my warriors. Most of my personal fighting force is hand-picked, you see? I have access to hundreds of warriors, so I'm at liberty to watch, to pick the best ones, to comprise the elite unit of Tenochtitlan's fighters." He shrugged. "I've yet to see you with weapons, of course. To watch you in all sorts of situations. But I like what I've seen so far. You may be worth the trouble of training you. You are quick, and your instincts are good. Also, you are brave and proud, and you seem to be able to think. Were you older, I would never have trapped you into revealing your lie." The Aztec's grin widened. "But you did. So now you will have to be honest with me. No more lies. Where are you from?"

Unable to take his eyes off the penetrating gaze, Kuini fought the strange urge to tell the truth. Despite his mocking arrogance, the man looked well-meaning and sincere. Yet, he was the leader of the fierce Mexicas, the enemies of his people. But then, Coyotl was also supposed to be his enemy, and they were good friends. He clenched his hands so tight he could not feel them anymore.

"You are really uncomfortable with this thing, aren't you?" The older man's words interrupted his thoughts. "Well, we'll leave it for a moment." The dark eyes narrowed. "Let me see. We will be staying here for a day or two. I'll give a few of my warriors the task of training you, to see what you can do. Then, before we go, I'll decide if you are worthy of my time. If I decide in your favor, you'll be trained to be an elite warrior. But if I decide to let you have this chance, you will have to be completely honest with me and tell me the dark secret of your origins." The man grinned. "It's a strange combination of those tattoos and piercings on such a Tepanec face as yours."

Kuini swallowed, studying the carvings upon the table. "If I want to… leave," he asked, stumbling over the words. "If I want to go home, can I do this?"

The man was taken aback, his eyes widening, puzzled. "What do you mean?"

Kuini bit his lower lip. "Am I a prisoner?" he asked quietly.

"Well," the Aztec shook his head, not amused anymore, "I suppose you are a prisoner as much as it concerns the people of Texcoco. As for us? No. You are not a prisoner. I don't see the sense in holding you among my elite warriors against your will. Too many men would give everything they have, their freedom and their lives, for a chance to be trained as such. I don't need unwilling people." The penetrating gaze grew cold. "You are free to go, boy. I'll even give a few warriors to escort you out of the city, in case those Texcoco Acolhua are still after your blood."

A maid came in, carrying a tray with dishes. The sight of a

sliced meat upon spread tortillas made Kuini's stomach rumble. Yet, he did not dare to reach for the food, the chill in the Aztec's eyes sending waves of alarm down his spine. The man attacked his plate heartily as if nothing else mattered, but his whole being now radiated cold indifference. And danger. *Like sitting next to a large jaguar that had already finished its meal,* he thought. *The one that would not necessarily attack you should you not make any sudden movement.*

He tried to think of something to say. Turning this man's incredibly generous offer down was not a wise thing to do. And it was a tempting offer, too. To be one of the elite warriors of those fierce Aztecs? To be a man praised and feared by all nations around the Great Lake and further to the East and the West?

He ground his teeth. What wild thoughts! Those Aztecs were his people's avowed enemies. Tenochtitlan's priests praised the hearts of his, Kuini's, people above anyone else. The captured Highlanders would be kept alive, to be sacrificed on special occasions, large festivals and celebrations. People like his father, his brothers, his friends, oh, even he himself when older. It was bizarre. He felt the eyes of the Aztec upon him, burning his skin.

"You are a strange cub, you know." The amusement crept back into the man's voice. "Like a caged animal, a young male jaguar, watching the people around with those blazing, haunted eyes, ready to pounce given the slightest chance." The lightly mocking grin was back in place. "I understand that you have just been beaten and tied and wounded, but still. One can relax, from time to time. And something is telling me that you are usually this way."

Kuini returned the man's gaze with an effort. Funny that they should have thought the same things about each other, he reflected randomly.

"You remind me of someone, and I'm trying to remember whom." The sliced meat finished, the man picked up the oily tortilla. "So you said your father was a Tepanec. Or was it your mother?"

Kuini tried to remember, his appetite gone again. "My mother," he muttered.

"A captive? A slave?"

Oh gods, why didn't he develop that story when loitering here the whole morning, thinking how to escape?

"I don't know. She never talked about her past." That's it. That should take care of his whole Tepanec history.

"Yes, the Tepanecs are usually that proud." The man reached for his cup. "So you know nothing of your Tepanec roots."

"No."

"Too bad."

The Aztec resumed his eating, not radiating too much danger anymore.

Kuini dared to lift his gaze. "There will be a war with the Tepanecs, yes?"

The Aztec grinned. "Yes, probably."

"Will Texcoco lose?"

"Well, it's difficult to say. They seem to think they will not." He shrugged. "We'll see. Soon enough, probably."

"But Tenochtitlan will fight too. Will it not?" Kuini glanced up, embarrassed by the open amusement in his older companion's gaze.

"Another thing that remains to be seen. Oh, those Acolhua people lack patience. Their Emperor thinks he can defeat the Tepanecs now, but he should have waited with his declaration of independence. Fancy talking new titles." The corners of the generous mouth lifted in a crooked sort of a grin. "His chances of repulsing the Tepanec invasion are fair, but they would be higher if he had waited. He doesn't know these people. Not the way I do. He thinks it will be enough to throw their warriors back into the Great Lake. But it won't stop another raid, and another. Tezozomoc will never stop, not until he wins. He will conquer Texcoco, if not this summer, then the next. Or the one after that. There is no stopping him. They should have waited until he is dead."

Kuini watched the darkening eyes wandering some remote distance, not noticing their audience anymore.

"My father also thinks that the Tepanecs are unstoppable. He fears their coming to these shores."

The Aztec's gaze focused. "Your father is a wise man. His intuition must be good. Or does he know about the Tepanec Empire more than his son does?"

"I don't know. He seems to know those Tepanecs, somehow. He knows so much about the Lowlands and their history. Even the other side of the Great Lake." Kuini paused to swallow a large chunk of meat. "He is a great leader."

"Leader of whom?"

He felt the meat sticking half way down his throat. Shivering, he gazed at his plate.

The laughter of the Aztec was hearty and unrestrained. "You are a mess, boy." He drank more of the water. "So what about that princess of yours? Who was she?"

"They say she is the First Daughter of the Emperor's Second Wife."

"Oh, the Second Wife. The cause of this whole war. Interesting." Eyes twinkling, the man watched Kuini over the rim of his goblet. "Take my advice, boy. Don't mess around with princesses. They are usually an arrogant lot who will cause you much trouble while giving you no satisfaction."

He remembered the girl, the way they had run up the main road together, with the yells of the incensed tortilla stand owner raging behind their backs.

"She is not like that," he said, then wished to swallow the words back. The mocking eyes of the older man made him wish to break something.

"I got into trouble over a princess too when about your age," said the man. "It was not worth it, believe me."

"Were you accused of kidnapping her?" It was difficult to imagine this dignified old man, the War Leader of the fierce Aztecs, getting into a trouble over a princess. They would give such a man princesses aplenty, should he indicate any willingness. Even the haughty Acolhua ones. This man must have twenty and more wives and concubines.

"Oh no, no kidnapping. But believe me, I was chased all over a palace too, and beaten, and yelled at, and accused of all sorts of things. And that was just the beginning." The grin of the man was irresistible. "Consider yourself getting off lightly."

Kuini stared at the man, fascinated. "Was she the daughter of the Revered Acamapichtli?"

"Oh no." The grin of the man did not waver. "She was the first niece of the Revered Tezozomoc." Laughing, the Warlord shook his head. "Oh yes, that was quite an adventure. You see, we, Tepanecs, are a very haughty lot. They say it about us all over both of the valleys and around the Great Lake. And they are quite correct, if you ask me."

Kuini fought his astonishment, trying not to gape. Eyes wide, he stared at the grinning face, his mind in a jumble. "I don't understand."

"What's there to understand?"

"You just said… you said… You are an Aztec, aren't you?"

The grinning eyes stared at him, sparkling, amused as if satisfied with the effect. "I am. Now, I am an Aztec. I lived in Tenochtitlan for more summers than you have seen. I'm the first Mexica Chief Warlord, appointed by Revered Acamapichtli himself. I've led the glorious warriors of Tenochtitlan for twenty and a half summers. But," one corner of the generous mouth lifted in a crooked grin. "I was born a Tepanec of Azcapotzalco. Before coming to Tenochtitlan, I was the Tepanec elite warrior for enough summers to earn a few scars and some captives." The man shrugged. "It's quite a forgotten past now. Not many people remember my origins. Acamapichtli is dead, and Huitzilihuitl, his successor, does not seem to remember. Or, maybe, he just doesn't want to. Sometimes, I keep forgetting myself."

Eyes wandering the depths of the forgotten past, the man seemed to appear older now, more tired and somehow sad. Kuini watched him, fascinated. The fierce, ruthless Aztec leader was not an Aztec at all. It was impossible to believe. Could it be true? Was this man really a Tepanec? And should those people land on this side of the Great Lake…

"Will you fight the Tepanecs if Tenochtitlan joins this war?" he asked, unable to hold his tongue.

The man looked up, startled. "I will, if I have to. I've been an Aztec leader for too long to let the past stand in my way." The sadness left the wrinkled face as the usual half-mocking twinkle reappeared. "You, with your Tepanec face and this name of yours, brought back such deeply buried memories." He shook his head, chuckling. "And I don't even know whether to thank you or to curse you for that."

Kuini finished his tortilla. "I'm sorry," he said. Then the curiosity got the better of him. "Do you have any family or friends left among the Tepanecs?"

The Aztec shook his head. "No. The people I cherished, my family, my friends, are all dead or scattered." He shrugged unperturbed, but the twinkle in the large eyes died once again. "I wish I knew what happened to them. If no one else, my brother should still be alive."

"Where was he when you last saw him?"

The mocking grin was back. "He was on his way to the wild areas of the highlands beyond Smoking Mountain, would you believe that?"

Smoking Mountain! The Highlands! Kuini's heart squeezed with a sudden longing for home.

But the Tepanecs? No, there were no Tepanecs among the towns and the villages and the people he knew. He tried to think of someone who may look like a Tepanec. No, there were no such people up there. Aside from Father, most didn't even speak the Lowlanders' Nahuatl.

"I hope you will meet your brother one day," he said, curiously unsettled. This Aztec, or Tepanec, was not a bad man.

CHAPTER 6

"The traitorous Aztecs are going to betray us!" called the Emperor's adviser angrily. "They will not send their forces to reinforce ours. They will leave the Acolhua people to fight this war alone and unaided."

Startled, Coyotl almost jumped. Standing beside the Emperor's chair, he listened intently, but the discussions with the warriors' leaders and the advisers had drifted on and on, people coming and going, talking endlessly as the sun slid down the western sky.

He shifted uneasily, his own worry mounting. He hadn't been able to talk to the Emperor privately, although he had tried to do so since the early morning. Iztac's troubles were not taken care of, and when he'd gone to see her, having been released from the official hall for the duration of the morning meal, he had been denied the right to enter her rooms. The slaves guarding the entrance were apologetic but firm. The Second Wife's orders were clear. No one was to see the First Daughter. She was to be kept alone, until her punishment was decided upon.

He ground his teeth. The filthy Second Wife had the right to do that. The girls were their mothers' responsibility. Even being the official heir, Coyotl could not go against her mother, unless permitted by the Emperor. And why would the Emperor pay attention to the troubles of one of his numerous daughters? He had more important things to do. Like preparing for the invasion of the Tepanec Empire that was out to conquer Texcoco.

And then, there was another worry. After the failure to reach his sister, Coyotl rushed out, scaling the well-familiar trail of the Tlaloc Hill. Yet, this trip turned out to be just as fruitless. Kuini was nowhere around their usual meeting place and, worst of all, the hill looked like no one had spent a night there. Had his friend headed home to his Highland town already? Although disappointed, Coyotl found himself wishing that to be the case. Yet, the worry kept nagging. What if his foreign-looking friend had not made it out of the city, after all? He, Coyotl, should not have agreed to leave him there in the marketplace. The Highlander might have gotten into all sorts of troubles, killed in many creative ways, and he wouldn't even hear about it, unless those were official or religious.

He frowned. One trouble at a time. Pressing his lips, he attempted to concentrate back on the Emperor's closest advisers, three elderly men, and their *altepetl*'s Chief Warlord, all four troubled and incensed.

"We can throw the Tepanecs back into the waters of the Great Lake without the help from the uncouth Aztecs," the other adviser was saying. He was a plump, stocky man of great dignity. "After all, what are they if not cheeky newcomers with no history or roots? Their warriors are fierce, but they have no finesse. We can do without them."

"In that case," cried the Chief Warlord hotly, "we will be preparing the invasion of their pitiful island the moment we are done with the Tepanecs. We—"

The Emperor raised his hand, cutting off the passionate speech.

"All of you may be underestimating the problem." The deep voice of Texcoco ruler rang strangely in the dimly lit hall. "What if the Aztecs will be throwing their fate in with the Tepanecs this time?"

A disturbing silence prevailed, and this time, Coyotl had no difficulty concentrating. Heart beating fast, he waited for the rest of the Emperor's speech, his stomach turning.

"What if they choose to reinforce the Tepanec forces?"

"Impossible, oh Revered Emperor," breathed the first adviser amidst the deep silence. "They would never do that."

"And what is to stop them? Their history with the Tepanecs until now is of cooperation and mutual wars and campaigns. Under Acamapichtli they were paying their heavy tribute without a murmur." The Emperor's gaze encircled them, heavy and penetrating. "Huitzilihuitl is craftier. He managed to acquire one of Tezozomoc's favorite daughters as his Chief Wife, and the cunning woman already made the mighty Tepanec Emperor cut the tribute down to fourth of what Tenochtitlan used to pay. Huitzilihuitl is careful not to offend his Tepanec overlords. And yet..." The Emperor paused, chewing his lower lip, his narrowing eyes thoughtful, staring at something indecipherable in the distance. "And yet, under the shiny coating of a perfect contentment, Huitzilihuitl may be cherishing the idea of Tenochtitlan's independence. His Chief Warlord, that unbearably arrogant, audacious man, may not be relating his emperor's entire mood. Or he may be relating his own thoughts, instead. He seems to be sure enough of himself to presume that his own judgment of the situation may be of importance. Acamapichtli has trusted this first Chief Warlord of his too much."

Coyotl watched his father's face, spellbound. Oh, what wisdom! What grasp! Under such an emperor Texcoco could not lose.

"Do you think Huitzilihuitl trusts this man as much as his father did, Oh Revered Emperor?" asked the second adviser, carefully.

The Emperor shrugged. "It is something I would rather have made sure of," he said, deep in thought. "This man may not have as much influence over the current Tenochtitlan's Emperor."

"I heard this Warlord has the Tepanec blood running in his veins," said the third man, who had kept quiet through the whole exchange. "His loyalty may be in doubt, if so."

"Many of our people have Tepanec blood, nobles and commoners alike," said the Texcoco Warlord impatiently. "This man, indeed, looks like a Tepanec, but it would account for nothing."

"I did not say this Aztec Warlord has a Tepanec mother or grandfather," answered the adviser calmly, eyes glittering. "Acamapichtli made this man his first Chief Warlord about twenty summers ago, after the series of successful raids led by this warrior against the southern shores of the Great Lake. Having taken plenty of their floating farms for the benefit of Tenochtitlan, this man was advanced into that exalted position, despite him not being a native of Tenochtitlan. In fact, this man seems to have no Mexica blood in him at all. Acamapichtli was unusually open-minded, his only goal - to advance Tenochtitlan whatever the cost. He didn't mind his Chief Warlord's origins as long as that one served his needs." The stocky man paused, looked up at his Emperor. "Oh Revered Emperor, I hope you forgive me, but yesterday, after listening to the insolent way this man talked to you over the evening meal, I made my point to inquire carefully, not among his warriors, but among his slaves."

The Emperor's eyes narrowed. "What did you find out?"

"This man may have been a full-blooded Tepanec, born in Azcapotzalco. He seems to come to Tenochtitlan already a warrior; an elite one. The Tepanec elite warrior, the owner of the brilliant-blue cloak. Some twenty and a half summers ago, he seemed to move to Tenochtitlan, turning into an Aztec warrior and leader. They say Acamapichtli relied on that man entirely, honoring him to the highest degree. They say he was, indeed, loyal to Acamapichtli, and they think he is loyal to Huitzilihuitl, his successor, as well. And yet..." The man shrugged, his glance shot at the Emperor deepening. "And yet, his loyalty could be doubted now that the first Mexica ruler is dead long since, and the Tepanecs are about to invade our shores."

Another deep silence prevailed, interrupted by a buzzing of insects near the shutters.

"A full-blooded Tepanec raised in Azcapotzalco? An elite warrior?" The Emperor's lips twisted unpleasantly. "That would account for this man's arrogance." The imperial gaze encircled them, heavily leaden, ominous. "Well, what would be your advice, my most trusted advisers?"

"Oh Revered Emperor, forgive me if my advice might be poor, but I think we should make him stay here for a few more dawns," said the first adviser. "And in the meanwhile, we should send a delegation to Huitzilihuitl."

"To complain of the insolence of his War Leader? To beg for his help? To do what?" The Emperor's eyes glittered strangely.

He already knew the answer, reflected Coyotl. But he wanted them to suggest it. To suggest what?

The second adviser licked his lips. "I agree with the advice of my colleague, Revered Emperor. Huitzilihuitl is young. He can be manipulated. He can be weaned off his father's War Leader and his advice. If done subtly, we can drive a wedge between Tenochtitlan's ruler and his Chief Warlord now that this man is here, his influence temporarily removed." The gaze of the man deepened. "If done subtly, the wedge we would drive would stay in place, widening with every passing day. This man's loyalty could be doubted now, with the war against his previous people nearing. His unwillingness to join this campaign is understandable, but his motives are personal, and they are not concerned with Tenochtitlan's welfare." The man shrugged. "Huitzilihuitl is no Acamapichtli. Once his Chief Warlord is removed, he may prove more cooperative."

"Removed, eh?" repeated the Emperor. "So you think that without the influence of this *Tepanec*, Tenochtitlan would join our case?"

"Yes, I think our chances to make them see the rightfulness of our case are greater, oh Revered Emperor."

The Chief Warlord took a deep breath. "The man should be executed for his arrogance," he said stiffly. "When he talked to you the way he did last night, oh Revered Emperor, I had a hard time restraining myself. He should not be allowed to live."

"We cannot execute ambassadors of our friendly neighbors and allies," said the Emperor lightly, but his gaze, resting upon his advisers, clouded. "We can only lodge our complaint with its Emperor, asking him to send here another of his most trusted people. Can we?"

The voice of the third adviser could be barely heard.

"Should something happen to this man while he is here..." The dark gaze dropped. "It would be most embarrassing, but with the war frenzy and so many foreign people around the city... Who knows? If the First Daughter of your Second Wife could be kidnapped in the middle of the day, Revered Emperor, I'm afraid even the Aztec Warlord would not be entirely safe here." He shrugged. "Anything could happen in such times."

Coyotl's heart missed a beat. So the Emperor knew about Iztac, but he thought she was kidnapped. *Oh gods, make him believe it,* he thought, trying to keep his anxiety off his face. *Please, don't let him punish her too severely.*

He watched the Emperor as the man nodded, seemingly unperturbed. "I understand. Please, make sure this man is guarded well. Send some of my most trusted warriors to reinforce his personal guards." The clouded gaze rested upon the adviser. "I trust you, and should you succeed you will be rewarded."

Another momentary silence, almost tangible in its heaviness. Then the Emperor's eyes lost their intensity, shifted to Coyotl.

"Nezahualcoyotl, go to the women's quarters. Tell the Second Wife to come here at once."

Coyotl swallowed. "Can I please talk to you privately, Revered Emperor?"

The cold eyes did not blink. "Not now. Go."

Seething, Coyotl rushed down the corridors, his worry overwhelming. Oh, but Iztac was in trouble, whether the Emperor believed the kidnapping story or not.

What will they do to her? he wondered, his steps heavy, echoing between the plastered walls. He knew the answer to that. Troublesome princesses were married off, hastily and with not much ceremony. She was of age; she would be given away with no additional thought.

Biting his lips, he thought about her sweet heart-shaped face, defiant, mischievous, sparkling with life. Or awash with tears like on the night before, when she worried not about herself, but about some boy she might have gotten in trouble. He clenched his teeth. She was special, and no one saw it, no one but him. There must be a way to help her!

"Honorable Master!" A pretty maid blocked his way, her cheeks blazing with dark red, eyes cast down.

He halted, looking her up and down curiously. "What do you want?"

"Please, Honorable Master. I am to give you this." The girl's hand trembled as she offered him a folded piece of bark-paper.

He took it, puzzled. The paper was small, torn carelessly from a larger piece, the drawing upon it clumsy and unclear. He brought it closer to his eyes, the afternoon light barely reaching the narrow corridor.

"What's this?"

The rough sketch depicted a kneeling figure of a man, probably a warrior judging by the topknot. The strong lines showed the figure's hands, tied behind its back. The head of the warrior was down. Despite the casual way the picture was done, despite the lack of coloring, the kneeling figure looked desperate. Unlike the proud colorful figures his friend had sent him only two days ago.

His heart missed a beat once again.

"Who gave you this?" he rasped, appalled.

The girl's face lost its color, becoming as faded as the picture he held. "I... I... Please, Honorable Master! The boy, he promised you wouldn't be angry."

He made an effort to calm down. "I'm not angry. You did nothing wrong. But tell me quickly. Who gave you this? What did he look like? Where did you see him?"

The maid took a convulsive breath. "I... He was just some boy, all blue with bruises. He said if I give you this you would reward me." She dropped her gaze. "I knew I should not agree."

"Where is he?"

"In the other wing of the Palace."

"He is here in the Palace?"

As the terrified girl took a step back, bumping her head against the wall, Coyotl became aware he was shouting.

"Listen!" He moderated his tone once again. "Just tell me exactly where he is, and I will reward you the way he promised."

"He is in the other... other wing of the Palace. Where the Mexica delegation was placed. The Aztec warriors are guarding him."

"What else?" demanded Coyotl, his head reeling. *How did the*

Aztecs get hold of him? And why would they bring him to the Texcocan Palace? It didn't make any sense.

"That's all," muttered the girl, eyes firm upon the floor. "He just pleaded with me to give you this."

Without a word, he turned around and rushed down the corridor, his heart beating fast. There were many servants going in and out of the various sets of room, but they all scattered out of his way. He didn't notice any of them. *The Aztecs? How had the Aztecs gotten him?* Oh gods, those savages would cut his heart out in a matter of heartbeats.

"What rooms were allocated to the Aztec delegation?" he asked a slave upon reaching the other side of the Palace. How stupid! He should have made the maid show him the way.

"Oh, downstairs, Honorable Master," mumbled the man carefully. "Just down the hall, beside the terrace."

"Take me there!"

The spotted cloaks of the Mexica warriors stood prominently against the whiteness of the plastered wall as the men squatted beside the wide doorway, playing beans.

Coyotl charged toward them. "Where is your master, the Chief Warlord?" he asked, his anxiety helping him to sound imperious.

One of the warriors rose to his feet.

"The Honorable Leader is not here." The man hesitated, measuring Coyotl with a glance. "He went to meet the Acolhua Chief Warlord and some other leaders."

"I want to see his prisoner. Is he here?"

The warriors exchanged quick glances. "What prisoner?"

"The boy he is holding here." Coyotl shoved his way toward the entrance. "Don't try playing games with me. As the Emperor's first son and the heir, the future Emperor of Texcoco, I know everything that is happening in this Palace!" He pushed the wooden screen aside. "And don't you think to follow me in. Stay here and keep your guard."

It came out well. As he entered the richly furnished rooms, he heard them staying behind, curiously subdued.

He crossed the room hurriedly, still finding it difficult to believe he would find his friend here, in the heart of the Palace, guarded by the elite Aztec warriors. Yet, there could be no mistake in the familiar figure squatting in the far corner, near the rectangular opening in the wall, crouching above another piece of bark-paper.

"So you did get my note?" The widely spaced eyes sparkled with amusement, radiating their usual challenging twinkle out of the broad, badly bruised and swollen face.

Coyotl just gaped, studying the marks, the cuts, the large crusted gash upon the wide forehead, another scab crossing the strong chin.

"Yes, I did," he muttered when able to talk. "You wild piece of meat, what happened to you?"

The smile widened. "All sorts of adventures, as you can see. But I did get to see the Palace."

"How? Did they catch you yesterday on the marketplace?" He eyed the sling holding his friend's arm in place, the painfully colorful patterns of bruises upon his limbs and around his ribs, naked except for the loincloth and sandals.

"Well, no. Not exactly. It's quite a long story, really." The smile kept spreading. "You should see yourself now. Staring at me all shocked and indignant, like a virgin shown a big one."

"I thought you were safely on your way home. When I didn't find you on the hill, I thought you just left." He flopped his hands in the air. "Stop laughing. It's not funny. How did you get into this mess?"

"It's a long story, and anyway, I'm on my way out of it, I think. The worst seems to be over."

"Not to me. You are in the Aztecs' hands, under the personal guard of their Chief Warlord. What can be worse than that?"

"Oh, all sorts of things. To be held by your people was far less pleasant, you know. All this colorful mess of my body was their doing, including the broken arm and the open head." He shrugged, still grinning. "Not that those Aztecs are any fonder of me, but their leader thinks I have potential, so they treat me nicely so far."

"The Chief Warlord?"

"Yes, him. A fascinating man."

"An arrogant, cheeky frog-eater!"

"Oh yes, that too," agreed Kuini good-naturedly.

"Did you get to talk to him?"

"Oh yes, quite a lot. He is a talkative one."

"What does he want with you?"

"Well, funnily enough, he seems to want to train me, to get me into his personal unit of warriors." The Highlander shrugged. "Not that I'll do it, but so far he keeps me safe from your people, so I'm not arguing."

"What did my people want to do with you?"

"Oh, they were toying with the idea of stoning me. I was told that this is what probably would happen, after the judge was through with me."

With disbelief, Coyotl eyed the unreserved amusement spilling out of his friend's eyes.

"Listen, if you won't stop making jokes, I'll leave. You don't make any sense, and you seem unable to comprehend the seriousness of your situation. It's not funny. You could be killed twenty times and more. And you are still in a grave danger, whatever that Aztec wants with you."

The pointy eyebrows lifted. "Believe me, I know. I have all these wounds and the broken arm to prove the seriousness of my situation. But whether it makes sense or not, I'm telling you the truth. I was led to the court upon the Plaza when that Aztec interfered. In this typical, arrogant way of his, I must say. But he did interfere and here I am, not stoned and even treated by a healer."

Coyotl squatted upon the same mat. "Why did they take you to the court? Why would they want to stone you? It's a punishment reserved for special crimes against the Palace and the royal family." He frowned. "A foreigner like you would be just strangled or handed over to the priests."

"Oh, that." The amusement was back in place. "I'm no foreigner, just to let you know. They all kept assuming I'm a Tepanec. The Tepanec boy from that district called Tepanecapan here in Texcoco. At some point, I became convinced of that myself. It felt safer."

Against his will, Coyotl grinned. "I told you that you looked like a Tepanec." He frowned. "It still does not explain the judge and the stoning."

"Oh, this part made the least sense of all. They said I kidnapped a princess. Imagine that!" Kuini's eyebrows jumped up again. "I talked to that girl on the Plaza. A nice girl. Very good looking. And the next thing I knew those warriors were upon us, dragging her away, beating me up, and when I came back to my senses, I was accused of kidnapping the princess." His grin wavered. "What? Why are you staring at me like that?"

"So it was you!" Coyotl tried to remember. At one point, he did suspect that it might be his friend, but then she said he was a Tepanec and that he called himself differently. Oh gods! "She told me that boy was a Tepanec and I didn't think. But of course—"

Suddenly, the broad face lost any trace of amusement. "What did she say?" The dark eyes sparkled dangerously. "Did the filthy *cihua* accuse me?"

Coyotl gasped, startled by his own surge of an overwhelming rage.

"She tried to tell them all you were not to blame," he hissed through his clenched teeth. "She called me in the middle of the night trying to make me go and save you. I didn't know she was talking about you, otherwise I would have done as she asked. But if you ever call her 'filthy *cihua*' again, I swear I'll kill you myself, and I'll take great pleasure in doing it!"

Trembling, he stared at the bruised face, seeing the uncertainty creeping into the dark eyes.

"Oh, I thought for a moment..." Kuini shrugged, dropping his gaze. "Sorry. I know she is anything but a filthy *cihua*."

A silence prevailed. Coyotl took a deep breath, trying to calm himself. "Forget it." He stared at the plastered wall. "Let us think how to get you out of here."

"Well," Kuini shrugged, grimacing with pain. "The damn arm," he muttered. "Listen, I think I can manage. I'll stay with this Aztec for a few dawns, until he has to go back. By then, I'll be much better, the arm and the head, with more chances of making my way home safely. It won't be difficult if he takes me out of the

Palace on his way to Tenochtitlan. Plenty of opportunities to go away. He says I'm not a prisoner. He told me I can go any time."

"And you trust him?" It was Coyotl's turn to lift his eyebrows. "Never trust an Aztec, particularly this one."

"Why this one in particular?"

"He is an arrogant bastard, ruthless and unpredictable. He has had this reputation for summers." Coyotl shrugged. "But maybe he is not destined to walk this Fifth World any longer."

Will they truly try to kill this man while here in Texcoco? he wondered suddenly, remembering the council held in the main hall. That could be a good solution to the cheeky old bastard, even if an unusual one.

"Listen," he said. "Let me try to smuggle you out of here. I think I can organize it after the next dawn or so. I should never have left you in the marketplace yesterday. It was stupid of me."

He saw his friend's smile flickering, open, unguarded.

"Oh well, I suppose I didn't think straight today. This Aztec, he is an interesting man, but you are right, I should get away from all of them." He grinned. "Thank you. You are a real friend."

"I was the one to get you into this mess, remember?" said Coyotl, embarrassed.

"Oh, yes." The twinkle crept back into the large eyes. "But it was interesting nevertheless. Bored I was not. And the Great Pyramid and the scrolls were well worth all of it and more."

"I'll let you visit here safely, for as long as you would like," said Coyotl gruffly, unsettled. "You'll be the most honored guest here the moment I'm the Emperor. Free to go wherever you like, to read every scroll, to enter every temple, to live in the best guests quarters of the Palace." He rose to his feet. "You'll get to tour the whole city in a litter, and the army of your bodyguards would be busy moving the crowds out of your way."

"Sounds good." The widely-spaced eyes did not twinkle, looking at him, holding a smile. "I'll make an offering for your people to win this war, so these times will come soon." He sighed. "I wish I could join you in the fighting."

"Maybe you will. Maybe your father will agree to send his warriors." Coyotl shook his head. "I'll be off now, to see what can be done. Stay low, and don't make the Aztec angry in the meanwhile."

Awkwardly, the Highlander got to his feet, clutching a piece of paper in his good arm.

"Will you give her this?" he asked, eyes avoiding Coyotl's questioning gaze. "The girl, the princess. I promised to send her a note. Before it all happened." The apprehensive gaze straightened. "Would you give her that if you see her?"

Coyotl hesitated, but only for a heartbeat. "I'll try to do that. She is being punished too, and no one can see her. Another prisoner in the other wing of the Palace, but on the second floor. I'll try to give it to one of her maids." He saw the frown, the concern in the dark eyes, and it puzzled him. "What happened between you two?"

The broad face closed. "Nothing. She was just nice and I promised her that."

Coyotl shook his head. "Funny that she liked you. We always thought alike, her and me. And she is quite a girl, I can tell you." He shrugged. "Don't fall in love with her, though. She'll be given away soon, hopefully to a nice man, but it surely will be a ruler or a very exalted nobleman."

CHAPTER 7

Unable to sleep, Kuini turned over once again, then buried his head under the blanket. What riches, he thought, relishing the touch of the soft cotton. The slaves who had come to prepare the outer room for the night had given him the expansive blanket with no second thought, along with a few pretty, colorful cushions. Unbelievable!

Yet, despite all the softness, he could not sleep. His body hurt, his head throbbed and the wooden planks fastened to his arm annoyed him.

He sat up, watching the sleeping warriors. The dull ache in his hand was neither better nor worse than before. The healer maintained it was cracked, but Kuini doubted the verdict. Being a highlander, he'd seen his share of broken limbs, remembering people twisting with pain or losing consciousness. Or screaming, shaming themselves. He shivered, recalling the sight of sharp, splinted bones peeking out of a bloody mess. No, his arm was damaged, but not broken. He could do without the stupid splint.

It took him what seemed like ages to release the ties. With no planks, his arm felt ridiculously light. Making no sound, he got onto his feet, watching the sleeping figures curled all around.

The moonlight streamed in through the large opening in the wall. He made his way there, treading carefully, aware of the warriors guarding the main entrance and the Chief Warlord sleeping in the next, very private and richly furnished, inner room. The bushes outside the window rustled gently, not far below, just a small jump. Grimacing with pain, he made it over the edge.

Landing carefully, he still felt the impact as it sent shafts of pain up his neck. Damn it, he thought, enraged. He would never make it anywhere with his wounds. He touched the bandage with his palm, then stood for a while, pondering. *What did he intend to do?* He had gone over the window on an impulse, thrilled with being unwatched for a change. But was it wise to try to run away? Would he make it over the Palace's wall?

Breathing the sweet night air, he relished the silence around him. He could take a careful walk, then climb back through that window, should no unguarded openings in the Palace's wall happen on his way.

Where was the other wing of this vast structure?

Sneaking behind the line of carefully planted trees, he felt more at ease. Here the shadows were deeper, the silvery moonlight not reaching through the thick branches, the torches – just a distant flickering. Walking the approximate line of the Palace, he turned when it seemed to be paralleled to the far edge of the building, and then made his way along the outer wall.

Ears pricked, senses sharp, he listened intently. To venture out of the trees and their safety was unwise. He should go back. It was insane to sneak around the Palace when its inhabitants were still after his blood. Should he get caught, he would be done for, this time for certain. He shivered, then shrugged and went out carefully, running along the open patch of the moonlit ground. Crouching behind the bushes, he relaxed a little. The Palace looked dark, unfriendly, glaring down at him, the cheeky intruder. Yet, one rectangular opening on the second floor flickered with a faint torchlight, glimmering kindly, invitingly. *The other wing. The second floor.*

He shrugged, but his heartbeat accelerated. What were the chances of this opening being hers? None, none at all. And anyway, no princess would be awake in the middle of the night, keeping a torch alive and blazing. Not the First Daughter of the Second Wife surely.

The wide-branched tree swayed in a comfortable proximity. He sneaked toward it, deep in thought. He could climb it and take a look with no one the wiser. Then he would go back into the safety of the Aztecs' quarters.

With only one good hand, it took him a long time to reach the higher branches, his damaged arm throbbing with pain, his breath coming in gasps. He tried to peer into the lit opening, but it was too far to see clearly.

Making it as close as he could, he crawled along the wide branch, clinging to it with all his might. An easy feat, but not with his stupid injuries, he thought, grinding his teeth, wincing with pain as the coarse bark brushed against his grazed limbs.

A silhouette moved and he froze, clinging to his slippery perch. Someone was crouching, probably on a mat, and now got up and moved about. A slender arm shot out, threw something against the wall.

His breath caught, he narrowed his eyes, peering through the darkness. The movement seemed familiar, yet he could not tell for certain, no matter how he strained his eyes. *Come on,* he thought. *Just come to the stupid opening.*

The figure sat there motionless for a while, then rose to her feet. Yes, definitely a woman. A young one. He thought he had recognized her abrupt, purposeful movements. She indeed neared the window, but then turned back, kicking something on her way, judging by the motion of her hips.

He slid his good arm up the branch, picking a small greenish fruit. It was difficult to direct his throw, clinging to the slippery bark with his damaged limb. The first fruit bounced off the wall, but the second went through.

He saw her jumping to her feet, stumbling over something. Oh yes, that must be her. He threw another fruit.

This time she reached the window, leaning out, peering into the darkness. Another missile went flying before he waved carefully, nearly losing his hold on the branch. He could hear her gasping, then putting a palm over her mouth.

Her next move startled him. With no hesitation, she pulled her skirt high and went over the windowsill. Eyes wide, he watched her long shapely legs finding the ledge, standing on it firmly, hands gripping the bulging stones of the wall. There was no clumsiness about her anymore. Like a small elegant lizard, graceful and full of confidence, she went down the wall as if she had done it before.

Stomach fluttering with anticipation, he climbed down hastily, not as graceful, or as fast, as she was. When his feet reached the wet grass, she was already there, eyes sparkling in the moonlight. Peering at him closely, she gasped, but again clasped her mouth with her palm, grabbing his arm with another, pulling him into the protectiveness of the darkness behind the trees.

His head reeled as he trailed after her, not understanding any of it. One moment he was on the tree, trying to see her through the only opening with a light, unsure of himself but protected; the next she was beside him, having scaled the wall in the most un-princess-like fashion, dragging him after her with the determination of a war leader. The strangeness of it enveloped him, made his skin prickle.

Deep in the safety of the Palace's gardens, she halted and turned around. In the darkness he could see only the soft outline of her face, the dark sparkle of her eyes, the black mass of her hair, now pulled up with many glittering pins and not sticking out everywhere and covered with dust.

"You shouldn't come here. It's too dangerous for you," she whispered breathlessly, her face so close he could smell the sweetmeats on her breath. "How did you manage to escape them?"

"I didn't," he said, trying to think straight, fighting the dreamlike sensation, fighting the urge to pull her closer. "I'm still a prisoner here."

"Oh, so am I." She giggled. "Two escapees."

"Did they punish you for running around the city?"

"Well, no. Not yet. But I'm locked in my rooms until they decide, and it's a real punishment. I hate being locked in the room!"

"But why? Didn't they blame me for kidnapping you?"

"Oh yes, they did!" He saw her frowning in the darkness, her eyebrows meeting each other across the smoothness of her forehead. "I tried to tell them, but no one listened to me. Only my brother, and I don't know if it helped."

"It doesn't matter," he said, warmed by her open worry. "I'm good now. But I don't understand why they blame you, if they already blamed me."

"Oh, I don't know. One can never understand these people. Everything they do is complicated and always to reach this or that goal. They must have a reason, but meanwhile, both of us are stuck here." Her frown deepened as she reached for his forehead. "They hurt you so! I can see it even in the darkness."

The touch of her fingers made him shiver, sending waves of excitement down his stomach.

"It's nothing," he said gruffly. "It'll pass."

"I'm so sorry. I tried to stop them." Her voice trembled. "They are beasts, every one of them. All the warriors. Why do they always have to be so... so aggressive, so bad-tempered, so cruel?"

That made him laugh. "That's what warriors do. I'm trained to be a warrior, too. You can't fight wars by being all cozy and soft."

"But you are not like that. You wouldn't hurt anyone who is not another warrior." She frowned. "I mean women, or children, or old people."

"I suppose not, but who knows?" He shrugged. "Remember the Aztec leader? You told me he is ruthless and cruel, your brother told me he is an arrogant bastard, but he was the one who saved me, for no reason at all. I should be dead by now. Your people wanted to execute me this morning, but he interfered." He peered at her. "You see what I mean? People are not always what we think they are. I never thought this way before, but now I do. He may be a bad man, but I don't see this side of him, and not because he saved me. I watched him and we talked." He shrugged again. "Maybe when I'm that old, they'll say bad things about me too, and maybe I'll be guilty of some of it."

She was peering at him, wide-eyed. "You talk strange, you know?"

He wanted to hit himself. What was he talking about? "Forget it."

"No, it was interesting. Strange and unsettling, but interesting. Fascinating. I wish we could talk more." Her face brightened. "And I received your note! Oh, how well you draw!"

He smiled, his pride welling. "Glad you liked it."

"Oh, I'll keep it until I'm very old! Those two people eating tortillas, oh what a beautiful drawing. I looked at this note, and I sent my maid to fetch me a tortilla with avocado right away, your drawing made me that hungry. And you know what?" She drew closer, peering at him, so near again he could smell her breath, sense the warmth of her body. "It was not as good as back on the marketplace. I have to get back there, to taste those tortillas again. They were incredible. Will you take me there sometime?"

He tried to concentrate, his thoughts rushing around, chasing each other with no consideration to his will.

"Yes, I will," he mumbled. "Somehow."

She beamed at him. "When?"

"I don't know. When can you get away again without them noticing?"

Her face fell and he sensed more than saw her elation evaporating. "Probably never."

Curiously unsettled, he tried to see her face. "Never is a long time. They won't be angry with you for that long. They'll drop their guard some time." As she kept staring at the ground, it felt only natural to put his hand under her chin in order to lift it. "You got away now. You are out here, see? You'll be able to do it again. What can they do to you after all? They can't kill you or even hurt you, I guess. You are a princess."

Her eyes glistened in the dim moonlight that managed to penetrate the thick foliage, the unshed tears held back stubbornly. She was not about to cry. No, not her.

"They will give me away soon," she said. "That way they can get rid of me and the nuisance I've always been."

"Give away? What do you mean? Where?"

"I don't know where, but I'm sure it won't be the place I would want to be." She shrugged, yet did not try to take her face away from his hands, still gazing at him, the enormous eyes glittering with a deep misery. "If not an appropriate ruler or emperor, then someone else, somewhere. All those noblemen are only too eager to add a princess to their collection of wives."

His heart twisted, remembering what Coyotl had said. She was destined for an emperor or a nobleman. But what sounded acceptable coming from his friend, looked like unnecessary cruelty, an unworthy punishment, coming off her lips. The sadness in her eyes tore at his chest.

"It won't be that bad," he said, pulling her closer with no additional thought. He just wanted to comfort her.

Yet, the feel of her body made his limbs tremble with tension; his nerves as tight as overstretched bowstrings. He saw her eyes changing. They still glittered like polished obsidian, but now there was additional glow to them. Her face shone at him, surprised and expectant, the moonlight sliding down the soft curve of her cheeks, inviting to touch it, to explore with his fingers.

He did just that, shivering with the sensation of the smooth softness under his fingertips. Her body tensed against his, but she did not make an effort to move away. She just kept staring at him, her bottomless eyes wide open as if mesmerized.

Her lips were slightly open and they felt soft against his. The uncertainty over, he pressed her closer, oblivious to the pain around his ribs. His body seemed to behave as if of its own accord, his hands seeking, lips demanding, making hers open further, not satisfied with the simple touch.

He had kissed girls from time to time, and there was that girl who had lain with him on the day before he left. Yet, never had his body been so demanding, so independent, so aware of the need. His mind, which always seemed to be controlling his actions, now just let go, went blank, gave up on the effort to control anything. His body was the one to set the tone now, commanding, claiming what was rightfully his.

Head reeling, he felt her body reacting, clinging to his, pressing closer, her lips opening, seeking, demanding too. The world around them swayed, blurred, disappeared. There was no Palace anymore, and no gushing *altepetl* outside its walls, no Great Lake and no Smoking Mountain. There was nothing but the sensation of their bodies pressed against each other and their mouths exploring, seeking, asking for more.

Their lips broke apart, but they didn't let each other go. Breathing heavily, he stared deeply into her eyes. The sounds of the breeze and the rustling trees began to return. Shutters screeched some distance away. Muffled voices neared.

He pressed her tightly, afraid to breathe. The footsteps on the nearby path were soft and careful. His hunter's instincts told him that there were three people out there, walking up the path, being careful to conceal their presence.

His eyes warned her to keep quiet, but she seemed in no need of such a warning. She was hardly breathing, her body tense against his touch, like a graceful animal, long legged and strong, ready to flee at the first alarm. He knew if she ran, she'd do it as elegantly, as efficiently, as she had been when climbing the wall. The clumsy girl from the marketplace was no more.

When the footsteps died away, they breathed again.

"That was close," she whispered, voice trembling with laughter, not afraid in the least.

He watched her glittering eyes, back to her mischievous self, his disappointment vast. The magic was gone. She pulled away and busied herself with her hair, fighting the glittering pins.

"Next time I come out to meet you, I'll make sure my hair is free of these pins," she said, beaming at him. "You messed up my hair."

He shrugged, angry, yet not understanding exactly why.

"What's wrong?" She came closer and peered at him, her excitement gone. "Was it the kiss? Did I kiss badly?"

"That was the best kiss I've ever had," he said, pulling her back, his mood improving.

She was still frowning. "You are only saying that to make me feel better." There was a childish, petulant tone to her voice now, and it made him laugh.

"You don't believe me? Then let me see again." He pushed her face up, despite her mild resistance. This time the kiss was not as breathtaking, but the sweetness was still there, making his body tremble with excitement. He felt her lips reacting, opening. It made his head spin.

Breathing heavily, they faced each other.

"See?" he whispered. "It was not a bad kiss."

Her eyes sparkled. "Will you meet me here again tomorrow

night?"

"Yes."

"Then I suppose we had better go back, before our captors notice that their caged birds flew out." But she made no effort to move away, snug in his embrace.

"You are not a bird," he said. "The way you climbed this wall, you would make a graceful lizard. A slender, exquisite serpent made out of gold."

He fought the urge to kiss her again, finding it difficult to restrain his hands from going under her blouse, the desire to explore her body overwhelming. Why wasn't she a simple village girl, just like that girl in his hometown, who had came out and lain with him with no additional fuss. Was he to go away satisfied with a kiss only? To meet her the next night for more kisses?

"We should go," he said, pulling away, busying himself with re-arranging his loincloth, embarrassed under her scrutinizing gaze.

"Have you done it with a girl before?" she asked, watching him, unabashed.

He turned away, angry with the amused curiosity her whole being radiated. "And you?"

"No, of course not! I haven't kissed before, either. We are not allowed to do these things."

He laughed. "You are doing many things that you are not allowed. Come, I'll take you back under your window. Can you climb it up as easily as down?"

"Yes, of course. I'm good at climbing. I always beat my brother to any wall or a treetop. When we were children we used to run around all the time." She sighed. "But since he has become an official heir, he has no time for me anymore."

"You must have plenty of other brothers and sisters."

"Not like him. I hate the rest of my family. And I hate this Palace, too. I had the best time ever on the marketplace with you."

"I'll take you there again, I promise," he said, the cavity in his stomach growing.

She turned to face him, eyes shining. "But before that, come to meet me here tomorrow, right after midnight."

He watched her climbing expertly, making it look like an easy feat. Her shapely shins shone in the dimming moonlight. When she disappeared behind her window, he still stood there, his thoughts rushing about.

The moon had dimmed considerably when he reached the other side of the Palace, craving to crawl back under the soft cotton blanket he had thrown away so impatiently some time ago. On the other side, many shutters were open, gaping darkly into the freshness of the night. He counted them, trying to remember which one he had left earlier tonight.

When he was about to charge through the open patch of a moonlit ground, his heart missed a beat, then froze. A silhouette moved along the wall, bending slightly, wearing only a loincloth and holding a knife, out and ready in its right palm. A curt gesture and another shadow separated from the darker side of the bushes, then another.

Kuini stopped breathing, pressing behind the thick trunk of a tree. Peeking out carefully, he saw the men crossing the moonlit patch, running hastily, making no sound. Under the wall opening next to the one he was supposed to climb back, they halted, catching their breath, regrouping.

The first man kept gesturing and one of his companions nodded, then took his knife between his teeth. Grabbing the bulging stones under the opening, the man pulled himself up quickly, effortlessly. For a heartbeat he poised on the ledge, peering into the room.

Kuini swallowed, his mouth dry. The opening in the wall had clearly led to the Aztec leader's richly furnished quarters. *Where the man slept alone, his warriors guarding the entrance or sleeping in the next room.*

He calculated fast. He could not reach it in time, and he could not do much against the obviously well prepared group of warriors. There was only one thing to do.

Eyes searching the ground, he rushed forward, picking up a large stone. Aiming as he ran, blessing the gods for leaving him his right arm good and useful, he hurled his missile straight through the gaping opening the moment the first man disappeared into its darkness.

Something fell, clattering. A sound of shattering pottery filled the night. The other man, already hanging upon the ledge, turned around, startled. As the third one, still upon the ground, rushed toward him, Kuini darted back into the protective darkness of the trees.

He didn't run in the direction he had come from, but turned to his left as if about to circumvent the Palace. The rasping breathing of his pursuer followed, growing nearer and nearer. Darting aside, he snatched another stone, slipping on the wet ground, but regaining his balance in time to duck the thrust of a knife.

A heavy hand grabbed his shoulder, but he twisted out of its grip, and while his attacker launched himself onto him, Kuini's right hand came out, the sharp edges of the stone hurting his palm. It smashed against the man's temple, and he winced at the sharp pain the blow sent up his arm.

His pursuer collapsed as if cut. Not wasting his time, Kuini fought the overwhelming urge to lean against a nearby tree. Out of breath, heart pounding insanely, he rushed back toward the Aztecs' quarters, anxious to reach them before the inhabitants of the Palace arrived.

He could hear noises. Many people talked excitedly as he pulled himself up the windowsill, but their voices died all at once. He didn't have time to see what was happening. Strong hands pulled him in, slamming him against the wall. His panic welling, he fought their pinning grip, then felt the sharp obsidian pressing against his throat.

"Wait!" he screamed.

Sweat rolled into his eyes, and he blinked, trying to see the broad face thrust into his view. The pressure of the knife lessened.

"Wait for what, little brat?" rasped the familiar voice. "Eh? Wait for your friends to come and help you?"

The face of the Aztec leader was barely recognizable, twisted with rage, smeared with sweat and blood, his cheekbone cut and still bleeding, his warrior's lock askew.

Kuini tried to stifle a cough. Unable to speak, he squirmed to ease away from the pressure of the knife, but the crushing grip upon his shoulder tightened, making his bones crack. The obsidian pressed harder. He could feel it nicking his skin.

"What do you have to say for yourself?"

He could not get enough air, but as the room swung, the pressure lessened again.

"Speak! What were you doing outside? Who were those people?"

He swallowed, trying to moisten his throat to make it work. "I saw people... they were outside..." He swallowed again. "I threw the stone."

"What stone?"

The pressure of the knife disappeared, and if not for the hand crushing his shoulder, he would have collapsed to the floor, his trembling legs unable to support him.

"The one that broke something in your room," he whispered.

The well-spaced eyes narrowed. "Come with me," tossed the man curtly, pulling away.

Kuini drew a convulsive breath, then another. It took him all his strength to straighten up, to walk after the Aztec, swaying, but holding on. As the warriors moved away, the hostility of their gazes followed him, burning his skin.

They entered the next room and, in spite of himself, he gasped, eyeing the terrible mess of broken pottery and shattered furniture. A low table lay overturned, and a half smashed podium covered a pile of torn mats and cushions, sprinkled with blood. The walls were covered with crimson as well.

His stomach turned as his gaze brushed past all these, lingering upon a dismembered body, aghast. On the raids that he had been allowed to follow for the past two summers, he had seen dead people, had encountered skulls that had been smashed to a pulp, broken bones, opened stomachs. Yet, never a bloody mess like the one he saw now. The man, or what was left of him, had been hacked into so many pieces that his flesh was literally splattered across the room.

His gaze drifted to the obsidian sword, still clutched tightly in the broad hand of the Aztec leader. What a marvelous, lethal weapon!

"Here!" A cup thrust into his hands. "Drink."

He drank it, ridiculously grateful, relishing the sensation of the clear water running down his tortured throat.

"Now tell me what happened. Why were you out there? Who were those people?"

Kuini met the dark gaze. "I went outside earlier," he whispered, then cleared his throat. "I couldn't sleep and I... I wanted to take a walk. Maybe to run away." He shrugged, wincing at the pain in his shoulder. "You told me I'm not a prisoner here."

The corner of the generous mouth lifted in a hint of a grin. "There are ways to go away. And no, those do not include running in the middle of the night or coming back with a bunch of dirty killers." The smile disappeared. "What happened next?"

"I came back and saw people crouching beneath your window." He paused. "Actually, when I think of it, I saw them earlier too, passing the other wing of the Palace, the opposite one. But I didn't pay them attention back then."

"Busy doing what?" The amused twinkle was back, glittering in the depths of the large eyes.

"Nothing."

"Go on."

Kuini took a deep breath, his throat still hurting. "I saw those people coming under your window. They were talking with signs. One went up, then the other. I threw a stone, to smash something, to wake you up. Then I ran, because the one who didn't go in ran after me. When I got rid of him, I came back here." He shrugged again. "I didn't want those Texcoco people laying their hands on me again. Without your protection, I suppose, they would still want to go on and execute me." His tiredness overwhelming, he slid against the wall, sitting on the floor, hugging his knees. "That's the whole story, and you can kill me if you don't believe me. I don't care anymore."

The dark gaze bore at him for another heartbeat.

"Rest here for a while."

As the heavy steps disappeared, he felt safe enough to shut his eyes, his limbs heavy, head spinning, throat hurting. The smell of death enveloped him, penetrating his nostrils with every breath. Such a stench!

He let the dizziness take him, loll him into a dreamless slumber, too tired to try to drag himself into the other room, which was full of people who had hated his guts, anyway.

CHAPTER 8

"What is the world coming to?"

The Emperor shook his head, reaching for a goblet that the servants rushed to fill with more *octli*. Sipping the spicy beverage, the heavyset man leaned back, comfortable upon his high, cushioned chair. "Despicable lowly murderers in the heart of my Palace. Difficult to comprehend!" The impenetrable gaze rested upon his guest, calm, perfectly composed.

"Oh, yes. I won't deny it. Even my warriors were surprised." The Aztec reached for his plate, his appetite seemingly not corrupted by the night's events that made the Palace agog with rumors.

Coyotl watched both men, fascinated, marveling at his father's calmness and the Aztec's ominous tranquility. The foreigner – Aztec or Tepanec – sat there as imposing, as arrogant, as always, eating heartily, conversing idly, unperturbed. But for a fresh cut upon his cheek and the scratches and bruises on his chest and upper arms, clearly visible under his spotted cloak, one might have assumed that no killers had tried to murder him in his sleep.

"The war with the Tepanecs will be over soon," said the Emperor, seemingly as unperturbed; yet Coyotl saw the dark shadows in his father's eyes, the thinly clasped lips. "After we finish them off, our lives will return to their normal state."

"What are your sources saying?" inquired the Aztec casually, devouring another tamale. "Does Tezozomoc plan on moving his forces any time soon?"

"He would do better coming here with no delay." The Emperor shrugged. "Otherwise my warriors would have to spend their time crossing the Great Lake."

The Aztec's eyebrows rose. "Oh, that would be an interesting development."

"Indeed." The Emperor drank more *octli*. "Maybe this would convince our worthwhile neighbors and allies to join our rightful war against the oppressor."

"It may happen," agreed the Aztec placidly, eyes blank. "I will be happy to relay your message when I reach Tenochtitlan." He picked his cup up. "I will be sorry to leave the hospitality of your Acolhua Capital."

"Oh, there is no need to hurry. It will take time to compose my message to my brother Revered Huitzilihuitl."

The Aztec's eyes narrowed. "How long will it take?" he asked somewhat abruptly.

"A few dawns." The Emperor's smile was wide and amiable. Exaggeratedly so, reflected Coyotl, watching his father. Oh, the Emperor longed to show the insolent Aztec. Or the Tepanec. Which one was this man?

"I would never dare to hurry the Revered Emperor," he heard the Aztec saying. "But I planned to be on my way this afternoon."

"So soon?" exclaimed the Emperor. "Oh, no. We could not let our guests leave in such a hurry. It's not every day we are honored with a visit of the most prominent warriors' leader of Tenochtitlan. You will have to stay for a little longer, Honorable Warlord."

The polite platitudes went on, as Coyotl listened, finding it hard to suppress a smile. Now the Aztec seemed to lose some of his appetite. Lips tight, eyes dark, he didn't go on arguing, but his concentration seemed to wander as the conversation turned back to politics.

Oh, the man understood it too well. He wouldn't get out of Texcoco easily, without committing himself to anything more tangible than a politely spoken words or a haughtily given advice. The arrogant bastard was trapped.

Coyotl's thoughts wandered to the meeting in the Emperor's private chamber prior to the morning meal. He remembered how thrilled he had been, summoned along with the closest advisers, making his way through the brightly lit corridors, still foggy with morning chill.

Yet, the meeting had been anything but merry. Furious with his most trusted adviser, the Emperor was snappy and prone to anger. The failed attempt on the Aztec leader was likely to turn into a great embarrassment. Either you succeed or you don't do this at all, was the great ruler's message, related through many flowery words. The adviser had been sent away in disgrace, while the rest of those present were informed curtly that the Tepanec forces, now definitely on the move, would most likely cross the Great Lake in a market interval or so. Couriers went running, and more of the war leaders were sent out to organize the warriors and to hurry the reinforcements.

Amidst all the excitement, Coyotl was informed that he would have to tour the provinces in a hurry, to rally the warriors.

"Nezahualcoyotl, you will go with the delegations," said the Emperor, eyeing his son almost kindly. "You have a market interval, no more than two, to bring back as many warriors as you can. I trust you with this mission. Do not disappoint me."

To go out as an official representative of the Capital? Oh, but for such a chance. Under his welling excitement, Coyotl lowered his gaze.

"I will not disappoint you, Revered Emperor. I thank you for your trust." He hesitated. "What about Tenochtitlan? Shall I go there as well?"

"No," said the Emperor thoughtfully. "The Aztecs problem will be solved differently." The heavyset man grinned and lifted his eyebrows. "Huitzilihuitl could use another wife of exalted origins. It will add some glamour to this dismal palace of his."

Coyotl felt his stomach tightening. "Not the First Daughter surely..." He swallowed, his voice trailing off.

"Yes, the First Daughter. She is suitable, of an age, and her blood is impeccable on both sides. Why, she could even rival Huitzilihuitl's Chief Wife, Tezozomoc's daughter. Her blood is as good, and her temper could prove an advantage. I heard Tezozomoc's daughter is wild enough."

"But Iztac-Ayotl is so young, and she deserves to be a chief wife, not a minor one," mumbled Coyotl, knowing he had no right to argue. She could have done worse, all things considered.

The Emperor's brows climbed higher. "Nezahualcoyotl, did I ask for your advice?"

"No, Revered Emperor."

"Then go. Attend the morning meal, then spend your time preparing your journey. I want you to go out tomorrow at midday, escorted by two times twenty of warriors."

And now, watching the Aztec's darkening face, Coyotl could not wait for the morning meal to be over. He had to talk to her and with no delay. It had to come from him, softened and presented as pleasantly as possible. She would be shocked badly as it was.

He frowned. On the positive side, Huitzilihuitl, the Aztec emperor, was still relatively young, a man that had seen no more than thirty summers, a kind and considerate person as rumor had it. On the other hand, Tenochtitlan's ruler had a dominant Chief Wife, the daughter of the mighty Tezozomoc. She was the one responsible for the considerably lessened tribute, having pleaded with her powerful father. She had given Huitzilihuitl an heir, a healthy boy of some summers, and was rumored to rule Tenochtitlan alongside her husband.

Would his wild, free-spirited, childish sister prosper in such a household? He grew uneasy at the troublesome thought, knowing the answer. She would not. If she was unhappy now, she would be a thousand folds unhappier in Tenochtitlan.

When the meal had finally ended and he was bidden to go, he made his way slowly down the corridors, his steps heavy. How should he break his news to her? Also he had to check on Kuini, another matter that could tolerate no delay. Could he take his friend along? To go out and travel the provinces would be enjoyable for both of them, and the Highlander would have every opportunity to leave for home whenever he wished to do so. He breathed with relief. One good turn.

"I want to see the First Daughter," he said to the slave guarding the entrance of the women's quarters. Frowning when the man hesitated, he barked imperiously. "Take me in now! This matter cannot wait."

Her maid squatted in the outer room, spinning a cotton thread. Surprised, she scrambled to her feet. "Oh, Revered First Son. It's such a pleasure to see you!"

"Where is she?" he demanded.

The woman's broad face spread in a wider smile. "She is still asleep. I checked on her only a little while ago."

"Still asleep?" cried out Coyotl. "What did she do all night?"

The woman shrugged, her narrow eyes crinkling with laughter. "You know how she is. Doesn't like sleeping at nights. Such a pretty, wild thing."

His heart squeezed, but he made an effort to stay calm. He had to be cheerful, for her sake. He had to make her see the positive side of it.

"Wake her up. I have to talk to her, urgently."

The woman frowned, but went in without an argument. He squatted on the mats, watching the room, taking in the pottery bowls, utensils, and spinning facilities scattered around low tables and podiums in cheerful disarray. Oh, but she was incurable. So boyish, so unfeminine. His grin wavered as he thought of her in Tenochtitlan, an exalted second or a third wife. Would she be allowed to bring her maids along?

Disheveled, she sailed out of the other room, her face puffy, undecorated gown askew. "You just had to wake me up, eh?" she demanded, eyes dancing, lips quivering with a smile.

He looked her up and down.

"You look greatly refreshed, oh Iztac-Ayotl, the First Daughter of the mighty Emperor. I could march you straight into the Emperor's official audience hall. His visitors would be awed by your beauty."

She picked a cushion and threw it at him, then dropped down on a vacant mat.

"Bring me a chocolate drink," she called toward the doorway. "And make it sweet." Turning to Coyotl, she smiled, then stretched luxuriously. "I had a most wonderful night, just so you know."

"Wonderful night? What did you do? Are you allowed to go

out?"

She shook her head vigorously. "No, of course not. But I had a wonderful night all the same."

"What happened?"

"Oh, nothing. Nothing special." She stretched once again, her smile spilling out of the blackness of her eyes.

"Iztac, you don't make any sense."

She rolled over the mat like a large animal, graceful and wonderfully feminine for a change. He watched her, wide-eyed.

"Tell me something," she asked, raising her head, one arm propped on an elbow, the other stretched. "Have you ever kissed a girl?"

"What?" He stared at her in disbelief. "Iztac, have you gone mad?"

"No, but I want to know," she went on unabashed. "Have you made love to a girl?"

He sprang to his feet. "Stop it. You can't ask me these things. What has come over you?" He glared at her, suddenly furious.

Her smile did not waver, but her eyes hardened, lost some of their previous gaiety.

"We used to know everything about each other," she said, frowning. "We used to spend so much time together. We shared everything." She shrugged. "I understand that you can't climb fences and trees anymore and we can't tell each other everything. But I wanted to know this thing. Why can't I ask you this? Maybe I have something to tell you."

He watched her uneasily, his stomach twisting. Since the Emperor had started treating him as an official heir, he had had no time for her, always busy, but happily so. While she? Well, she had stayed behind, doing her best to entertain herself, getting into all those troubles. She was right. They used to know everything about each other. And when she was sent to Tenochtitlan, he would lose her entirely.

His stomach as tight as a rubber ball, he studied her gentle heart-shaped face, skin creamy and as smooth as a golden mask, the dark eyes wide-open and glittering. He bit his lower lip.

"Listen," he said, sitting beside her. "Those things change, and we are not children anymore. I have to tell you something, and you should not take it badly. It's actually a good thing, all things considered."

She straightened abruptly. "Have you talked to the Emperor?"

"Yes. I tried to talk to him yesterday, but he wouldn't listen. But this morning he brought the matter up himself."

The color left her cheeks all at once as her eyes lost their spark. "What is he going to do with me?"

He took her shoulders between his arms, pulling her closer, but she squirmed out of his embrace.

"What? What is he going to do? Is he giving me away?"

"Yes," he said, unable to shift his gaze, yet wishing to look anywhere but at her twisted, haunted face.

"Where?"

"Tenochtitlan."

"What? Why Tenochtitlan?" She moved farther away, until her back was against the wall. "No! Not the Aztecs. I hate them!"

"Listen, Iztac. They are not that bad, and their Emperor is still quite a young man. They say he is really nice, considerate and all. You could be given to an old province ruler with half of twenty fat wives. Think about it."

She took a convulsive breath. "I don't want to think about it. And I don't want to go to Tenochtitlan!"

He saw her biting her lips, trying to control herself. His heart squeezed harder. "You would have been given to this or that ruler one day. This one is not a bad man, at least."

He reached for her hand, but she snatched it away.

"Don't touch me! I don't want anyone touching me from now on." She jumped to her feet. "So that's it, eh? Is it final? When do I go?"

"Well, he didn't tell me that. I tried to argue, and he just told me that it's not my place to comment." A sudden thought occurred to him. "But maybe he just thought about it. Maybe he didn't ask the Aztec yet. If so, you will probably have plenty of time until it's settled, don't you think?" It was awkward to look at her from the floor. He got up. "It will take time and, who knows, maybe Huitzilihuitl will refuse." Seeing a flicker of interest in the dark desperation of her eyes, he went on, clinging to this only hope. "The Aztecs don't want to go to war together with us. They seem to prefer to stay neutral. So maybe their Emperor would not want a princess of Texcoco."

It was difficult to stand the look in those black, bottomless eyes, but before he dropped his gaze she took hers away. Listlessly, she went back, sitting upon the mat, slow and careful, as though afraid to break something.

Not knowing what to do, now that he could not even hug her, he welcomed the interruption as two maids came in, carrying a tray with chocolate and tortillas.

"Put it here and leave," he told them curtly, angry with their wondering glances. "Come, Iztac. Drink your chocolate."

But she just sat there, staring at the floor, her shoulders sagging.

"Please," he said, sitting beside her. "It's not that bad. It may not happen, but if it does, it won't be that bad. You'll see."

"You were right," she muttered. "You warned me. You told me they would give me away if I got caught."

His heart made strange leaps inside his chest.

"No, that has nothing to do with it. Really, Iztac. Look at me!" She stared at the floor stubbornly, so he lifted her face, touching her chin only lightly. The misery in her eyes made his stomach turn. "Listen, it has nothing to do with your marketplace adventures. The Emperor wants another alliance with the Aztecs. You are the most available princess, that's all. Your blood is impeccable, better than mine even. Think about it. Acolhua on one side and Tepanec on the other, with a sprinkle of the Toltec blood even. You are the granddaughter of Tezozomoc himself, do you realize that? I should be honoring you with all sorts of titles before daring to converse with you. Think about it." Seeing the sparkle of amusement passing through the depths of the obsidian vastness, he picked up a tortilla. "Am I allowed to eat the food that the revered gaze of the Toltec princess has rested upon? I'll cherish the moment and will tell my children about it."

"Stop it!" She frowned, stifling a giggle. "You are impossible. I wish they would make *you* marry the Aztec Emperor."

"Huitzilihuitl wouldn't want me. I'm not as pretty as you are, and my Mexica blood is nothing to him." Encouraged with the effect, he grinned. "And anyway, see, I'm half an Aztec too, so stop badmouthing us, the Aztecs. We are not that bad."

She shoved an elbow into his ribs. "You are not an Aztec. You are an Acolhua nobleman, the First Son of the Emperor. The future Emperor of Texcoco, the greatest of them all, the one that will be remembered for generations." She looked at him searchingly. "And I'm not joking. I know you will be all of that."

The warm tide washed over his face. Embarrassed, he released her and went toward the table.

"We have to defeat the Tepanecs first," he said, busying himself with the food. "So I'll be able to ascend that throne one day, to do all those things you were prophesying just now."

She sat beside him. "We will defeat them, won't we?"

Coyotl shrugged, frowning at the sweetened tortilla. "The Aztec Warlord seems to think we won't. Such a self-assured bastard! I wish they had killed him last night."

"Well, it's a strange wish." She picked up her cup and drank a little, her face twisting. "That chocolate is bitter. Didn't they have enough sense to put some vanilla in it?" Glancing at him, she grinned. "This Aztec Warlord may not be that bad. I heard he can be nice, too."

"Where did you hear that? He is a heartless beast. With no nice sides to him."

She looked mysterious. "I have my sources of information, and he did one good thing."

"What?"

"He saved that boy from the marketplace."

"He did not save him for nothing. I bet you ten cocoa beans he saw a way to use him. And it won't be anything good, believe me!"

Her face fell. "Then you have to help him get away!" she cried out, clutching onto her cup.

He watched her knuckles wrapped around the prettily painted pottery going white. "You get mighty upset, sister." Raising his eyebrows, he saw her golden cheeks turning dark. "You liked that boy, eh?"

"No! It just that..." She stood his gaze for a while, then dropped her eyes. "He is nice and... I wish they would give me to him."

He chuckled. "No chance of that, unless the savages from the Highlands conquer the Lowlands. Then you may be given to him, as his father is some sort of a mighty war leader or something. I suppose he could be considered nobility up there in the mountains."

She gaped at him, eyes wide, mouth open. "He is a highlander? A savage?"

"Yes, of course. Didn't you notice the tattoos? And the way he behaves? You are dense!" He laughed into her face. "You should see yourself now, sister. What a sight! I should get Kuini to draw your likeness looking like that. On the best quality bark-paper, with all the colors only he knows how to apply best."

"Kuini?"

"Yes, that's his name. Means jaguar in their strange-sounding tongue." He sobered. "And he *is* a jaguar. A tremendous boy. I've known him for summers."

Her jaw dropped. "How?"

Pleased with the effect, he laughed. "It's a long story. I'll tell you one day."

Her face fell again. "You won't have a chance. I'll be in Tenochtitlan, a minor wife to the annoying Aztec Emperor."

He clasped her hand. "I'll find a way to bring you back if you are unhappy there. I promise!"

Kuini jumped, startled as the gentle hand touched his shoulder. For a moment his heart leaped, but the face peering at him from above was round and homely, not heart-shaped and as if chiseled out of polished wood. The eyes staring at him were brown and bright, not as black as obsidian.

He blinked, finding it difficult to adjust to the strong

midmorning light.

"What?" he asked, wishing to close his eyes again.

"I brought you food," said the girl. "The midmorning meal. Don't you want to eat?"

"Maybe." He rubbed his face, wincing when his palms brushed against the crust on his brow, remembering the healer coming to check on him sometime during the early morning, studying his wounds, clicking with his tongue. Again, the treatment was unpleasantly painful, and the man kept shaking his head, murmuring as he inspected the grazed bruises on Kuini's throat. He shrugged, hardly remembering any of that. He had just wanted to return to sleep, and he wanted to do it now as well.

"Well?" asked the maid. "Won't you get up or something? Am I to feed you like a baby?"

"Leave the food somewhere around," he said, closing his eyes.

"But I'm to serve you!" She stood there, hands firmly on her tray, legs wide apart, planted into the floor as if readying for his attempt to throw her out by force.

Grimacing, he sat up, leaning against the wall. "I don't need you to serve me. I can eat all by myself, you know?" He looked her up and down grimly, wishing her to go away.

"Oh, I know you are not an emperor. But they told me to serve you the food, so that's what I will do."

Kneeling, she put her tray down, then went away. He watched her bending to lift a low table on the other side of the room. A heavy thing, he reflected, watching her face turning red, glittering with sweat. Awkwardly, she carried it across the room.

"I'm beginning to feel like an emperor," he said, when she arranged the plates with hot tamales and fruit, making sure the slices of avocado scattered prettily around the dishes. His stomach grumbled.

"Well, don't get used to it. I'm sure it's a temporary thing."

"Why? Who told you to serve me?"

"The Aztec Warlord, who else?" She eyed him mischievously. "The Emperor is too busy to bother with foreigners."

"What foreigners?"

"Any foreigners. You and your stupid Aztecs."

He picked up a tamale. "Careful with your tongue. They'll chop you into twenty little pieces with those obsidian swords of theirs if they hear you talking about them like that."

She knelt opposite to him, holding a flask and a cup. "I heard one of the people who tried to sneak in here during the night was cut into so many pieces they had a difficult time scrubbing him off the walls."

His stomach turned at the memory. "Yes. He looked like an elk after a pack of wolves feasted on him for a whole night."

She gaped at him. "Did you see it?"

"Oh, yes."

"A pack of wolves feasting on elk?"

He glanced at her, startled. "Well, yes, that too."

"Where are you from?"

"It doesn't matter."

"Didn't you come with them from Tenochtitlan?"

He frowned. "Just leave it. Serve me that food if you must, but stop talking."

She glared at him, then poured a cup of water and banged it pointedly upon the table. He paid her no attention.

So, the Aztec had made sure he was taken care of, being served food like an emperor, he thought, hiding a smile. The man did understand that he, Kuini, was trustworthy, and that his throwing a stone might have helped. Good.

He devoured the last of the tamales and grinned. So, now, it all might be quite simple. When the Aztecs left, he'd go out with them, and so would leave the Palace and this accursed *altepetl*, safe and protected. Then, he would go home. Leave openly or run away, should the Aztec turn a liar and try to take him with them against his will. Oh, it would work out either way.

"Don't you have any *octli*?" he asked the girl as she refilled his cup.

"*Octli*? At this time of the day? You all must be hopeless drunkards in your Tenochtitlan."

He lifted his eyebrows. "We manage."

Amused, he stared her down. So, now, he was presumed to be an Aztec, not a Tepanec. Next he'd be taken for a Big-Headed

Mayan. He wanted to laugh, lightheaded and replete with food. The people of the Lowlands, Texcoco Acolhua in particular, were incredibly silly.

The rasping voices brought him down from his cloud of euphoria. While the girl jumped to her feet and busied herself with cleaning the table, the leading Aztec, his face closed and grim, burst into the room, followed by a few of his warriors.

Kuini stared at them, his elation evaporating. Tearing the imposing headdress off, the Aztec hurled it into the far corner. Next came the massive necklace, flying across the room. The man shifted his shoulders as though relishing the sudden freedom of movement.

"Go away," he said curtly, noticing the maid.

As the girl scampered off, the dark and indifferent glance lingered on Kuini, but only for a little while, moving on to encircle the room. The warriors stood behind their leader, apprehensive, expectant somehow.

"Well," said the Warlord finally, "as we are not leaving today, make yourself busy with some training. Find out where their training grounds are around the Palace, then let me know. I need a good exercise as well." His gaze encircled them, heavy with meaning. "Is that clear? Find the training ground, send me word and wait for me there." The well-spaced eyes lingered on Kuini. "Go with them."

"But Honorable Warlord— " protested one of the warriors.

The dark stare made the man drop his gaze. "This boy saved my life. He is to be trusted. Treat him as such." He turned to leave. "Train him a little until I come. Go easy on him with his wounds, but find out what he can do and with what weapons." The narrowed eyes bore into Kuini. "Have you trained with a sword before?"

"No." Kuini cleared his throat, curiously upset with the flicker of disappointment in the older man's face. "But I was taught to handle a club, and I can use a spear and a sling."

"Those are not good enough." The man turned to the tall bulky warrior. "Teach him to use the sword. Let him try one of yours for a time." His gaze darkened. "And I want to have him back in one piece and unharmed. Is that clear?"

"Yes, Honorable Leader," said the man, but the glance he shot at Kuini was anything but friendly.

He got to his feet slowly, trying to conceal his fear. Yet, as they began pouring out of the room, the Aztec's voice startled them again.

"On second thought, stay!" He gestured curtly. "The rest of you go and train, and send for me right away."

Afraid to breathe with relief as yet, Kuini waited for the last of the warriors to pour out. The silence prevailed. The Warlord stared out of the open window, deep in thought.

"Filthy bastards," he hissed finally. "Stinky, dirty, pest-ridden manure-eaters!" Kicking the low table so viciously it toppled over, the man turned abruptly and disappeared into the other room.

It took Kuini a while before he dared to breathe again. *What had come over the bad-tempered beast?* He strolled toward the same window. Was it the aftershock of the nighttime attack? No, not likely. The man had looked his old derisively amused self when leaving that morning, after the healer had finished smearing an ointment over his cut cheek.

He stared at the bushes below, remembering the way he had run there, the way that stone had felt in his hand. He should have left last night, sneaking away through one of the entrances. The girl could have shown him the way out, he thought, aware of the warmth spreading below his chest. With her ability to climb and her experience in running away, she could have helped him tremendously.

He suppressed a smile. Would she wait there for him at midnight as promised? It could be a perfect solution. She would be able to guide him out, but not before another one or two of those breathtaking kisses of hers.

The footsteps erupted again and he tensed. Peering at the long sheet of bark paper, the Aztec came back, still deep in thought.

"How well do you know the areas around Texcoco?" he asked, voice low but calm and well in control once again. The man was changing fast.

"I know some of it," admitted Kuini carefully.

"If you want to leave Texcoco on foot, heading southward, what would be the safest way to do this?"

A paper thrust into Kuini's hands. He studied it, wide-eyed. The painting was colorful, drawn with strong, decisive lines, like the scrolls Coyotl had shown him back in the temple – had it happened only two dawns ago? – but in a sort of a large picture, instead of many small ones. A solid part of a drawing was painted dark purple, with a few figures in it. The rest was unpainted and full of images of people, animals, and other creatures with multiple heads and limbs.

"See here?" The large finger pointed at the images to the right of the purple area. "Do you know these areas? Can people pass there without venturing into the Highlands?"

Kuini blinked. "I don't understand."

"The Highlands," repeated the Aztec impatiently. "If you want to go down, southwards along the Great Lake, can you do this without venturing into the lands of the savages?" The finger invaded the purple area. "I want to end up here, but I need to make some of my way over the land."

"You want to go out of Texcoco—"

"Would you shut up?" The man flung his arms in the air. "You don't have to repeat everything I say. Let alone yell it at the top of your voice." He took a deep breath and lowered his own voice once again. "Just answer this. Have you ever traveled around Texcoco?"

"Yes." Oh, he should have run away through the previous night. This man was insane.

"Then can you, or can you not, show us the best way to move southwards?"

"I think so." This time Kuini kept his voice as low. "I know the areas to the east best, but I happened to go southwards a few times. There are comfortable roads down there."

"And if I want to avoid the roads?"

"Oh then, well, you'll still find enough trails, I suppose." He knew there were enough trails. His people never used the roads of the Lowlanders.

The man peered back into the sheet. "Where exactly? Show me

the way you would use."

Kuini stared into the picture. "What? Here?"

Suddenly, the broad face crinkled with laughter. "Oh, I see." He stared at Kuini, amused. "It's a map. It's a picture that is showing some of the areas and their roads and settlements. Haven't you seen one before?"

"I... No, I don't think so. I saw a calendar."

"Yes, calendars are good. But I need you to help me with this map now. Come here." The Aztec went to the overturned table. Pulling it into an upright position, he spread the long sheet of paper upon in. "This purple thing here, in the far corner, is the Great Lake. See? Here, on this spot, nearer to the left, is Tenochtitlan." The wide palm moved upward. "Out there, on the better side of the lake, you see? This is Azcapotzalco, the capital of the Tepanecs. No brackish water on these shores." The palm shot backward, crossed the purple vastness, halted on the opposite edge. "And here is Texcoco. See this figure? That's their Acolhua symbol."

Kuini stared at the painting, mesmerized. The calendar, the accounts of battles, even the engineers' drawings were nothing compared to this. Here was the map of the whole Great Lake. Being able to draw something like that, one wouldn't even need a scout, he thought, his heart beating fast. You would just draw your way and give it to the person you wanted to guide. He tried to grasp it.

"What do the other figures mean?" he asked, his throat dry. "Over there, for example."

"Oh, this is Tlacopan. A large Tepanec province and the tributary of Azcapotzalco, of course."

Kuini found the capital of the Tepanecs again. "So, they would have to cross all the way up here?" he asked, pointing toward the symbol of Texcoco.

"Correct." The Aztec glanced at him, eyes twinkling. "You learn fast, boy. And I promise to give you this drawing to study and to show you more of these things. But now, I need you to concentrate." He pointed back at the symbolic Texcoco. "Can you guide us up here without making us stumble into the Highlands?"

"I can, but not all the way. I've never been too far away to the south." He peered at the purple shape where it split as if parted by an invisible boundary. "What's this?"

"That's another lake. Lake Chalco." The Aztec grinned dreamily. "Many campaigns up there. Many memories. We almost finished them off, those Chalcoans, a few summers ago." He frowned. "Tezozomoc didn't like it. He forced us to retreat, to leave the Chalco *altepetl* alone, when we could have just taken them all, like a ripe fruit. And what do you think your righteous Acolhua of Texcoco did? Sided with the Tepanec Emperor, no more and no less. But now? Oh, now they are all indignant with our inclination to keep out of their precious war with this same Tezozomoc. Filthy bastards!"

Kuini hardly listened, his eyes drinking in the precious scroll, unable to get enough, leaping from image to image, from *altepetl* to *altepetl*.

"So you want to go all the way up the lake Chalco, and then cross there?"

The Aztec studied the map, then grinned, openly amused. "No. It would be too long of a walk. But it's not a bad plan, jaguar cub. Not bad at all, and under regular circumstances I might have considered it. But now..." He looked up sharply, then got to his feet and began folding the map. "Now, we stop talking and will go out to do some training."

Kuini ground his teeth. He didn't hurry to jump to his feet, but as the Aztec finished folding the sheet, rising voices caught their attention. People were arguing outside the entrance.

Abruptly, the Aztec straightened up. Paces long and springy like those of a jaguar on a hunting path, he went toward the doorway in time to meet one of his warriors, coming in hesitantly.

"Honorable Warlord, the Emperor's First Son is here. He is insisting on meeting you."

"The First Son? The heir?" The Aztec looked genuinely surprised. "What would that slimy bastard want with me?" He hesitated and looked around, amused and doubtful all at once. "Well, let him in. We can't have the next Texcoco Emperor thrown out of my quarters with force, can we?"

Kuini found it difficult to breathe. *Coyotl? Here?* It could mean only one thing. He wished his friend would come later, when the Aztec was not here, or even when both of them would be away on the training session.

Heart pounding, he watched Coyotl coming in, lingering at the doorway, unsure of himself, despite the attempt to look otherwise. He must have been counting on the Warlord being elsewhere, like yesterday, but could not back away when informed otherwise.

Kuini rose to his feet, his mind refusing to think. He had to do *something*.

"Well, what a surprise," he heard the Aztec saying, the mocking tone in the deep voice more pronounced than usual. "The Revered First Son himself. I can't say I'm not honored."

Coyotl hesitated, clearly thrown off balance. "Greetings, Honorable Warlord," he said finally.

The large eyes of the Aztec twinkled. "Please, come on in," he said, his exaggerated politeness bordering on an outright offense. "What can I do for you, oh future Emperor?"

Coyotl's eyes sparkled. "I came to relieve you of the burden of your prisoner."

"What?" The surprise of the man was genuine this time.

"I came to take your prisoner away," repeated Coyotl, suddenly more sure of himself.

The eyebrows of the Aztec climbed high. "Is this what the duties of the Emperor's heir have come to? To run around, collecting the offenders who didn't make it to the court in time? Is the royal house of Texcoco that thirsty for the blood of this boy?"

"No!" said Coyotl angrily. He shifted his weight from one foot to another. "This case is exceptional, and I will be responsible for this boy from now on, personally."

"Will you stone him personally too? Or will you just strangle him with your own hands?"

Coyotl gasped. "He will not be executed!"

"Then what do you want with him?"

"I don't have to tell you. You are a guest in this Palace. You cannot take people of Texcoco just like that. We are not in Tenochtitlan."

"This boy is not from Texcoco, and your people wanted to kill him anyway. It doesn't look like any of you will miss him."

"And what do *you* want with him?"

The Aztec shook his head calmly, but his eyes grew dangerously cold. "I don't have to tell you that, either."

Kuini's gaze leaped from one face to the other, aghast. "Stop it," he said quietly. "Please stop arguing."

They turned to him at once, astounded, wide eyed, as if a statue in the far corner of the room had just opened its mouth.

He licked his lips. "Please, stop arguing about me."

"What?" called the Aztec, clearly thrown out of his usual mocking self-assurance.

Kuini clasped his palms tight. "I know it sounds strange," he said, licking his lips once again. "And I'm sorry about that. It's all just a huge misunderstanding, you see? Funny as it may sound, I know both of you mean well and..." He swallowed. "I'll go and talk to the Honorable First Son outside, if both of you don't mind."

He wanted to laugh at the sight of the Aztec's face, so dumbfounded, so astounded the man looked. Clenching his teeth, he proceeded to the doorway, praying that the warriors at the entrance would not try to stop him, hoping that Coyotl would follow promptly.

Leaning against the plastered wall, he tried to contain his trembling. What now? The warriors eyed him suspiciously, but said nothing. He fought the temptation to walk away, to put as much distance between them and himself as he could, until Coyotl stumbled into the corridor, looking grim.

"Well?" he asked, stopping at some distance, sounding challenging.

"Shall we go and talk outside?"

"Is it safe for you now?"

"I don't know."

"Well, I suppose, as long as you are with me..." His friend's tone softened.

They stepped into the early afternoon heat and headed down the wide stairs.

"So," said Coyotl, halting at the bottom of the staircase. "You seem to be on quite good terms with the Aztec Warlord now."

Kuini shrugged. "Well, yes. He is all right."

The dark gaze was his answer. "I suppose you'll be heading for Tenochtitlan now, en-route to becoming an Aztec yourself."

"No, I'm not!" He glared at his friend, suddenly very angry. "I'm trying to find my way out of this mess, that's all. You were the one to insist that I should come here, remember? So stop acting like I did something wrong, like I betrayed you or something!"

Eyes narrow, lips pursed, Coyotl stared back. "The Aztecs seem as though about to betray us, so if you go with them, you *will* betray me."

"I'm going home the moment I step out of this Palace, this way or another. I'm not about to get into any of *your* wars, whichever way they go. Acolhua people, Aztecs or Tepanecs, they are all the same to me, they all want to kill me or my people, so I'm out of here, out of this mess, out of your wars and politics. I should never have come here in the first place!"

Breathing heavily, they glared at each other, oblivious of the people's stares. Then Coyotl's eyes focused, lost their fierceness.

"Well, I suppose I should wish you well," he said through his clasped lips.

Kuini's stomach turned, finding it difficult to see the hurt in the familiar face. Coyotl was a friend of many summers, maybe the only friend he had. The boys from his town and the villages of his homeland were nothing but playmates, never close enough to share more than rough jokes and messing around.

He dropped his gaze. "I'm sorry. I didn't mean it this way." Clenching his palms together, he looked at the groomed paths and the carefully planted trees that were swaying ahead, seeing none of it. "I'm just tired of being tossed around. Tired and confused. I need to go home and think about all this. Then I can decide." He looked at his friend searchingly. "Will you understand?"

Coyotl's face softened. "Yes, of course. I still wish you would come to fight with me."

"Maybe I will. I do have some time, don't I? The Tepanecs are not here yet."

"They are on their way."

He hated the small wave of fear that rushed through his chest. "Are they?"

"Well, yes. It's a secret yet, so don't tell anyone. But they will be crossing the Great Lake soon."

He remembered the map, the purple drawing of the Great Lake, the symbolic *altepetl*s.

"I'm to go out, to rush around the provinces, to gather the promised warriors forces," he heard his friend saying. "The Tepanecs should be here in a market interval or two. At long last! So I'll be heading out of the city tomorrow, and I'll be able to smuggle you along. Then you'll go home with no trouble." Coyotl's smile widened. "Or you could stay with me, and we'll gather those warriors together, to rush back, maybe straight into a battle."

"How will we explain my presence there?"

"Oh, we'll find a way."

He watched his friend's glowing face, cheerful once again, full of its usual lighthearted confidence. It could be a wonderful adventure, he thought. Just one single battle and then he would be off for home, with no one the wiser.

"If you think it's possible..." He frowned. "The Aztecs are leaving as well. So I suppose I can sneak out with you tomorrow with not much trouble."

"The Aztecs won't leave anytime soon," said Coyotl abruptly, his frown startling in its suddenness. "So don't count on it."

"No, they are definitely leaving. They are ..." Something in his friend's face made Kuini bite his tongue. "Oh, well, maybe I got it all wrong."

"No, you didn't get it all wrong. They may be thinking they'll leave, but they won't. Not anytime soon. Their filthy manure-eater of a leader needs to be taught a good lesson in manners and politics, and the Acolhua Emperor is just the man to do that." Coyotl's pleasant face twisted and lost any trace of its usual pleasantness. "I wish I was here to see it, but neither of us will be in Texcoco by that time. So be ready tomorrow, through the first part of a day. Will you?"

They saw a spotted cloak rushing toward the staircase.

"Speaking of bad spirits," murmured Coyotl, then peered at Kuini again. "Be ready."

"Yes, I will." Kuini smiled. "Thank you. You are a great friend."

"Wait and see until we fight together. It will be grand!"

He watched Coyotl's tall figure rushing down the stairs, his thoughts scattering in disarray. The glance of the passing Aztec warrior made him uneasy.

What to do?

CHAPTER 9

It was already well past midnight when he managed to sneak out, having waited for the Aztecs to fall asleep. The warriors were not a problem, but the Warlord turned out to be difficult. The man refused to submit to tiredness, although he obviously hadn't slept much through the previous night that included an attempt on his life.

Exhausted as well, Kuini found it difficult to stay awake, the afternoon of intense training with the Aztec having taken much of his precious energy. Grinning, he recalled the feeling of holding a real obsidian sword for the first time in his life – a heavy, uncomfortably long affair of solid wood, adorned by viciously sparkling, razor-sharp obsidian on both sides. He had a difficult time trying to just hold onto it, let alone hack or block the blows. But the Aztec was relentless. Pushing and demanding, he made Kuini work hard, expecting his pupil to excel from the very beginning, indifferent to the fact that he had never dealt with a real sword before.

There was another reason for this particular training session, Kuini had discovered, while not busy trying to survive. From time to time, the Aztec would let his trainee rest, going to the other warriors, conversing with them, seemingly idle. Yet, Kuini could not help but notice the alert, tense bearing of people trying to concentrate, making sure not to miss a word of what was being said, but afraid of being overheard. The shreds of conversations would reach him sometimes, so toward the later afternoon, exhausted and scratched all over, he had gathered that the Aztecs planned to leave on foot, just like the man had told him earlier, but probably unannounced. And unauthorized – was Kuini's conclusion.

Why?

He didn't have to think hard to figure out the answer to that. Coyotl had said that the Emperor wanted to teach the arrogant Aztec a lesson, and clearly the Warlord was too wise of a man and not that arrogant to stay and face that particular battle.

So the Aztecs were about to sneak away, thought Kuini, rushing toward the protection of the dark trees, retracing the way he had gone last night. The evening was pleasant, even chilly, and the moon shone more strongly than it had on the night before.

He shivered. It would be difficult to climb that tree under her window in such illumination. But maybe she'd be waiting outside. His stomach twisted with anticipation. It was she who had told him to come. He hadn't asked her. Or had he?

Hastening his step, he glanced at the sky. If she was outside, she would be mighty upset with him being so late. He shrugged. A few more of her breathtaking kisses, and then he would go back and think about what to do.

His stomach twisted again, but this time uneasily. The Aztec had counted on him, Kuini, to guide his people through the Lowlands, at least part of the way. Could he disappoint this man by leaving with Coyotl? To go with his friend, the boy he had known, the boy he had trusted for summers, was the most appropriate of solutions. He owed the fierce Aztec nothing. He had known the man for a few dawns at the most.

To grind his teeth didn't help. Yes, he did owe this man something. He owed the Aztec his life. The Warlord had undoubtedly saved him that first time, and he had been kind to him ever since. Short-tempered and rude, but kind and well-meaning nevertheless. They kept saying the man was a ruthless, cruel, heartless bastard, but he, Kuini, had seen the other side of the Warlord so far. Why, he had actually come to like this formidable Aztec Leader. How bizarre!

Reaching the opposite wing of the Palace, he paused, his heart twisting with disappointment. The opening above the wide-branched tree was as dark as the rest of them, looking blankly into the silvery night, its shutters half-closed.

Pressing his lips, he tried to contain his frustration. So there would be no silly talk tonight and no kisses. She might have not been able to make it for twenty and more causes, he reasoned, but his anger kept growing, speculating that maybe she had just gotten enough of adventures with foreigners and commoners.

Undecided, he eyed the dark window. Maybe it was for the best. This girl, while being exciting, had brought him nothing but trouble. He was better off without her wild, pretty, delightfully untamed presence.

Carefully, he sneaked out and crossed the moonlit ground, heading for the protection of *her* tree. He could just take a look; see if there was a way to climb it. Maybe she did wait and was just afraid to light a torch. Or, maybe, she had fallen asleep, and he could still wake her up by throwing something into her window.

A shadow separated from the thick trunk, and his heart missed a beat, then burst out into unrestrained pounding. The familiar slender form pounced on him, grabbing his arm.

"What took you so long?" she whispered angrily. "I waited forever. This is no midnight!"

"Calm down," he breathed. "You'll wake them all with your shouting."

"I'm not shouting, and you *are* late!"

He watched her animated, defiant face, hard put not to laugh.

"So I'm guilty of being late," he whispered. "What now?"

She shrugged, glaring at him from under her brow, looking again like a petulant child. He pulled her closer, and she resisted, but only a little.

"So, am I kissing you right here in the moonlight for the whole Palace to see or will we go somewhere quieter?"

She giggled. "I suppose somewhere quieter would do."

Her nearness made his head swim as his nostrils took in her scent – sweetmeats and another something, belonging only to her. His hands told him she was wearing a different gown, the warmth of her body reaching through the thinner material.

They made it back into the darkness of the gardens, but this time she pulled him on, leading deeper into the depths of the artificial forest as if following an invisible path.

"Where are we going?" he asked, having difficulty concentrating with her so near.

"You'll see. The best place in this whole Palace."

She refused to slow down until they reached a small clearing that was facing a pond, its flicker dim in the moonlight, unable to penetrate the thickness of the trees surrounding it. The large trunks guarded it like stern warriors, forming a circle around the stony borders. He gazed at it, appreciative.

"Pretty, isn't it?" she asked, her eyes flickering mischievously. "And very, very secluded."

He watched her, suddenly dizzy with desire. She stepped closer, standing next to him, eyes black and gleaming, reflecting the sparse light. Her face seemed sharp and more defined in the darkness, a mask chiseled out of stone, or maybe out of solid gold. But a mask with warmth and a scent belonging to a young woman.

Unable to fight the temptation, he pulled her closer, kissing her forcefully, the way he had done on the night before, losing control, needing her badly. She reacted by pressing against him, opening her lips to welcome his. It made his head spin, his limbs going liquid, having a life of their own. The warmth of her body was intoxicating, making him mad with desire. The kiss was not enough.

With the last of his strength he pulled away.

"Wait!" He could not recognize his own voice, so strident and hoarse it sounded.

"What?" She didn't make an attempt to move. Pressing closer, she leaned against him, her face brushing next to his, lips caressing, not kissing but only touching. It made his head reel.

"Why no kissing?" she asked again, eyes glittering, teasing.

He swallowed. "Because, you know... kissing is not... not enough."

She didn't blink, didn't move away. The same beautiful statue kept gazing at him, but something had changed. The look in the obsidian eyes deepened.

"What else would you want to do with me?" she asked, voice

calm, but low and throaty.

He took a step back, bumping his head against a tree. His heart made strange leaps inside his chest. She laughed, but it was a nervous laughter, and it did not break the spell.

"We can't do this," he said, gazing at her, his chest hurting.

"Why not?"

He swallowed again. "Because, you know… you are a princess, the first daughter or whatever. Princesses don't do this."

Suddenly, something in her face changed. Right before his eyes it hardened, lost some of its innocent, sweet, girlish look. All of a sudden, she looked older, more mature, not the mischievous girl he had known for two days. The dark eyes returned his gaze, suddenly empty, their unhappiness bottomless. The generous lips stretched into a mirthless smile.

"Yes, princesses are to be kept pure," she said bitterly. "To be given and taken like pretty pottery. To be sold for the convenience of their *altepetls*, like the last of the slaves."

He stared into the depths of her eyes, now dark with anger, seeing her lips quivering, her hands clenching into fists. His heart went out to her.

"It may not happen that fast," he said, helplessly. "There is no sense in thinking about it until it happens."

She stared at him for another heartbeat, then turned around and went toward the stone adorning the pond's edges. As she knelt beside it, her palm reached the dark water, playing with it, creating small waves. So fragile-looking, so defenseless. Her sagging shoulders made his chest tighten, as did the sight of her gentle neck, unprotected, with her hair pulled up fashionably, in many elaborately woven braids. Only now he noticed the way her hair was arranged as if for a special occasion, her gown flimsy and prettily embroidered. He wondered how she had managed to climb down the wall without tearing the light material up.

Squatting beside her, he watched her fingers making strange patterns on the transparent water, trying to think of what to say.

"It will happen fast enough," she said quietly. "I'm to be offered to the Emperor of Tenochtitlan."

"Tenochtitlan?" He looked at her, wide-eyed. "Why

Tenochtitlan? I've gathered that your royal house is rather displeased with the Aztecs."

"Oh yes, they are displeased with them. Mightily at that." She sounded surprisingly calm. "But they need those ferocious barbarians all the same. Hence the marriage offering."

"I'm sorry," he said helplessly.

She turned and faced him so suddenly it startled him. Darker than usual, her eyes peered at him, unsettling, making his stomach flutter.

"Will you make love to me?"

The sounds of the night disappeared all of a sudden. Even his heart, which was beating wildly, seemed to stop. He stared into her eyes, taking in the tension, the desperation they held. Also, the suppressed anger, the resentment. No, there was nothing enticing about that gaze. She had looked at him differently before.

"No," he said.

Her eyes widened as the blood drained from her face. Even in the dim moonlight, he could see her paling visibly.

"Why not?" she asked gruffly.

He shrugged, shifting his gaze back toward the pond.

"You have to tell me!" Her voice rose, then shook. "I was good enough to kiss. Why not to make love?"

He clenched his palms so tight he could not feel them anymore. "Because you want to use it as a way to get back at them. And that's not why people make love."

He peered at the water, following silhouettes of small fish darting everywhere. They looked so busy, so purposeful. He clenched his teeth, then came the chuckling sound.

"Oh, you highlanders are so proud," she said, and her voice shook with laughter.

Startled, he turned his head. Eyes twinkling, she watched him, smile wide, crinkling with mirth. No more dark shadows, only the usual teasing, mischievous amusement. How quickly she was changing.

A slender palm came up, reaching for his face, running down his cheek, lingering, sending waves of excitement through his stomach. He didn't fight his need anymore. Pulling her closer, he kissed her again, and this time with no misgivings.

Her scent enveloped him, intoxicating, something sweetish and bitter at the same time, some sort of a flower, maybe. His lips slipped down her neck, following that scent. She shivered and tensed, but relaxed when he pressed her stronger. Her palms slid along his back, caressing, leaving strips of warmth in their wake.

He didn't remember how, but at some point they moved away from the pond, toward the welcoming softness of the early summer's grass. He pulled her gown up, and as she tensed, he stopped, but only to straighten into an upright position.

"No," he said, pushing her back gently, when she tried to sit up as well. "Stay like that."

She complied readily but shyly, her eyes enormous, shining brighter than the moon. He remembered making love to that girl from his town, the way he had pulled her skirt up, making it hastily to what was below. But oh no! What was good for some girls was not good enough for *her*. His fingers found the ties of her gown, and it took him ages to untie them, but he didn't care, not in a hurry.

"No," he said when she resisted while he pulled the light material off. "You should let me see you."

"Why?" she asked softly, helping him to push her clothes away.

"Because you are a goddess. I know you are a goddess, but I have to see it for myself."

Her smile took his breath away. This, and the sight of her body, gleaming softly in the moonlight, slender and thin, but perfectly shaped, her breasts small and round, her stomach golden and smooth.

"You see," he said, running his palms along her soft angular curves, liking the way her skin tensed under his touch. "My people worship the Moon Goddess. She is one of our main deities." His finger encircled her breast, enjoying the way her nipple hardened, so dark it looked black, but not like her eyes. "I always imagined her slender and tall, but silvery. But now I know I was wrong. The Moon Goddess is golden, and her eyes are as black as obsidian. But the rest is just like I thought."

The look in her eyes made him forget the last of his qualms. He reclined beside her and let her body welcome his, confident in losing control, just as when kissing her. When he entered her she gasped and he stopped, but she clutched him tighter, her arms strong and demanding.

"Did it hurt?" he asked, but she shut his mouth with a kiss, and he let the wave of pleasure take him, confident and trusting, knowing it was the right thing to do.

Spent, they lay on the grass, ignoring the stones jutting against their limbs, floating in the silvery magic. When she moved, he pulled her closer, making her comfortable against his body, although the bruises adorning his ribs still hurt.

"You were right," she whispered dreamily. "Now I know why people make love."

"Why?" He opened his eyes, blessing the darkness around them. He didn't want to see anything, not even the sky. It would take his attention away from the perfect world where there was nothing but them and the feel of her skin against his.

"You make love to your chosen mate, to that one perfect person that was made by the gods especially for you." She paused, and he could sense her sudden sadness. "To make it with someone else would be to lay with them and nothing more. I wish there was a way to avoid it."

He peered at the sky, seeking a familiar arrangement of stars. "I should have kidnapped you for real."

He could hear her chuckling, a soft, lilting sound. "Back on the marketplace?"

"Yes. It would have saved me much trouble."

"Would you have carried me to the Highlands?"

"Yes. Right up the treacherous paths of our Smoking Mountain. No one would find us there. Not even my people."

"And we would make love day and night." She raised her head, leaning on her elbow, gazing at him, her face aglow with excitement. "But what would we eat?"

"I would hunt things, and you would cook them." He grinned. "I'm afraid there would be no maids with tortillas, and no tamales, either."

She wrinkled her nose. "Oh, I can live without those. But you would have to go down here to get me the chocolate drink. This one I really need every morning."

"No, no chocolate drinks," he said firmly. "Sorry, but you've been kidnapped, princess. So, no luxury of the capital for you."

She lifted her eyebrows, eyes twinkling, challenging his authority. "Oh, we'll see." Her grin widened. "So, what else would we do for countless summers upon countless summers in your mountains? Make love, hunt and cook... What else?"

He shrugged. "Make more love." Then he brightened. "Oh, and you'll have all those canyon walls to climb. We'll see who beats whom on climbing."

"It's no competition," she said smugly. "I climb better. Yesterday it took you half a night to get down that tree."

"I was wounded and exhausted," he protested. "After I kidnap you, we'll find a trail with a suitable wall, and we'll see who climbs better."

"I bet you ten cocoa beans I'll win."

He laughed and pulled her back down so her head rested on his shoulder, her disheveled braids tickling his chin.

"How did you know where I'm coming from?" he asked idly.

She giggled. "I know everything."

"Last time we talked about my origins, you thought I was a Tepanec."

"But now I know you are a wild Highlander. One who looks like a Tepanec, though." She stretched and turned to her side, running her fingers along his chest, making rays of pleasure to spread like waves across his skin. "My brother told me. He told me he has known you for many summers. He thinks highly of you."

"Does he know about us?"

"No." She chuckled. "I almost told him. But then... Well, then we got to the less pleasant part of the conversation. He tried to make me feel better about Tenochtitlan, to make me see the good in it."

"Is there anything good in it?"

She shrugged. "He says their Emperor is nice."

He could feel her sadness, the way her head now lay listlessly upon his shoulder, her body tense and unresponsive. He felt it coming in waves, bleak and desperate, corrupting the wonderful freshness of the night.

"I wish I could do something," he murmured, pressing her tightly against him.

"Why don't you kidnap me for real?" Her whisper was so soft it hardly reached his ear, brushing against his cheek like a gentle breeze.

He caught his breath. "Would you..." He swallowed. "Would you really want that?" Stomach fluttering, he cleared his throat. "It's so different up there. The life, I mean. It's nothing you would know or recognize." He shifted uncomfortably. "It's not an easy life, you see?"

She was silent for a long while, and he bit his lips, annoyed with the sense of acute disappointment welling in his chest.

"I think you don't know how this kidnapping works," she said finally. "You don't report to the princess the conditions of her future life, like an emperor's adviser would. You just take the woman you fancy and go away. It's that simple."

He lifted his head and watched her, laying there, lips quivering, eyes glittering, teasing.

"That simple, eh?" he repeated, finding it difficult to contain his excitement. "Well, maybe I'll do just that."

Her eyes shone at him, so dark he could see the sparkle of moonlight reflecting in them. He cupped her face in his palms, a new sense of ownership welling. She was his, truly his, and he would make sure she belonged to no one else.

"I'll take you away, I promise," he said, when able to control his voice. "You will be mine, and mine alone."

The sparkle of laughter disappeared, replaced by a different glow. Her face glimmered, dominating the surrounding night, taking away the Palace, the Lowlands and the Highlands, the Aztecs and the Tepanecs. The boiling conflict around the Great Lake disappeared, replaced by an eternal tranquility, by the peacefulness of the night, by the perfect feeling of their bodies, already familiar with each other, and their mutual future, so bright it shone.

"How many dawns do we have?" he asked as they washed in the pond, having finished with more kissing. He wanted to make more love, but knew better than to press her. Everyone knew that the girls would hurt and even bleed for the first time, unable to do it again right away.

"What do you mean?" she asked, splashing in the dark water.

"Until you should be sent to Tenochtitlan."

"Oh, I think a few market intervals at the very least. My brother says they may not reach an agreement for quite a while, maybe never even." She shrugged. "But we better hurry. In case they reach it fast."

"How long is this market interval?" he asked thoughtfully, tying his loincloth as he left the water.

She looked surprised. "Five, six dawns. Didn't you know that? Don't you have markets up there in the mountains?"

"No," he said curtly, slightly embarrassed. "Not like your markets, anyway." He frowned at her. "I told you it would be quite different. So make up your mind now, before it's too late."

Her cupped palm shot out, sprinkling him with drops of water. "I told you I don't mind. I insist only on the chocolate drink. And I also wish it to be sweetened thoroughly."

He leaned forward, trying to reach for her, but she was fast, leaping backward, retreating deeper into the pond.

"I'll be stuck with a willful princess, oh gods." He laughed, sprinkling her with more water as best as he could before getting back to his now-wet loincloth. "Anyway, your brother is going to smuggle me out of the city tomorrow. So, let me see. Two dawns for my way there, three to get back. One market interval." He frowned. "Can you get out of the Palace, so I could meet you somewhere out there? Say, on the Plaza or something. I would rather not enter that Palace again; in my entire life if I can help it."

"Oh yes, I can do that. But how do I know when you'll be there? On what day exactly?" She climbed back out of the pond and stood there, naked and dripping, beautiful in the moonlight. He caught his breath. When she bent to pick up her gown, he had a hard time restraining himself.

"I'll send you a note," he said, concentrating with effort. "When you receive it, just make it out to the Plaza the moment you can. Don't worry if it takes you a day, or two, even. I'll wait." Unable to resist, he came closer, catching her in his embrace, squeezing hard. "I will wait even if it takes you moons to come out. You are mine. You are the gift of the gods, and you belong to me only."

Her eyes made his heart beat faster. Unguarded, they beamed at him with so much love, so much innocent trustfulness, he knew he would do anything to keep his promise.

CHAPTER 10

The night was still deep when he made his way back to the Aztecs' quarters. Having watched her climbing the wall, sure-footed and confident, he found himself sneaking into the shadows smiling, deep in thought.

Oh, she would fit the ridges of Huexotzinco, his home town, perfectly, enjoy the life up there. Texcoco or Tenochtitlan had nothing to offer her, while the Highlands, and a certain Highlander, would make her happy and free.

All the soft summer grass around the river, he thought, grinning. So many places to make love, and then to climb rocks and jump into the river. Did she know how to swim?

He climbed into the window easily, the dull pain in his arm almost unnoticeable now. One market interval. Five or six dawns. Oh yes, he could make it.

Jumping into the room, he froze, unable to breathe. The warriors squatted around the low table, about half of twenty, fully dressed, including their cloaks, their swords attached to their girdles along with the rest of their bundles. Immersed in observing what lay on the table, they now sat straight, looking at him, their surprise and their open displeasure made worse by the single torchlight lighting the darkness.

He took a step back, felt the smoothness of the wall behind it, his eyes seeking the Aztec leader, seeing the man's broad face, tired and pale, looking older in the dancing light, his imposing headdress thrown carelessly upon the nearby mat.

"Well, is it not our wild boy, wandering through the night?" The large eyes twinkled, observing the intruder, less surprised than the warriors, almost amused. One corner of the generous mouth lifted in a sort of a crooked grin, cold but not entirely unfriendly. "Had difficulty sleeping once again?"

Kuini licked his lips, unable to think. He should be saying something now, answering, probably explaining. He stared at the man, speechless.

"Well, boy, you returned in time. Come here." The curt nod invited Kuini to near the table.

With his legs heavy, difficult to control, he made his way toward them slowly, still ready to flee should any of the warriors try to get up. He had nowhere to go and no way to leap over the windowsill quickly enough. Still, he would try to get away, he decided. With those unpredictable bastards one never knew.

The scroll on the table spread long and creased, well-used, evidently folded and unfolded many times. Kuini studied the images, his mind refusing to work. The drawing resembled the map of the Great Lake the Aztec had shown him earlier, but this time the purple area was smaller, tucked at the upper corner of the picture, while the rest was unpainted and covered with large and small symbols.

"See, here." The rough finger pointed at one image, placed under the drawing Kuini recognized as the symbolic Texcoco he had seen on the other map. "Can you guide us there? Or maybe even there?" The finger moved down the borderline, pointing at another image.

"I... umm... what are those?" asked Kuini, painfully aware of the helplessness of his question.

"Coatlinchan," said the Aztec, unperturbed, moving back to the first image. The rest of the warriors raised their eyebrows. "And this one, this one is..." He turned to one of his men. "What do they call that town?"

"Chimalhuacan," said the man. His dark gaze rested on Kuini, skeptical, full of disdain. "Honorable Leader, he doesn't even know what the pictures on the map are. How could he guide us?"

"He knows what they look like for real," said the Aztec. He looked at Kuini, one eyebrow raised. "Don't you?"

"I've been around Coatlinchan, yes," muttered Kuini.

"Is it close to the Great Lake's shores?"

"Well, yes. It's on the mainland, but it's not really far away from the lake."

"Good." The Aztec turned back to his companions. "So all we have to do is to reach this Coatlinchan. As quickly as possible. The boy is the best guide we can have for the moment, so he'll do." He rose to his feet. "Let us move. We still have to get out of this filthy *altepetl* before dawn breaks."

Paces long and determined, the man headed for the window, full of purpose and looking somewhat younger again. The rest of the warriors came in. Kuini counted about twenty more.

"Keep an eye on the boy," said the Warlord to one of the warriors, a young man with a badly scarred face. Nimbly, he disappeared into the darkness outside the window, leaping over the edge with the agility of a much younger person.

So much for "you are not a prisoner," thought Kuini, enraged, jumping back into the familiar ground. *How many times had he gone over this window?*

The darkness had turned chilly and the stars dimmed. It was well into the second part of the night, although the dawn was still far away. Soundless and sure of himself, the Aztec led them into the darkness of the Palace's groves as if familiar with the place. The warriors followed, making no sound upon the wet grass.

Circumventing the Palace, but from the site opposite to the one Kuini used to walk, they reached the wall and kept moving alongside it, soundless and lethal, jaguar-like in their spotted cloaks. When their leader halted, Kuini recognized the place, his heartbeat accelerating. They were just a few tens of paces from the pond. He tried to keep his face blank.

The Aztec nodded, and two of the warriors leaped into the darkness, while the wave of the man's hand made the rest wait. After some time, the warriors returned, gesturing, their nods reassuring.

"Is it guarded?" breathed the Aztec, almost inaudibly.

The warriors nodded once again, the question in their faces obvious.

"Get rid of them, but don't leave the bodies. There is a pond somewhere around. Throw them there."

No, not the pond, thought Kuini, clenching his teeth. Somewhere else, but not in *their* pond. He could picture her coming here through the next morning, to re-live some of the night, maybe. It would be so much like her to do so. And what would she find there? Floating, mutilated bodies!

Then he remembered her punishment and breathed with relief as the warriors began moving again. She wouldn't be coming to the pond with the dawn. She was not allowed out of her rooms.

Oh mighty Camaxtli, he thought fervently. *Please let me get away from those Aztecs and be back in time.*

A market interval, five to six dawns. Yes, he should have plenty of time, he thought, passing the narrow gates, his elation welling. He was out of the accursed Palace and still alive, and in one piece.

The Emperor paced the reception hall, his steps long, his elaborately decorated cloak swirling angrily. The man was beyond any regular stage of rage.

"Disappeared just like that?" he bellowed once again.

The kneeling advisers cringed, and even Coyotl, standing behind the Emperor's chair, fought an urge to flee. He had never seen his father so enraged.

"Oh, what a traitorous, dirty, arrogant lowlife!" exclaimed the Emperor once again, clenching his fists. "Just went away, sneaking under the cover of the night, while my warriors must have been sleeping, snug under their blankets!" He turned to the Chief Warlord. "Are the gates of my Palace not guarded?"

"Many of your faithful warriors are guarding the gates day and night, Revered Emperor," muttered the veteran warrior, off balance for a change. He looked up imploringly. "The dirty Aztecs didn't use the gates."

"Then how did they get out?"

"They must have scaled the wall." The man almost stuttered

over his words.

"That warlord is an old man!" exclaimed the Emperor. He turned around, resuming his angry pacing. "No, they must have used one of the gates."

Surprised with the open dismay of the usually short-tempered leader of the warriors, Coyotl just stared, his own worry nagging. What about Kuini? Did the filthy Aztecs drag his friend along? They must have done just that, filthy bastards. But then, it might have been for the best, he reasoned, suppressing a shrug. The Highlander was capable of sneaking away once back in his element.

"Has the delegation to Tenochtitlan left yesterday as planned?" The Emperor's voice broke into his thoughts.

"Oh, yes, Revered Emperor," answered one of the advisers hastily. "Composed and instructed exactly the way you wished."

"So, they will still reach Huitzilihuitl before his Chief Warlord will." He turned back to the kneeling warrior. "Have you checked the shores? Those Aztecs may still be busy around the wharfs."

"Yes, Revered Emperor. They did not attempt to sail out of the city. Their long canoes are still here."

The Emperor stomped his foot. "Then where did they go?"

"I think they may try to go away by land," mumbled the Warriors' Leader from the floor.

"They cannot reach Tenochtitlan by land!"

"Maybe they will attempt to sail from another location."

"Get up."

The warrior jumped to his feet hastily.

"Send a group of warriors – a large group! – to comb the countryside, to search for their traces. How many warriors were they?"

"About twenty or so, Revered Emperor."

"Send twice as many men. No, three times!"

"What would be their instructions?"'

"Kill them to the last man." The Emperor frowned, then looked as if fighting a smile. "It is not safe to roam around our countryside in the time of war. The highlanders may have attacked them. Those savages are just the people to do that and leave no survivors." The smile showed eventually, a mirthless grin. "This man will yet wish he did not try to outsmart me."

As the Chief Warlord disappeared hastily, the rest of the people present breathed with relief, but Coyotl back's was covered with cold sweat despite the pleasant midmorning breeze. *Oh mighty Tlaloc, let Kuini get away from the Aztecs before our people reach them.*

"Nezahualcoyotl!" His father's voice startled him. "You go out into the provinces as planned. Leave now, with no delay. How many warriors are you taking with you?"

"Two times twenty of warriors, Revered Emperor," said Coyotl, heart beating fast.

"Leave with no delay, and be back in a market interval."

"Yes, Revered Emperor."

Relieved to be out of the tension-filled imperial chamber, Coyotl rushed along the long corridors, his thoughts still in a jumble. One market interval? No, he'd never manage. Six dawns to cover five provinces. Impossible. And yet the Emperor was not in the mood to anger him any further. When the Tepanecs arrived, Texcoco would need every warrior it could gather.

However, his day did not get any better. The leader of the Palace's guards stared at him, unsettled, even afraid.

"I kept your warriors ready for the midday, as you requested, Honorable First Son," he said, raising his hands in a somewhat defensive manner. "But the Honorable Chief Warlord recruited them for another mission."

"When?" cried out Coyotl, appalled.

"Not very long ago." The warrior shrugged, apologetic.

"So, how many warriors are left to escort me to the provinces."

"Half of twenty, Honorable First Son."

"Am I, the First Son, the Emperor's heir, to travel the countryside that is facing a great war with such a small entourage?" He felt like striking something or someone. "This is unbelievable! Those were my warriors. How could the Chief Warlord just take them?"

"Please, Honorable Master," pleaded the warrior. "Of course you cannot travel with such a small escort. In half a day you will have your two times twenty warriors again, I promise you that personally. Please, be patient."

"But I cannot wait!" Coyotl punched the wooden plank adorning the doorway, wincing at the pain in his fist. "I'm to go away *now*, to return in a market interval!" He tried to control his temper. "Listen, give me the warriors you have and gather the rest throughout the day. We will be heading for the north first, so make sure those warriors reach me at the town of Acolman, no later than the nightfall."

"Oh, Honorable First Son, you should wait for those reinforcements. It is not safe to travel with so little escort."

Coyotl turned around, kicking a basket lying on his path. "What choice do I have?"

Angrily, he stormed out, back into the realm of the sun. Everything was going wrong, everything! He was supposed to go out in great spirits, with his two times twenty of warriors and his friend by his side, having two market intervals to travel leisurely, taking much pleasure out of this mission.

But now? Now, he was to rush all over the Acolhua lands, with hardly a handful of warriors, while the invincible Tepanecs approached his *altepetl* like a lethal wave. Oh, may they all go to the lowest level of the Underworld!

He eyed the warriors pouring out of the building as the bushes behind his back rustled, causing him turn abruptly, startled. Not again! Iztac's face beamed at him, fresh and shiny in the strong morning light.

"What's amiss?" she asked breathlessly. "Everyone is running around like the world is all amok. Are the Tepanecs here?"

He blinked, eyeing her, his breath caught. Her hair was pulled high in elaborately woven braids, revealing her face entirely, to shine against the morning sun like a golden statue. The bright greenish blouse and skirt set off her coppery skin to perfection, with the matching necklace and turquoise earrings enhancing the effect.

"No, not yet," he said, clearing his throat. "It's just... Well, there are all sorts of things amiss, but nothing that should concern you in particular."

"Are you going away now?" She peeked at the warriors behind his back.

"Yes, I am."

"Oh." Her gaze lingered, straying toward the wooden construction as if expecting someone to come out of it.

"Iztac-Ayotl," he said, still staring. "What are you doing here?"

"Oh, nothing," she said, returning his gaze, eyes innocent, exaggeratedly so. "It was just so crazy this morning, with everyone running around nervous and agitated. So I wanted to know what's going on."

"Are you allowed to go out now?"

Her smile widened. "What do you think?"

"Oh, Iztac, you are impossible. Go back, quickly. It's broad daylight, and you are not even disguised. You'll get punished all over again."

She wrinkled her nose. "What can they do to me? I got punished already, didn't I? What would they do? Send me to Tenochtitlan tied and on foot?"

He could not suppress his grin. "That would serve you right."

"So, you are off now?" Her eyes strayed again, scanning the surroundings.

"Yes." He eyed the warriors too, annoyed with their glances, the way they measured her greedily from head to toe. "Iztac, go back to the women's quarters."

"When are you coming back?" she asked, ignoring his demand.

"In a market interval."

Her eyes lit. "Oh, a market interval. It's good. I should like to see you in a market interval." She smiled widely. "Make sure you are not late."

"Oh, not you too," he cried out, amused and annoyed at the same time. "The Emperor insists that I cover five provinces in six days. And now you. I'll be back, don't worry."

Her laughter rang out like a pair of coppery rings, attracting the attention of the warriors once again.

"Just be back in time. It's important. I'll tell you why when you return." She peeked behind his back once again. "So you are off now, aren't you?"

"Yes, I'm off. You've asked me that about twenty times already." He peered at her. "What do you want, sister? Just spill it out."

"Oh, nothing, nothing. I'll go back now, I guess." She hesitated. "Your Highlander is coming with you, isn't he?"

"No, he is not. I think he left with the Aztecs."

"Oh!" Her face fell. "I thought he was supposed to..." She frowned. "Oh well, I should go back." She peered back at him. "When did the Aztecs leave?"

He laughed. "This is the question that made the whole Palace agog. Somewhere around the dead of the night is anybody's guess."

Her grin puzzled him. "Not the dead of the night surely. But maybe through the second part of it." She shook her head. "Well, I'll be off now, brother. Have a safe journey, and come back quickly. I'll be waiting for your return, but not if it takes you more than a market interval."

He watched her hurrying down the well-swept path, a merry spot of bright green and gold. *What has come over everyone?* he wondered. *Has everyone just gone mad?*

CHAPTER 11

Coatlinchan turned out to be quite a large town, spread not far away from the muddy shores of the Great Lake.

Curious, Kuini watched the narrow alleys running between the scattered one and two-story houses, wooden or cane-and-reed made. In such a place, the superiority of his Acolhua enemies was hardly showing. Save for a few two-story high pyramids, this town looked no better than any settlement of the Highlands. Texcoco provinces were not much to look at, he decided, satisfied.

They reached the town toward the end of the day, having covered much distance on foot. Had they taken the wide, well-kept road, they would have moved much faster, but the Aztec leader insisted on avoiding the regular paths, and Kuini was more than happy to comply. He didn't know the roads as well as he knew the tracks and the shortcuts, having traveled those with his brothers, on an occasional foray.

Elated to be outside, his freedom at his fingertips, he led them confidently, pleased with their growing appreciation. The warriors' attitude thawed, and no more dark or disdainful glances were shot at him, while the Warlord seemed to be outright proud of his protégée. Kuini grinned to himself. This man was such a mix of good and bad.

Startled, the governor of Coatlinchan seemed at a loss as to how to proceed when over twenty arrogant, dangerously armed and determined visitors descended upon his palace-like dwelling. Pale and afraid, the elderly man tried to keep the remnants of his dignity by offering the best guest quarters upon the spacious grounds – a large, prettily set cottage in the artificial groves near the wall. With his entourage of advisers and warriors following, he tried to understand the unusual sort of mission the Aztec high official was on.

"What we need the most is to commandeer a small fleet of your best boats," said the Warlord, strolling through the gardens arrogantly, ahead of his hosts. "With dawn we are to sail to Tenochtitlan. Our journey is urgent and extremely important, so I would appreciate if the boats were prepared this very evening." He glanced at his host, eyes cold and firm, but amiable. Oh, the man knew he would be obeyed, reflected Kuini, watching with admiration. "For now of course, a bath and a good meal for me and my people will do. We appreciate your hospitality. My personal gratitude, and that of my Emperor, will know no bounds. In such difficult war times all settlements on this side of the Great Lake should support each other with no reservations."

Kuini wanted to laugh. Flowery pleasantries said in a tone that brooked no argument; a ridiculous combination that clearly had the desired effect on the local ruler. Their mats in the pretty cottage among the trees of the secluded part of the gardens were soft, their blankets of the best quality, their meal rich, and their bath scorching hot.

He tried not to wince, fighting the urge to run away, breathing with difficulty in the thick fumes, having never entered the baths of the lowlanders before. What a strange way to clean oneself, he thought, sweating in the profuse heat, at a loss for what to do with a bunch of twigs thrust into his hands.

The other warriors seemed to enjoy themselves, squatting comfortably, scrubbing the dirt and accumulating sweat off their naked bodies. Hardly visible in the clouds of mist, which kept spreading every time a slave with a bucket would come in, splashing more water on the red-hot glowing wall, they laughed and joked with each other and their leader, content and perfectly at ease.

"A nice way to finish a long day," said the Aztec as they reclined around the low tables, devouring their food with enjoyment. "I wish through each day of every campaign some provincial town would be there to serve and to entertain. Do you think this petty ruler will have enough sense to send us a pretty slave girl or two, or twenty for that matter, to finish the perfect day?"

The warriors laughed.

"Twenty-one," said the tall warrior, whom the Aztec had told to keep an eye on Kuini on the previous night, when leaving Texcoco. "Our guide is also a person and not such a young boy as not to enjoy a pretty girl." He grinned at Kuini. "Aren't you?"

"Oh, how inconsiderate of me," laughed the Warlord. "Yes, jaguar cub, you'll get the prettiest one of them all. You did well." He turned to the others, grinning. "See? One doesn't need to read maps to be a perfect guide. I keep wondering how one learns all the invisible trails around those settlements." The large eyes bore into Kuini, but as if sensing his growing uneasiness, the man winked and turned away. "So tomorrow afternoon we are back in Tenochtitlan, with the filthy Texcoco Emperor tearing out his hair and about to get a good beating from the none-less-filthy Tezozomoc."

"Don't you think they have a fair chance of pushing the Tepanecs back, with this entire side of the Great Lake behind them?" asked one of the warriors, a heavyset man with a smooth round face. He hesitated, then added with a grin. "Honorable Leader."

The title sounded out of place in the general atmosphere of comradeship that filled the cozy room, so different from the Texcoco Palace, where the Warlord would dine alone or in the company of a chosen few. They all laughed.

"I do think they have a fair chance of throwing the Tepanecs back, oh Honorable Warrior," said the Warlord, amidst a new outburst of laughter. He sobered. "But this immediate victory would not help them. Tezozomoc has the empire, with all its imminent resources and manpower at his fingertips. He is an able leader. And a greedy one. Texcoco people cannot beat him in the long run. They should have waited for the death of this particular emperor, which, considering his very advanced age, could not be too far away. Then they should act. With our ardent help, most probably."

Kuini watched the man, fascinated. He could see the warriors listening avidly, hanging on every word. This man was the undisputed leader of those elite noblemen, the best warriors of the Lowlands, he reflected, awed. Even should he choose to brush honorific titles aside for one unordinary evening.

His eyelids were heavy, and he fought the sleepiness, reaching for another tortilla. He should stay awake, wait for them to fall asleep, then go away. Sailing to Tenochtitlan was definitely not a part of his plan, although those Aztecs were warming to him and were he just a boy from Texcoco, he might have considered their Warlord's generous offer. However, as it was, he had to go away quickly. He now had less than five days to reach home and be back in Texcoco.

His stomach twisted at the thought of *her*, waiting on the Plaza, disguised as a commoner girl again, with her hair braided and her long legs covered by a maguey skirt, her black eyes glittering, expectant and impatient, a mischievous smile in place.

Aware of the growing excitement he wished to conceal, he got up quietly and went to the small opening in the wall. Running away with her would put an end to the hope of fighting the Tepanecs with Coyotl. Too bad he could not postpone it until after the Tepanec invasion. Would the Lowlanders lose eventually, as the Aztec Warlord assumed they would?

He shuddered. What would become of Coyotl then? There had to be a way to fight the Tepanecs with his friend. But maybe she could be placed with his family, until he returned...

He bit his lips so hard it hurt. Returned from what? From fighting with the Lowlanders, the enemies of his people? Oh gods, but he was truly a mess. He had to go home and forget all about the great capital, *all of it*.

Quietly, he made his way toward the nearby mat. He'd wait until they fell asleep, then he'd be gone. Back to the Highlands, back to normality, to his countryfolk, to his family, to the familiar mountains and customs, where people would bathe in a river and not in strange heated constructions.

He must have fallen asleep after all, as in the dead of the night, he jumped up, his heart pounding. Someone rushed past him, a pair of sandaled feet.

"The Warlord," he heard the urgent whispering.

"What is it?" The Aztec's voice sounded wide awake, calm and in full control, but pressing.

"There are warriors in the gardens. We counted about twenty of them, sneaking between the trees."

Kuini's heart pounded in his ears, so strong he could not hear the words properly. More people were awake now, their whispering tearing through the darkness.

"We wait here," said the Warlord, jumping to his feet. Snatching up his girdle, the man busied himself with tying it up. "Let the manure-eaters make the first move, thinking we are snugly asleep."

Careful not to near any wall opening, he went between the warriors, talking to them quietly, explaining, encouraging.

"They'll try to get in by stealth, so watch the doorway and the wall openings."

A knife landed beside Kuini.

"Use this, boy. For now. You'll get a better weapon quickly enough. I'll see to that." The large eyes twinkled, measuring him up, penetrating, as though looking into his deepest thoughts, as though amused and appreciative of what they saw there. "You'll do well. I loved what you managed to do with that sword yesterday while training. So just remember what I taught you and trust your instincts."

Their tension welled. A quiet whispering reached them from time to time, brought into the room by a light breeze. Then, finally, the careful footsteps, heading for the doorway. Oh, but these were warriors, no assassins, reflected Kuini. They wanted to storm the place, and they would have done it anyway, although the temptation to surprise the sleeping enemy was evidently great.

The first pair that entered the room died instantly, cut by the knives of the warriors on both sides. Two spotted cloaks pounced soundlessly, dragging in another pair of men, killing them as swiftly while their peers pulled the first bodies in.

The silence prevailed, interrupted by a slight rustling of the bushes outside. No one moved. Then the voices rose, and they could hear people running.

An arrow flew in, hissing at the quietness of the room. Mesmerized, Kuini watched it penetrating the wood of the opposite wall, its colorful feathering trembling. More of the enemy warriors poured through the doorway, all to die as quickly as they entered.

"Stupid manure-eaters," he heard the Aztec muttering. There was no place to maneuver in the crowdedness of the room, and the enemy's advantage in numbers was wasted.

After a short time filled with more doorway-fighting, a fire-arrow came in.

"Very well. Time to go out and show them," declared the Warlord calmly. "Follow me and stay close to each other. Guard each other's backs until we know how many of the dung-filled frog-eaters are out there. Hear me! Don't scatter. Stay close." He slipped through the doorway without waiting for an answer and without looking back.

Kuini watched the warriors following quickly, disappearing into the darkness. His excitement welled. To wait in the closeness of the room was nerve-wracking, but the opportunity to go out, even if toward an enemy eager to kill, was exciting, liberating.

He breathed the night air deeply, then rushed into the shadow as an arrow slipped by his ear, reminding him of the battle. People were fighting all around him, their swords clashing, the wooden handles of their weaponry creaking against each other. He heard the swishing of a club and ducked, stumbling and almost falling over a sprawling body. Clutching his dagger tight, he dove into the protective darkness behind the cottage.

The man with the club followed. He could hear the heavy breathing behind his back. Darting aside, Kuini turned sharply and the club swished beside his ear, pushing against his shoulder. It made him lose his balance, and he flipped his hands in the air, groping for something to steady himself. His palm clutched the rim of his pursuer's cloak, and the man swayed too, suddenly close, momentarily exposed. The dagger, still grasped tightly in his right fist, came to life on its own. Slippery in his sweating palm, it made its way swiftly, shooting upwards, forcing its path through the soft tissue under his assailant's ribs.

The weight of the warrior was suddenly upon him, squashing, impossible to hold against. His back hit the ground heavily, hurting his damaged arm. He felt the man's palms making their way toward his throat, while warm, sticky liquid trickled down his own ribs.

He kicked fiercely, unable to breathe, his panic welling. The man groaned, trying to grab his stomach, his body limp, pressing, choking in its stench of sweat mixed with fresh blood.

Unable even to scream, Kuini pushed with the last of his strength, crawling from under the squirming enemy. Scrambling onto his feet, still panicked, he rushed back into the moonlit clamor of clashing sounds and screaming people, not bothering to retrieve his knife.

The body he had stumbled upon earlier was still there, blocking his way, and this time he slipped and crashed on top of it. However, the fall refreshed him, somehow, made his head work again.

Pushing himself up, he noticed the sword still clutched tightly in the dead man's hand. Fighting the grip of the limp fingers, he pulled on the carved wooden handle. It came out easily, and he hurried onto his feet, suddenly elated, the proud owner of an obsidian sword.

The battle raged all over the moonlit ground and the surrounding patches of darkness. He saw the Aztec hacking his sword fiercely, powerfully, a lethal weapon in his broad confident hands. The other spotted-cloaks swirled all around, but their enemies were still numerous, pressing their attack, springing out from all over the place, more men pouring in from the darkness of the palace's gardens.

Clutching the heavy sword in both hands, he did not duck as a tall, thickset man attacked him. Their weapons met, pressing against each other, and Kuini's hands shook, the pressure in his left arm increasing, sending shafts of pain up his shoulder. His opponent was infinitely stronger.

Disengage and leap aside. The voice of the Aztec echoed in his

head, along with the memory of the training grounds back in the
Texcoco Palace. He did just that, wavering, managing to catch his
balance, avoiding the razor-sharp touch of his attacker's obsidian,
but barely.

Attack, he remembered the man repeating. *Always attack. Don't
let them put you on the defensive.*

He hacked his sword again, reaching for his tall opponent. The
man stepped aside too, and then pressed on, clearly seeking an
opportunity to engage their swords anew.

Kuini leaped backwards, but the rough trunk of a tree blocked
his way, scratching his back. Having no way to avoid the
confrontation, he blocked another attack with his sword, grinding
his teeth in an attempt to hold on. It didn't help. He had no chance
against his much stronger rival.

Sweat rolled down his face, stinging his eyes. The pain in his
arm became unbearable. He almost stopped breathing in an
attempt to hold on, to prevent the inevitable, to slow the
approaching obsidian spikes, hating the way they continued
moving closer toward his face. His chest was empty, and he could
not get enough air, his whole being concentrated on the effort to
hold on.

The enemy laughed. He could see the squinted eyes sparkling,
the broad face gleaming with a sense of a victory. Gritting his
teeth, he felt them nearly crushing against each other, yet all of a
sudden, the man's face changed. An expression of surprise swept
over it, reflected in the widening eyes. The pressure of the sword
lessened, then disappeared, as his attacker went down, toppling to
his side.

Kuini moved his arms, trying to make them work. He could
hardly feel them anymore. Taking a deep breath, he blinked as the
Aztec's face swam into his view, grinning.

"Good work, jaguar cub," The voice reached his ears, full of
amusement, as always. "But make sure to choose your rivals more
carefully. You were too young for that one. In a few years I would
bet on you, but not yet." The large eyes twinkled, moved away.
"Come with me."

He followed obediently, his legs trembling, the aftershock of the confrontation difficult to cope with. The moonlit night was full of spotted cloaks now, but a few were lying on the ground, among the multitude of wounded and killed warriors.

"How many of them got away?" asked the Aztec, walking briskly among the bodies, studying them.

The rest of the warriors, blood-smeared and exhausted, but elated nevertheless, followed.

"Maybe half of twenty," said someone.

"I think more," argued another.

"Here is one pretty healthy manure-eater." One of the spotted cloaks dragged out a stunned warrior, bloodied, but not overly so.

The Warlord grabbed the man by the cloak, pulled him up roughly, slammed him against a tree. "Where did you come from? Who sent you?" he barked.

The man said nothing, his face twisting with pain, eyes widening at the sight of a dagger that came up seemingly out of nowhere. Glazed, they followed the glittering blade as it pounced toward his face. The cut it made was long and vicious.

"Tell me now," demanded the Aztec once again. "Before I take your eye out."

The man swallowed.

"Wait!" he screamed, when the razor-sharp obsidian nicked his eyelid.

The knife stopped. "Where are you from?"

"Texcoco."

"How many people?"

"I... I don't know... No!" The warrior screamed when the knife pressed again. "Two times twenty of warriors!"

"What else are you not telling me?"

The man gulped.

This time the knife pressed against his throat. "We are not at war with your people, however dirty your Emperor is trying to play. So I won't take you as my captive. Your blood won't be welcomed by our gods." The knife pressed harder. "I can either kill you or let you go, and I don't have time for this. Tell me what are you not telling me and do it now."

The man coughed as the pressure of the knife lessened. "More warriors... more warriors are waiting..." A gurgle. "On the shores here... On the way to Chimalhuacan too... many warriors."

The Warlord pushed his victim away, to waver and fall on his back.

"Well, I suppose we are not as welcome here as we had previously thought," he said, curiously unperturbed. "Let us take care of our wounded, then we'll be off." Frowning, he led the way back toward the cottage. "We have not enough warriors to fight for their canoes, so we'll have to make it for Chimalhuacan," he said quietly once inside. The narrowing eyes turned to Kuini. "We'll need more of your circumventing paths, boy. Can you help us with those?"

Kuini took a deep breath. "I think I can find the way to Chimalhuacan, but..." He hesitated. "We will have to go up into the mountains a little way."

The warriors around him murmured.

"How little? How much time will we spend in the Highlands?" asked the Aztec sharply.

"About half a day, I think."

"Do you know these places well?"

Kuini swallowed, too tired to think. He didn't care anymore. "Yes, I know these places well."

The penetrating gaze bore into him for a heartbeat, then moved away.

"I won't ask you how you know these places," declared the Warlord with a sudden chuckle. "I'm not sure I want to know." He straightened up abruptly. "Hurry up. Let us move before they thought of blocking our way out of this place."

CHAPTER 12

The sun managed to slip through the clouds toward the late afternoon, as they made their way down the slope. Green with the early summer grass, the trail was not difficult, nothing like the roads and paths leading to Huexotzinco, Kuini's hometown.

Yet, their progress was painfully slow. Careful not to make too much noise, exhausted by lack of sleep, hindered by their wounded, the warriors made their way gradually up the moderate slopes.

Kuini sighed. No, they would never make it back to the Great Lake's shores before nightfall, not at such a slow pace. But then, with the fresh Acolhua forces hot on their heels was it not safer to pass the night here, on the low ridges of the Highlands' edge?

He eyed the Warlord slowing his pace wearily, talking to a warrior behind him. Their leader was tired too, that much was obvious. His posture still straight, his bearing as imposing, the leading Aztec's shoulders sagged imperceptibly, and his lips were clasped a little too tightly, his face gray with fatigue. With all the impressive willpower and strength, with all the experience and sparkle, the man was old, reflected Kuini; and maybe also spoiled by many summers of the luxury belonging to his high position.

"How long before we are out of these ridges? I trust we won't have to pass the night here."

Kuini swallowed. "Yes, it may happen. We are too slow."

"Oh, curse them all into the lowest level of the Underworld!" exclaimed the man, inhaling loudly through his clenched teeth. "I can't believe it. I swear I'll make the filthy Texcoco Emperor pay for this!"

"I'm sorry," said Kuini, pitying the redoubtable leader. "Maybe, if we hurry up now..." He measured the sun. "There are only two more ridges to pass." He shrugged helplessly. *No, they would never manage.*

The Aztec's eyes reflected the same thought. "It doesn't matter," he said, making a visible effort to calm down. "Maybe we are safer up here, with those filthy Texcocans proving more efficient than I thought." He shrugged. "Never make a mistake of underestimating your enemies, boy. A person who does it would lose, and he would deserve it greatly, too."

"You haven't lost yet."

The man's eyebrows lifted. "No, but they've got me on the run, and I don't like it in the least. I haven't run from anyone for twenty summers and more. Not that fast, anyway." He sobered again. "I didn't think they could be so efficient, those Acolhua manure-eaters. Who knows? Maybe they can beat the Tepanecs, after all."

"I hope they do," muttered Kuini, thinking of Coyotl.

"Why?"

Uneasy under the suddenly penetrating gaze, Kuini shrugged.

"I like Texcoco," he said finally. "It's beautiful and, I don't know, it's full of many great things. The pyramids and the temples and the scrolls. And some Acolhua people are good." He dropped his gaze. "I don't know."

"Some Acolhua people are good, eh?" The Aztec's lips stretched into a wide grin. "You are a highlander, aren't you boy? With a Tepanec for a mother, but still a wild highlander."

Kuini straightened his gaze. "Does it matter?" he asked, not afraid anymore. They were in the Highlands now, and he could get away from these people in a heartbeat, leaving the fierce Aztecs to fight the mountain trails all by themselves. They depended on him now. He was returning the Aztec a favor. Life for life.

"Oh, it does, of course it does. But mostly because you made me curious. You can be a Big-Headed Mayan as far as I'm concerned."

"Then you've still got it all wrong. I lied. My mother was no

Tepanec and she has never been a slave. She is a Chichimec and so is my father!"

The wide eyes glanced at him, startled. "It doesn't make sense. You look like a Tepanec, and you speak a Tepanec-accented Nahuatl. You can't be a pure Highlander."

"But I am. I am that!" Kuini took a deep breath, suddenly annoyed. "I don't know why I look like this, but I have nothing to do with the Lowlanders of either side of the Great Lake. I should never have come to Texcoco. After all this is over, I'll go home, back to Huexotzinco, never to return."

He stared at the distant ridges, glowing with the purple of the setting sun. His chest hurt. Oh, but he should never have come to the shores of the Great Lake, never. Coyotl, the Aztec Warlord, even her, the First Daughter of the Second Wife - they were all enemies of his people. He should have kept away from them.

His stomach tightened at the thought of *her*, naked in the moonlight or climbing the wall, or laughing into his eyes, so pretty and lacking any pretense, so trusting and innocent. She would be waiting for him after the market interval was over. She'd trust him to come back as he had promised. And he didn't even know her name, he realized, a stony fist squeezing his chest. The First Daughter of the Second Wife. They had shared so much in those two days in the Palace, they made love and planned their future together, and he didn't even know her name. He clenched his teeth tight, turning his face away from the penetrating gaze of the older man.

"You are a mess, boy," he heard the man saying, and there was a smile in his voice. "But weren't we all at your age?"

They spent the night in the small clearing, keeping their fire low, feasting on berries and roots that Kuini had found. He could have tried to hunt something, but the Warlord decided against it. To hunt and cook would create noises and smells he wished to avoid while roaming the enemy's countryside with less than twenty warriors, some of them wounded.

Although hungry, they slept well, taking turns watching the surroundings. Refreshed and full of purpose, they resumed their journey with dawn, spending no time watching the beautiful sunrise that painted the ridges in a variety of magnificent colors.

Yet, Kuini's mood did not improve. A strange feeling of being watched haunted him, nagging in the back of his mind. It made his skin crawl.

The Warlord seemed to be gloomy as well. He walked ahead of the party, watchful and tense, face closed, lips pursed, not his talkative old self.

Refusing to relax their pace, they made fair progress, reaching the first of the two passes leading back toward the Great Lake and the town of Chimalhuacan. The Warlord hesitated, eyeing the narrow gorge suspiciously, straining his eyes against the glow of the midmorning sun.

"I don't like this pass," he muttered, frowning. "Too easy to trap a bunch of tired warriors like us. As a matter of fact, a fresh and bloodthirsty force of ten times twenty men could be trapped here as efficiently." His frown deepened. "Is there another path that would allow us to detour this ravine?"

Kuini glanced at the ridges around them, uncertain. Yes, this pass was deep and narrow, adorned by cliffs with footholds aplenty, dark and ominously calm, as though watching the foreigners, as though daring them to try to enter.

"We can climb this cliff and try to make our way up there," he said, hesitating.

The Aztec measured the steep rocks with a glance. "We can't get the wounded up there, and I'm not sure about the rest of my warriors as well. They are no mountain goats to hop up these cliffs with no trail." He grinned. "They are no highlanders." Sobering, he watched the pass, his eyes narrow. "Well, it's not such a long walk and there is this cluster of rocks over there. If someone is waiting to shoot at us from behind those ridges, we can take cover behind the rocks." Resolutely, the man straightened up. "Let us get it over with. If we had any choice or any scouts to send, we could have gone on deliberating."

Tall and purposeful, filled with his usual cheerful authority, he went between his men, talking to them, encouraging, instructing.

Kuini's stomach churned. If only there was a way to detour this pass...

The sunlight dimmed as they proceeded down the trail, the steep cliffs towering from both sides, dark, threatening, scowling at the careless intruders. The wind grew, shifting dry leaves and broken branches, raising clouds of dust.

Kuini looked up, his stomach twisting. They had been watched, now he was sure of it. Not all of the noises were being made by the wind. He glanced at the Aztec, walking alongside, peering at the cliffs around, tense as an overstretched bowstring. Then a decisive expression washed over the broad face.

"Move faster," he cried out abruptly. "Keep distance from each other, but head for these rocks as fast as you can. Move!"

They hastened their step, uncomfortable with the strange request of keeping distance. They were used to doing the opposite, but Kuini could see the Warlord's reason. Spread thinly, they would make more difficult targets. The Aztec seemed to know everything, just everything. But for a chance to learn from such a man! He glanced at the wide back and hurried.

The arrows came shortly thereafter, with vicious hiss tearing the air, followed by darts and stones aplenty. The air was suddenly heavy, difficult to breath, full of flying objects, swishing shrilly, seeking their victims.

"Behind the rocks!" yelled the Warlord. "Run behind the rocks."

The warriors needed no reminder. They darted for the cover, but did not run straight. Veteran fighters, they raced in zigzags, struggling to make difficult targets.

His heart racing, Kuini hesitated, then dashed after them, heedless of reason. The heavy sword made his progress cumbersome, but he refused to drop it, clutching it in both hands. What would the Aztec think of him if he dropped his sword?

The nearest rock towered ahead when a powerful blow sent him sprawling. Astounded, he pushed himself up, surprised when his right arm refused to react. Clumsily, still clutching his sword, he got to his knees and swayed, the pain in his shoulder exploding, making him gasp.

There were footsteps and a strong arm pulled him to his feet, dragged him, swaying, ahead, dumping him behind the nearest rock.

"Stay here," gasped the Aztec. "I'll take a look at you in a short while."

The man was gone, not solving the mystery.

What happened?

Clenching his teeth against the pain, Kuini reached for the source of it until his hand met a wooden shaft, smooth and pleasant to touch, sticking out of his back. In disbelief, his fingers followed it, reaching the point where the polished wood turned warm and sticky, pulsating with pain. He tried to think.

The warriors all around him rushed about, talking urgently. Yet, some lay on the ground or sat, gripping their bleeding limbs, their faces twisting with pain.

He clasped his lips tight, the realization dawning. So he was shot. He had an arrow in his back, but it was not that painful. Maybe he would be all right, after all. He twisted his head, trying to reach for the annoying thing again. The agony exploded, and he gasped, giving up on the effort.

The attempt to get up was crowned with more success. Avoiding sharp movements and sudden turns of his upper body, he discovered that he could walk quite steadily.

He peeked out from behind his rock. Warriors, unmistakably Highlanders with their dark war paint and flowing hair, stood now upon the opposite ridge, waving their clubs, victorious. He could hear them laughing, catching the fragments of their conversation as they stood there, not attempting to climb down. *Why?*

He knew the answer to that even before bothering to turn his head. Another group of warriors descended the path from the direction they were heading. His breath caught. There would be another force closing their way back, he knew. Oh, but there was only one leader who would bother to trap his enemy so thoroughly. The rest would just charge, but his father was the War Leader of the United Clans for a reason.

He saw the Aztec passing by, his face drawn, eyes blazing, lips clasped tight.

"We'll keep moving behind those rocks. Maybe those would

spread for long enough to bring us to the end of this pass." He shook his head briskly, going from wounded to wounded. "Come on! Get up. You can walk well enough. Look at this boy with an arrow in his back and looking like nothing happened." He winked at Kuini, then turned around and peeked from behind the rocks once again. A loud expletive escaped his lips. "Change of plan," he said finally. "Looks like we are to make our stand here." He shrugged. "Well, let us show them what the elite Mexica warriors can do, even when trapped."

He went between his men, organizing those still capable of fighting.

"No need to keep back to back," he said cheerfully. "Those cliffs will do. And no need to keep those gloomy faces. The flowery fields of the eastern sky would welcome us readily. Think of this beautiful place, the tranquility. But before that, fight like wild jaguars. Don't give up until there is no trace of strength left in your bodies, until the last heartbeat, the last drop of blood. Remember that only real warriors can reach the eastern sky's paradise."

His gaze brushed past Kuini, lingering. "Come." He nodded and headed toward the opposite edge of the rocks.

Swaying with dizziness, Kuini followed.

"Listen, jaguar cub," said the man when well away from the hearing range. "You did your best, and I'm grateful for that. Now, go away. Climb those rocks and be off. Can you do that with this stupid arrow? You seem to be able to walk well enough."

Having difficulty breathing, Kuini stared at the broad, dust-covered face, taking in the strong cheekbones, the generous mouth, the dark well-spaced eyes that, even now, could not hide that typical light twinkle.

He swallowed, his throat dry. This man was going to die, and he was not suppose to feel sorry, but somehow his heart pounded wildly, and he could not just go away.

"I can't," he whispered.

The full lips twisted into a familiar, mischievous grin. "What's wrong with you, boy?" The man laughed. "Those are your people out there. We are just a bunch of intruders, and no one will miss us, not in your parts of the land." The warm palm rested upon his good shoulder, giving him strength. "Climb this cliff and wait for the battle to be over. Then go to your people. You'll make a great warrior one day. A great warrior and a great leader. Trust me. I've seen enough young men to be able to tell. But now go. We'll meet in the eastern sky paradise one day."

His breath caught, Kuini stared at the man for another heartbeat, then turned around and peeked onto the dusted road. The warriors were nearer now, strolling ahead confidently. He could see their painted faces, their combed oily hair. Through the recent days he'd grown so accustomed to the partly shaved heads and the warriors' locks of the Lowlanders, he found it strange to watch his people's unshaved skulls. He thought he had recognized the short, dominant figure in a headdress, walking ahead, leading them.

"My father will be the one in the lead," he said. "I'll go and talk to him."

A hand grabbed his good shoulder. "No!"

He shook it off without turning back. To take a deep breath became a necessity, but he walked out stubbornly, praying that he would make it as far as his people without losing his strength. To fall in the middle of the road between the two fighting forces would be embarrassing, he knew, aware of his pounding heart. The sword hindered his progress, clasped in his left arm now. It seemed heavier than before and unnecessary, yet he could not drop it. Not with the Aztec watching.

The road stretched ahead, long and twisted. The attacking Highlanders were still far away. He could hear their voices, if barely. However, the voices to his right carried clearly through the dusted air.

It took him an effort to turn his head, to glance at the cliff and the archers and slingers upon it. The pain in his shoulder grew.

"Don't shoot!" he cried out, finding it curiously strange to talk in his own tongue now. He had no strength to raise either of his arms, one wounded and the other burdened by the sword. It would take too much of his dwindling strength. Yet, they must have heard him as no arrows came.

The Highlanders were closer now. They slowed their pace and watched him, undecided. He could see their faces, their paint running in the midmorning heat. He tried to recognize them, but his eyes were blurry, head spinning and empty of thoughts. He fought the urge to lean on the sword.

Someone shouted. A figure parted from the crowd of the painted faces. Paces long and urgent, the man rushed forward, covering the distance in a few powerful leaps. He felt strong hands grabbing him and almost sighed with relief, leaning against the familiar strength. Blinking, he tried to concentrate as Father's narrow, sun-burned face swam into his view, the man's eyes wide open, enormously large in the strong wrinkled face, mouth gaping. Oh, the formidable leaded looked unbecomingly surprised. Kuini wanted to laugh hysterically.

"What are you doing here?" gasped Father.

"I... I can explain."

He saw the large eyes filling with amusement, so very familiar by now.

"He can explain," said Father to the warriors, who had surrounded them, chuckling. "I'm sure that story would be entertaining to listen to." The man straightened up, sobering. "Take him back there and see what can be done with that arrow of his. But wait for the healer if it's stuck too deeply." He frowned. "On second thought, just make him rest until we are back. Come, let us finish with those arrogant dung-eaters first."

Kuini listened, surprised with the effort it took him to understand. He had heard nothing but Lowlanders' Nahuatl for the past few days, and it felt strange to listen to his people's tongue once again.

"Father, wait!"

The man frowned with impatience, but something in his son's face had probably caught his attention. The large eyes narrowed.

"Please," Kuini licked his lips, hearing nothing but the wild pounding of his heart resonating through his ears. Swaying, he straightened up, clenching his fists tight. "Don't attack them."

"What?" The narrow jaw tightened along with the hardening gaze.

Kuini swallowed. "Please, those people, they did not invade here, they didn't come to fight. I brought them here to avoid some of the Lowlanders' roads. They didn't mean to come here." He swallowed again, but it brought no relief. His mouth was so dry he could feel the sides of his throat clinging to each other. "Please, let them go."

The warriors around them went silent. He could see their faces staring at him, astounded, their disapproval unconcealed.

Father's face closed. "Take him back," he said curtly. "Take care of his wounds."

He fought the grip upon his arm, ignoring the pain exploding in his shoulder.

"Father!" he said, stepping onto the man's path. "If you attack them, I'm going back there."

The narrowed eyes flashed, boring into him. As the man took a deep breath, the air hissed, coming through the widening nostrils.

"If you want to go back, go back," Father's voice was hard, cutting like the sharpest obsidian. "If you want to fight with the enemies of your people, the enemies you led here for some reason, you are at liberty to do just that."

He stared at the blackness of those eyes, seeing the rage and the frustration. His chest tightened. This man was his father, and he was a great leader and a great man. Why would he do this to him?

"Please, Father," he said quietly. "I'll go to them, but not because I want to betray you... or our people. This Aztec Warlord... he saved my life... more than once. I owe it to him. I can't let him die like that." He swallowed again. "I'm sorry."

He narrowed his eyes against the dizziness. It was difficult to see clearly. His father's face was changing, or was it his imagination? He saw the clasped lips opening, the set jaw relaxing, the rage in the dark eyes retreating, giving way to an astounded, even somewhat frightened, expression.

The man took a convulsive breath. "The Aztec Warlord," he repeated, licking his lips in his turn, eyes widening, flooding with... fear? "The Chief Warlord?"

"Yes," mumbled Kuini.

The clasped lips parted with difficulty. "What's his name?"

"I don't know."

"What does he look like?" It came out curtly, like an order. Was he now a prisoner to be tortured for information? He remembered the warrior from the previous night, and the knife slicing the man's frightened face.

"I… What does it matter?"

"Tall? Broad shoulders?" continued his interrogator, oblivious of Kuini's question.

"Yes."

The man turned around abruptly. "Come with me!"

His dizziness growing, Kuini followed, glad to get away from the warriors, who'd also followed, hurrying after their leader. What was Father going to do? Would he thank the Aztec for saving his son's life before killing him? Would he tell him everything he thought about Tenochtitlan and the filthy Aztecs and Tepanecs? Would he try to take him alive, a prisoner, such a prominent leader making a worthy sacrifice in the Sacred Grove's temples? Yes, that must be it. Oh gods. He shouldn't have tried to interfere. He'd made the matter so much worse.

"Stay here," said Father curtly, addressing the warriors when the rocks and the people crouching behind were again clearly visible in the midday sun.

A few began arguing, but he silenced them with a short gesture of his hand. Alone and imposing, despite his lack of height, he proceeded down the road, the feathers of his headdress swaying lightly, even calmly, in the strong breeze.

His heart swelling with pride along with his mounting worry, Kuini watched, his breath caught. How much strength, how much will-power! Oh, but his father was a worthy rival to the formidable Aztec. Were they going to fight each other, hand-to-hand?

His chest tightened, and it made his dizziness worse. The pain pulsating in his shoulder grew, coming in waves, each stronger than the other. He let his sword rest against the ground, unable to hold its weight anymore. The temptation to lean on it was great, yet he fought it, eyes on the rocks, a light mist blurring his vision.

He saw Father halting, standing there, in the middle of the

road, legs wide apart.

"Come out, Chief Warlord of the Aztecs," he cried out in Nahuatl, and his voice rolled between the cliffs, strong and challenging.

Kuini saw the Aztec's tall figure springing from behind the rocks, not waiting for another invitation. As imposing, as dignified, the Warlord strolled toward his rival, radiating power and no fear. Oh, this man had welcomed the challenge. One could be sure of that. It was easy to imagine the derisive sparkle in those large, widely spaced eyes.

Hardly noticing what he was doing, his legs took him closer, although it made the pain in his back so much worse, bringing more grayish mist to the corners of his eyes. Now he could see the Aztec more clearly, but what he saw in the familiar face made him gape. No derisive sparkle and no fierce challenge reflected in the dark eyes, now wide-open and growing larger and larger, almost popping out of their sockets. The broad face paled, the same almost frightened expression flooding it, the same expression Kuini had seen on his father's face such a short time ago. The generous mouth opened and closed, but no sound came out. The man looked as if about to faint.

Kuini blinked, trying to make sense of what he saw.

"I told you not to venture anywhere near *her* people's lands, oh Honorable Leader of the barbarian Aztecs," he heard Father saying, and the man's voice shook with laughter.

The Aztec's eyes sparkled. He inhaled loudly, then shook his head too, his own mirth spilling.

"I can't believe it," he said, when able to speak. "Oh, I knew you would go far, little brother. But that far?"

This time Kuini leaned on his sword, without noticing it. The sun seemed to grow stronger, making the grayish mist spread.

He didn't blink, didn't try to banish it. It felt only natural now to slip onto the ground, to dive into the merciful fog, away from the sunlit world that did not make any sense.

CHAPTER 13

It was bright and relatively quiet, and he didn't hurry to open his eyes, floating in the pleasant fogginess, allowing the waves to loll him back into sleep. He remembered surfacing and diving into this blissful obliviousness, hot and cold, and hot again. It was a strange feeling, but a calming one.

Yet, this time the fogginess dispersed before he had managed to go down. Almost sorry, he lay there, refusing to open his eyes.

His senses reached out, not anxious but calm, probing idly, unhurriedly. It was quiet outside, and he lay on something soft, but unpleasantly wet.

As he realized that, he shuddered and opened his eyes, trying to sit up. The motion released much pain in his chest, or his back, he couldn't tell. He gasped and gave up on the effort. Peacefulness gone, he turned his head carefully, afraid to bring the pain back. It hurt, but bearably so.

He narrowed his eyes against the light flickering in the far corner. The room was familiar. He knew were the torch was fastened; knew what the low table standing underneath it would hold. He had known this place since he was a child, the wooden one-story house of his father, with plenty of rooms and a large patio. The room he was laying in was his alone since his four grown up brothers had moved into their own houses, starting families of their own.

Carefully, he shifted again. Kicking away the wet blanket, he rolled onto his side, away from the pain, trying to push himself up using his hands only. It was a difficult task, and he was again covered with sheen of perspiration before he managed to remain upright.

Breathing heavily, he sat there, feeling victorious. The room swayed, but not too badly.

He took his hand toward the source of the pain behind his right shoulder. It came back sticky with ointments. The smell hit his nostrils. But of course. Mother's ointments would always stink to the skies. Yet, they usually did the work. And so did her potions. He winced, remembering the bitter taste of the things he was made to drink when feverish. He had been made to drink those potions now too, he remembered vaguely. Between the bouts of sleepiness, when it became too cold.

So he was sick, he thought. Sick and wounded. The arrow in his back was to blame, of course.

He frowned, the memories flooding in. He had been guiding the Aztecs through that stupid accursed pass, and then Father had been there and some fighting had ensued. Then Father was acting strange, and the Aztec was acting strange.

He pressed his lips together, refusing to think about it. *Those last words of the Aztec.* No, this could not be true. He must have been getting sick already with all the mist and the dizziness. His mind was already leaving for the other realms to roam, so he must have imagined the man saying what he had.

He looked up as the door creaked and hurried paces crossed the outer room. The small figure of his mother burst in, as always, brisk and purposeful.

She saw him sitting and gasped.

"Oh, you are back with us!" she cried out, not her usual reserved self.

Rushing toward him, she brushed his tangled hair off his face, her palm lingering upon his forehead, feeling it out.

"You made us worried," she added with a smile, apparently satisfied with what her palm related to her.

"I'm sorry." He smiled, liking her touch. "How long was I like that?"

"Oh, since they brought you in, almost three dawns." She squatted beside him. "You worried all of us this time. First, you disappear for so many dawns; then, you are brought back with all these wounds, your mind elsewhere, your body burning." Her palm reached out, brushing against his cheek, caressing. "Why would you do all these things?"

He shrugged, but it made the pain attack his chest anew. Biting his lips, he looked away.

Her hand moved up, caressing his hair. "Did you like it there in Texcoco?"

Afraid to shrug again, he just motioned with his head.

"You can tell me," she insisted. "It's a pretty place. I've been there once."

He studied her face, suspicious. "When?"

"Very, very long time ago. Thirty summers and more. Another lifetime."

"What did you do there?"

Her face darkened. "Nothing worth mentioning."

She looked at him searchingly, her strikingly bright eyes penetrating, as though looking into his mind. She was the priestess of the Great Obsidian Butterfly Goddess, her high priestess. The priestess with the yellow, cat-like, unsettling eyes. Many people feared her.

"There are some memories a person would prefer to forget," she said. "Everyone's life has secrets. Only that one person's secrets might be small and unimportant, while another's could be quite deep."

"How deep is yours?" he asked, refusing to meet her gaze.

"Mine? Mine is deep enough. But not that deep."

He pursed his lips. "And Father's?"

"Well, Father's is deeper." She fell silent. "You see, your father is a great man. He was always like that, even when as young as you are now. When I first met him. He has been our people's leader for so many summers. Not every man deserves that honor."

"Especially if he is a foreigner, eh?" His anger was so sudden it almost choked him. "Who is he? An Aztec? A Tepanec? A filthy Acolhua Lowlander? Who is this man?"

She didn't move, didn't take her gaze away, the brightness of her eyes turning sad, filling with compassion.

"He was born a Tepanec, a nobleman of Azcapotzalco. But his mother came from the Far North, hence his foreign looks." Her mouth tightened. "He left his people of his free will. He came here, to live with me and my people, and he dedicated his whole life to making our fortune better. We were a defeated people. Now we are proud and warlike. We didn't take back our lands, but we are still here, with our pride intact. Thanks to the people like your Father, Kuini. Think about it." She looked at him searchingly. "What does his past, his origins, matter? He did nothing wrong. He was always what he is now, a kind, brave, strong person, a great warrior and a great leader. Why would you hold his origins against him now that you know his secret?"

"And the Aztec?" he asked, refusing to be pacified. She was right, of course she was right. What would his father's origins matter? But his anger kept growing, impossible to control.

"What Aztec?" she asked, genuinely bewildered.

"The Aztec. The Chief Warlord. The man who had called him 'little brother.'"

"Oh, that man." She narrowed her eyes as if attempting to collect her thoughts. "This man indeed is your father's older brother. He is a good man, too. Not like your father, but good enough."

"Do you know him?"

"Yes. He saved my life once."

"Oh, how exciting!" He heard his own voice growing louder, dripping with disdain. He could not stop himself. But for the wound, he would jump to his feet and run away, never to return. "What a lifesaver. He saved mine too, you know? Such a benevolent spirit, watching over our family. I'm sure he'll be there if Nihi or the others would get into trouble, leaping from behind a tree or a rock, to save their lives, as well."

"Kuini, stop it!" she said sharply. "I'm talking to you as to a grown person, and you are acting like a child."

He clenched his fists, welcoming the pain in his shoulder this time.

"Because I'm tired of this," he hissed through his clenched teeth. "Because I grew up like a regular Chichimec of the

Highlands, and now I'm discovering that what I really am is a filthy Tepanec and what-not. In Texcoco they all kept taking me for a Tepanec, and now I understand why. I am that! The filthy Tepanec. Maybe I'll go back to the Lowlands and join Tezozomoc's warriors now that they are landing on Texcoco shores. At least I'll be fighting with my people! I'm sure they'll be delighted to enlist me, a son of a nobleman from their filthy *altepetl*, whatever it's called."

She jumped onto her feet. "I don't have to listen to this!" Her chest rising high with every breath, she glared at him, making a visible effort to control her temper. "I'll bring you your ointments and food, and some water to wash up. You rest in the meanwhile. Rest and try to get back to your senses!"

Her steps were swift, hissing angrily upon the earthen floor. He shut his eyes. May they all go to the lowest level of the Underworld! To that lifeless vastness one had to cross if one did not die properly, the warrior's death; that place where the obsidian rocks would clash against each other, threatening to squash the careless passerby. He could imagine his father making his way in the grayish nothingness, against the slashing wind and the swirling dust.

Trembling, he opened his eyes. Did the man deserve that for being born a filthy Tepanec? No. But he deserved that for lying about it. He, Kuini, had grown up surrounded by lies, knowing nothing about the people who brought him to this world of the Fifth Sun. And Mother, too! What was she doing in Texcoco those twenty and a half summers ago? *Nothing worth mentioning.* Of course. He believed her on that. Another dark secret that would probably make him feel even worse.

There was a small pottery bowl full of water. Hands trembling, he snatched it, then threw it against the wall, watching it break into many pieces. The pain in his back exploded, but he welcomed it, grinding his teeth. It took the edge off his rage, if only for a little while. He stared at the wet blanket and his loincloth. He should have drunk the water first.

The sight of his loincloth sprinkled with drops of water brought back the memory of the pond and *her*, naked and laughing, splashing him out of its depths. He caught his breath. How many dawns had passed? Mother said he had been sick for three dawns, then another two or three while on the journey. Oh gods! The market interval was over. He was supposed to have been there on the Plaza today, or maybe even on the day before.

He bit his lower lip until it hurt. *All right*, he thought. *Think.* There was no need to panic, not yet. He was late, but she would still be there in the Palace. She wouldn't be sent to Tenochtitlan that fast. So even if late, he will find a way to reach her, to let her know.

Wincing with pain, he got to his feet with difficulty, leaning against the wall, pausing, desperate to regain his strength. No, he was in no condition to make his way to Texcoco, but then in a day or two, or maybe three, he would recover. He was late anyway, so a few more dawns wouldn't matter. She would have to wait just a little longer.

Unsteadily, he went into the main room, suddenly hungry. Eyeing the simple interior of the familiar house, he felt his rage returning. It was all so pleasant and simple once upon a time, before he went to Texcoco. This house, this town, the Highlands, his family, all familiar, *trustworthy*. But now? Now, it all changed. Or was it him? He took a deep breath. Yes, it must be he who had changed.

He thought about Coyotl, unable to suppress a grin. His friend would be stunned when he told him. He could picture the slender face of the emperor's heir, eyes wide, mouth gaping. He had been the first to state that Kuini looked like a Tepanec. How ridiculously correct he had been.

He hit the wall with his fist. He'd go back and join Coyotl in his fight against the Tepanec invasion. That was it! He had wanted to do it all along, but was afraid to betray his people should his father, the Leader of the Warriors, decide not to join this war. Oh, but the honorable leader turned out to be not as pure, not as honorable as previously thought. So he, Kuini, had no obligations to that man anymore.

He smiled bitterly. There was nothing to stand in his way now. Hitting the wall once again hurt. He winced with pain.

"I suppose it was built to hold up against all this pounding."

Gasping, Kuini turned around, recognizing the amused derisiveness of the familiar voice. The Aztec stood in the doorway, arms folded, legs wide apart, blocking the late afternoon sun with his broad shoulders, tall and even more imposing without his cloak, the necklace upon his wide chest glittering. Well rested, refreshed and sunburned, the man looked younger than his years again. Not the same person Kuini had remembered last seeing, old and exhausted, gray with fatigue, preparing to die.

"Glad to see you back among the living, boy," said the Aztec, coming in unhurriedly. "Even if spitting with rage, attacking those helpless walls." Squatting beside a low table, he reached for an unpainted flask, filling two cups, nodding at Kuini. "Come. Sit and have a drink. I wish it was *octli*, but your people seem to be fond of *pulque*, and I wouldn't touch that drink even had it been the last beverage left in the whole Fifth World."

Clasping his lips tight and trying not to sway, Kuini crossed the room and sat on the opposite mat, almost weak with relief. He needed to recover his strength and fast.

"I see you didn't take well to all this family history revealed to you under somewhat dubious circumstances." The man drank thirstily. "I can understand you, you know. It was too much and not in the best timing. I was feeling like fainting myself, I have to admit."

Oh yes, he remembered that, the face of the Warlord, lifeless, covered with dust and drained of blood, thrown off his usual confident self. He remembered thinking that the man would faint any moment. Another meal, shared with this man, surfaced.

"You told me you had a brother somewhere around our Smoking Mountain," he said quietly. "But I never thought..." He shrugged, forgetting his wounded shoulder.

"Oh, neither did I. Although, upon reflection, you looked familiar, almost painfully so. But I was too busy to think about it. The filthy Acolhua Emperor took my mind off the wild market boy." The amused grin widened. "If you looked more like your father, I would have noticed. But when a boy looks like a reflection of yourself, one tends to miss the connection all together."

To take his thoughts off this new realization, Kuini reached for his cup. The water refreshed him, taking away the bitter taste in his mouth.

"I'm going to join Texcoco in their war against the Tepanecs," he said, studying the cracks upon the old table.

"Why would you do that?" There was no trace of amusement in the Aztec's voice now.

Kuini looked up. "Because I owe nothing to any of you now. Because the only person who was honest with me is now facing this war, and I want to help him, if for no other reason than because he has never lied to me, never told me half-truths." He stood the hardening gaze. "Yes, the First Son, the heir, Nezahualcoyotl, my friend of many summers, the only person who never lied to me." He tried to stop his hands from trembling, his rage welling, impossible to control. "So yes, I will fight those Tepanecs, yours and my father's people."

The Aztec's grin returned slowly. "Oh, you *are* an interesting thing, jaguar cub." The twinkle crept back into the well-spaced eyes. "But I suppose it'll do you good, you know? To go away on this campaign. You have great potential. You are brave and fearless, and your instincts are good. Yes, you'll make a good warrior, and I suppose it's about time to start your training for real." The man's grin widened. "I would have taken you with me to Tenochtitlan, but in the state your mind is in now, you won't have it. Although, it could be a perfect solution." He shrugged, gulping the last of the water. "While away, you will see that your father did nothing wrong. You are frustrated, wounded, and you came to discover your family secrets at the worst timing, so now you are taking your anger out on him. But it'll change." The grin disappeared. "Your father is a great man. He did a remarkable thing. With unusual courage, he left his own people for the sake of the unknown. I left too, but I went to Tenochtitlan, another well-known *altepetl*, almost the same customs, almost the same people. While your father switched a winning nation for the defeated one. The Highlanders were defeated, scattered by the Tepanecs, who had done this for the sake of their Acolhua cousins. The slaves markets were bursting back then with all those Chichimec women and children. Ask your mother." He shrugged. "They are still not an empire, those Nahua and Chichimec Highlanders, but they are better off now. And your father played a considerable part in this recovery. He is not the Leader of the United Clans for nothing, boy. Think about it." The hard eyes held Kuini's gaze, penetrating. "After so many summers of being a highlander and a leader he must have forgotten his past all together. Why should he remember? Why should he repeat the old story all over again to each of his numerous sons, informing them of some irrelevant, forgotten past?" The dark eyes narrowed, this time accompanied by a slight grin. "Your brothers seem to take it not badly, you know? In fact, they couldn't care less. They were living the regular lives of the highlanders, and they'll go on doing just that. While you," the piercing gaze bore at him, difficult to stand. "You were different from the very beginning, sneaking around the Lowlands, gaping at Texcoco *altepetl*, attracted to its majesty, striking up friendships with people who are irrelevant to you. You did whatever you pleased, boy. And you will go on doing just that. I can see it. But don't blame your father for this. His revelations would change nothing for you. You played with the idea of joining Acolhua forces or even going with me to Tenochtitlan for days now. Do you think I didn't notice? Nothing changed, jaguar cub. Nothing at all. Only now, you have found an excuse to blame someone else for your frustrations. And as tempting as it may be, get it out of your head, boy. Your father has nothing to do with it." The grin widened. "Go away and find your own path. But talk to your father before you go. I'm sure he'll be only too happy to supply you with good weapons and good advice."

"I have my own weapons," muttered Kuini. "I have the obsidian sword now."

"Oh, yes. That you have." The Aztec smiled. "And I was impressed, I can tell you. You got your first sword through your first battle, and you used it well, all things considered. Quite a feat for a boy of your age." The grin widened. "So just forget your frustrations and go and turn yourself into a warrior. But talk to your father first. Be brave enough to face him."

"And what about you?" muttered Kuini.

"What about me?"

"Will you go back to Tenochtitlan?"

"Oh, yes. We are leaving tomorrow at dawn. It was a nice diversion, this pastime in the Highlands, but one must go back to his duties. Regretfully so." The twinkle was back, sparkling out of the dark eyes, derisive, challenging. "If my Emperor decides to honor his obligations to the Tepanec Empire, I may be facing you on the battlefield, come to think of it. A dangerous prospect, with you and that sword of yours."

Kuini stared at the man, perplexed. "It can't be. The Aztecs would never do that to their allies."

The Warlord shrugged. "Well, we won't join that war in force," he said, thoughtfully. "But some groups of our warriors may be found on those Texcoco shores, to keep Tezozomoc at peace. Nothing to warrant the presence of the Chief Warlord, though, so there is no need to worry. We won't be fighting each other. Therefore, just keep yourself safe, and I'm sure we will meet again. I should like to meet you in a few summers as a seasoned warrior." He shook his head as if waking from a daydream. "Is it not the time for an evening meal? I am starving. The air in the Highlands makes one hungry."

With a surprising agility for his years, the Warlord sprang to his feet.

"I should visit here more often, now that I know I won't be sacrificed on your altars right away," he said with a laugh, heading for the doorway. "Get yourself together, jaguar cub, before your family gathers here. Your brothers were quite anxious to make sure you were well again. Especially that huge, broad-shouldered fellow, the oldest one. He would make a good elite warrior as well." Another merry chuckle. "I swear you Highlanders have tremendous potential."

As the man's wide back disappeared behind the doorway, Kuini let himself lean against the wall, exhausted, his stomach rumbling, head empty of thoughts.

That man was all right, he reflected randomly. And he did speak some sense. Much sense, to be honest. He was wise, and brave and good at everything. He was all right for an Aztec. Or a Tepanec.

Then the realization struck and he cursed aloud. The damn man was his uncle, curse his eyes into the lowest level of the Underworld.

CHAPTER 14

Posing upon the top of a hill, Coyotl watched the Great Lake, his breath caught. From his vantage point, he could see the distant shore swarming with warriors while the muddy waters of the lake swarmed with canoes.

So many of those! Twenty times of twenty vessels and more. Twice as many warriors, if so. His eyes kept counting and recounting, unable to follow. He never thought the Tepanecs would come in such force.

He glanced at his warriors, those who had followed him here. They stood there, peering down at the lake, their strained faces reflecting his feelings.

Oh mighty Tezcatlipoca, he thought. *Please give our warriors strength. Please fortify their spirits. Please make us strong in minds and firm in bodies, let us face the upcoming struggle with joy, let us kill many enemy warriors and sacrifice more of them for you to feed upon their life forces.* He shut his eyes. *Please, help us win,* he added quickly, knowing he should not ask the mighty deity for something as personal.

The Acolhua warriors were spread between the two nearby hills, presented in even greater numbers. Two days before, coming straight from the Great Capital, bringing along the reinforcements he had managed to gather on his mad dash through the provinces, Coyotl was impressed. Near to a thousand warriors and auxiliaries. How could they lose with so many people? He alone had brought almost twenty times of twenty warriors from five provinces. Admittedly, it took him much longer than a market interval, more than two in fact, but what he did pleased the

Emperor greatly. They would throw the Tepanecs back into the Great Lake, achieving an enormous victory, killing many and capturing more.

However now, looking at the colorful gathering down below, at the multitude of the foreigners wandering their shores as if already possessing them, the obsidian of their swords sparkling, their plain or brilliant-blue cloaks swirling, he felt a twinge of anxiety. Those Tepanecs lost very few battles, if any. They had ruled many areas around the Great Lake for so many summers the elders could not remember when the land had not been dominated by them.

He shook his head. *Stop thinking about it!* he ordered himself. *You are not going into a battle, thinking how to lose it. You think only of the fighting itself, of the joy a good hand-to-hand provides, of the glorious victories, of the glorious death upon the battlefield, the paradise of the eastern sky there and waiting, beckoning.*

"Let us go back to our people," he said, turning to the warriors.

They followed sullenly, not yet accustomed to their duty as the Emperor's heir's personal guards. Coming straight from the Capital, they wanted to fight with their fellow Texcocans, Coyotl knew. However, he was responsible for the warriors of the provinces. Not to lead them, of course, but to organize, to keep everything in order until the battle would ensue.

He smiled to himself, enjoying his new duties. Good at organizing things, he had made his tour of the provinces run smoothly, bringing back more men than expected. Many more. The greatly pleased Emperor praised his First Son and made him responsible for those twenty times twenty of warriors, hinting that should he manage, he would be entrusted with even greater responsibilities.

He made an effort to hide his smile. The Emperor, otherwise irritable and edgy, was pleased for a few heartbeats. What an achievement! He could see the sentiment reflecting in the faces of the advisers, and it made him wish to laugh, nervously so. What was amiss this time, besides the Tepanecs swarming their shores?

Still the very same Aztecs, he was quick to discover. The untrustworthy neighbors and so-called allies would not send a single warrior to fight the invaders. The Acolhua envoys delegated two market intervals ago came back just ahead of Coyotl. Bypassing the arrogant Aztec Warlord did not help. Huitzilihuitl was adamant. In so many flowery words and protestations of sympathy and good will, the Aztec Emperor said no. Tenochtitlan would not fight the Tepanecs. Tezozomoc was Huitzilihuitl's father-in-law and Tenochtitlan had many obligations to Azcapotzalco. Both *altepetls* had had a long history of cooperation. As if Texcoco had no history with Tenochtitlan whatsoever. Oh, the filthy Aztecs!

The Acolhua Emperor fumed, but could not do anything to relieve his anger. Not yet. Maybe one day, but now he still needed to keep the Aztecs happy as, at least, Huitzilihuitl promised not to send his warriors to fight with the Tepanecs against Texcoco. He would send a small amount to keep Tezozomoc happy, but nothing more would be done. So the marriage proposal to seal the ties between the two *altepetls* proceeded as planned, accepted graciously.

Iztac-Ayotl! Coyotl shivered, remembering how he had rushed to her quarters, only to meet a firm refusal. She was not allowed to receive visitors. Not even the Emperor's First Son, the official heir, her half-brother.

He tried to argue, to no avail. She had a whole new set of maids, no doubt appointed by her mother, tough hags each and every one of them. From the circulating rumors he gathered that she had been caught again wandering the Plaza only a market interval ago. Well, that would explain the firmness of her imprisonment this time, he thought, his heart twisting. Oh, she was incurable. Why would she do something like that?

He sighed, remembering that he had been lucky enough to say his farewells, after all. On the next day, when he was leaving to take his freshly recruited forces to join the Emperor's, he had met her palanquin heading down the main road. Palace's guards and officials, Emperor's wives and concubines, musicians and many people dressed in their best regalia, surrounded it, proceeding with great pomp. The First Daughter of the mighty Emperor was sent away, to be given to another Emperor in all the splendor her status ensured.

Making his warriors wait, Coyotl had followed the procession, hoping against hope to catch a glimpse of her until his effort paid off. Upon reaching the Plaza, the procession stopped. The music piqued, and the groups of dancers began their performance.

He peered at the palanquin, wishing the curtain to move aside. Yet, when it did, he gaped, blinking, finding it difficult to recognize the imposing figure perching on the edge of the cushions, frozen like a marble statue.

Dismayed, he came closer, pushed his way through the crowds, oblivious to their grumbling. While the rest of those present watched the performance, he stared at her, trying to make out the familiar features under the huge headdress made of exquisite feathers and sparkling jewelry.

She looked ill, small and pale below the colorful magnificence, with her hands lying lifelessly in her lap, as if they were difficult to move under the weight of so much splendor, her thin arms burdened by glittering bracelets, her slender fingers overloaded with rings. She was sparkling like a golden statue, but her real sparkle was gone.

He came closer, pushing her maids aside firmly. They tried to block his way, but he glared at them, grateful that the Second Wife's attention was distracted by the performers.

"Iztac," he called softly, uncomfortable with looking at her from below.

She turned her head slowly, with an effort, as if afraid to make a sharp movement. Thinner than he remembered, her face looked at him, drawn and pinched, lacking in color, lacking in expression. The dark eyes watched him, empty, indifferent, reflecting no emotion. The generous mouth did not move.

"Iztac, it's me," he said, at a loss, not sure if she recognized him at all. "Sister, how are you?"

The corner of her mouth moved slightly. "I'm well."

"I'm sorry I couldn't make it back sooner." Unable to stand the stare of those black empty eyes, he bit his lower lip. "Are you angry with me?"

"No."

"You look beautiful," he labored on, trying to break through this ghastly indifference. "You are the center of this event. The next Empress of Tenochtitlan. No more a meaningless princess."

Something flickered in the dark gaze, but he could not be sure what as she turned her head away quickly.

"Please, Iztac," he pleaded, wishing they could be alone, even for a few heartbeats. "Please, say something. Don't go away like that."

She looked down as much as her imposing headdress would allow her, watching her bejeweled palms, lifeless in her lap.

"I wish you a happy life," she whispered. "Keep yourself safe in the battle. Don't let anything happen to you."

He swallowed to banish the knot forming in his throat. "I will," he said. "We will beat those Tepanecs, and then, I'll come to Tenochtitlan. You'll show me all around this famous island-city. Will you?"

She didn't answer, staring at her palms, again motionless like a statue. Her, of all people. His heart squeezed.

"I have to go now," he said, when able to speak. "But I will visit you, I promise. Please, don't be so sad. It will all be good, you'll see. I'll make sure you are well. You can trust me."

She didn't move, didn't say a word, but the bracelets encircling her arms rang softly as her shoulders shook. He reached for her palm, squeezed the cold, slender fingers.

"Please, sister, cheer up. I will come to Tenochtitlan as soon as I can," he forced out, beginning to ease away.

"Coyotl!"

He turned back sharply, bumping into one of her maids.

Her eyes were back upon him, black and glittering, not empty anymore. "If you see your Highlander again, tell him that a market interval is five to six days. Not half a moon. He was learning so fast, but that one he got wrong, so badly wrong."

Her lips quivered as she turned away. One slender palm shot up, pulled at the curtain hurriedly. He noticed it was trembling, too.

What market interval? he wondered, his sadness welling. The thrill of the flutes hit his ears, suddenly ugly, annoying in its

persistence. What were they all so excited about? The Aztecs
would not help them; the unreliable neighbors agreed not to
betray their Texcoco allies, nothing more. She was sacrificed for
nothing.

Dusk was nearing when Coyotl came out of the Emperor's tent,
having spent a whole afternoon listening to the warrior's leaders
and advisers. His head pounded, and his stomach churned,
although it was full, replete with refreshments served to the
Emperor's entourage aplenty.

Tomorrow with dawn they would attack, he knew, his heart
beating fast. Tomorrow they would engage in a great battle
against the mighty Tepanecs.

Oh gods, let us win, he thought fervently. *Let us throw the greedy
Tepanecs back into the Great Lake. Let us defend Texcoco against the
ruthless, insatiable enemy.*

A servant sprang onto his path, startling him.

"What do you want?" asked Coyotl angrily.

"Oh, Honorable Master, I apologize for startling you."

"You didn't startle me. What do you want?"

The man hesitated. "I am to give you this." A coarse palm came
out, offering Coyotl a folded piece of *amate*-paper.

His heart piqued. Fighting his impatience, he unfolded the
sheet carefully. In the remnants of the daylight the picture looked
beautiful, vivid with its strong coloring, showing a warrior with
an obsidian sword, standing proudly, watching a purple spot that
looked like a depiction of the lake on the maps. He eyed the
warrior's sword, magnificent, wonderfully detailed, its obsidian
spikes almost sparkling, as black as the moonless night.

"Where is the youth who gave you this?" He found it difficult
to control his voice.

"Over there, Honorable Master," said the slave, pointing
toward the hill Coyotl had ascended earlier in the day to watch
the Tepanecs.

"Take me there!"

The path curved upward, passing another vantage point, then turning deeper into the woods. He sent his guide away, then made his way hurriedly, his grin widening with every step.

"Oh, that was fast!"

The Highlander stood upon the edge of the cliff, outlined against the darkening sky, as always oblivious to the height and the possibility of a long fall. Legs wide apart, arms folded, he watched Coyotl, his usual amused, slightly challenging self.

Yet, something was different. Whether it was the new scar upon the wide forehead, or the way the broad chest seemed to fill, his friend had changed, reflected Coyotl, taking in the wide, proudly straightened shoulders, the new self-assured sparkle in the well-spaced eyes.

"What happened to you, you wild adventurer?" he called out, his eyes taking in the sword tied to a new decorated girdle. "It can't be!"

"Oh yes, it can." Kuini's laughter rolled down the hill.

"How?"

"That story is too long to tell it all now. But to make it short, here I am, ready to serve you with my sword, oh Honorable First Son."

"Oh, shut up. You are impossible. What happened?"

Kuini laughed again. "So many wild things you would never believe a half of them, if I told you." He came closer, put an arm on Coyotl's shoulder. "But the main thing is that I came to fight with you. No more silly thoughts and no more misgivings. We'll fight together. I trust you to find the way to smuggle me into your forces safely, with no filthy warriors dragging me into filthy courts."

Coyotl wanted to whoop with joy. "The easiest thing!" He clasped his friend's arm. "It will be tremendous!"

"Oh yes, it will."

Grinning, they turned to watch the Great Lake spreading far below their feet, still covered with busily moving warriors, ant-sized from such a height; and as purposeful.

Kuini shook his head. "Quite a sight."

"Oh, yes. I watched them the whole afternoon as they ran down there, so busy, like stupid ants. I can't wait to fight the bastards!"

"They are so many. I've never seen that many warriors before. I mean, one's head spins trying to count them."

"Easy. Twenty times twenty of canoes. Two, three warriors per canoe. It comes to, well, a lot."

"And your people?"

"Much more than that!" exclaimed Coyotl proudly. "The provinces yielded more than expected." He glanced at his friend. "Nothing to worry about."

"I'm not worried."

Coyotl squatted upon the dry grass. "So, how was it with the Aztecs?"

"Insane. Unbelievable. Impossible."

"I told you, you should have come with me."

"It's not like I had much choice, with them bolting for the back gates in the darkest of the night." Kuini dropped beside him, making himself comfortable, half laying upon the damp earth.

"So they *did* go through the gates. The back gates?"

"Yes, the small gate behind the pond."

"Oh, then the Chief Warlord was right. You should have seen the Emperor, blue with rage and the Chief Warlord shaking on the floor."

"I've seen enough of the Palace guards blue with rage, mostly with me." Kuini chuckled. "I don't want to see the Emperor, whatever color he takes when angry."

Coyotl laughed, then shook his head. "No, I suppose you are right. You don't need to be anywhere near the Emperor." He thought about the Aztecs sneaking away in the dead of the night. "But there should have been warriors guarding the gates, I would think. There were guards out there, weren't there?"

"Yes, of course, there were a few. For a while, at least."

"Oh, what a dirty manure-eater!" Surprised by the suddenness of his own anger, Coyotl looked away. That Chief Aztec Warlord was beyond words. "So, what happened next?"

"Oh, many things. But the Aztec Warlord did make it to

Tenochtitlan, eventually. I know you would rather he did not, but I have to tell you that. I came to like that man. So careful with your tongue when I'm around and we are on that subject."

Coyotl raised his eyebrows, but his elation refused to give way to anger. "Oh, you get your sword and now you are presuming to tell me what to talk about?" He poked his elbow into his friend's ribs. "So how did you get away?"

"Easily." Kuini flashed one of his open, unguarded smiles. "I'll tell it all to you one day, after this battle is over and we are feasting on some of those wonderful tamales and drinking *octli* like real warriors." He rolled onto his back and watched the sky, smiling contentedly. "There is another thing," he said quietly. "And I'll need your help with that."

"What?"

"Oh, nothing special." The Highlander stretched, but there was a tension in his pose now. "It can wait until after the battle. Until we are back in that pretty *altepetl* of yours."

Coyotl shut his eyes, pitting his face against the breeze coming from the lake.

"We won't be back in a hurry," he said, enjoying the rare peacefulness. "If we beat those Tepanecs..." He paused briefly. "*When* we beat those Tepanecs off, Father is planning to invade their side of the Great Lake. So we are in for a long campaign."

"Oh." There was a note of disappointment to his friend's voice.

"What's wrong?"

"No, nothing. Nothing at all." More sky observing. "Do you think it's wise, to tempt the beast like that?"

"What beast?"

"The Tepanecs. You have to fight them now, I understand that. But to cross into their lands would be sort of pushing it, no? They are quite an empire and, well, won't they get angry for real?"

"We have more people!" stated Coyotl hotly. "And we are angrier now than they ever could get. We'll take many of their towns, and we'll lay siege to Azcapotzalco. You'll see." He glared at his friend, but his glare was quite wasted as the Highlander still sprawled on his back, gaze wandering the skies. "You will see."

"Oh, I'm sure I will. And I do wish you luck with the crossing."

Coyotl straightened up. "Won't you be coming with us? What a coward!"

"Shut up," growled Kuini, refusing to take offense. "I would love to, but I have some things to do. Something to settle at home."

"What? Did you come here to fight with us without your father's consent?" He chuckled. "The delegation from the Highlands returned a few days ago, and quite angry they were. The Chief Warlord was near to exploding. He is sure to piss boiling water for some time."

"No, nothing to do with my father. Or the problems of the Texcoco Warlord to relieve himself." Kuini was silent for a long time. "I need your help with something."

"What?"

"I passed through your *altepetl* this morning. That's how I found out where you were. And I need to ask you for a favor. But I want you to promise you won't get angry with me asking you that."

"Ask away."

"Would you deliver a note to that girl? The princess. That sister of yours." More silence. "I promised her and, well, I can't send her notes if I don't get into the Palace. And it didn't seem possible this morning."

Coyotl swallowed, remembering the last time he had seen Iztac, with her heart-shaped face so taut, so lifeless under the splendor of her new elevated status. Unable to speak, he watched Kuini sitting up abruptly.

"Are you angry because of that?"

Coyotl just shook his head. "You can't send her notes anymore. She is not in the Palace."

"What? Where is she?" The dark eyes stared at him, filling with fear. "Don't tell me..." The wide shoulders sagged of a sudden. "Tenochtitlan?"

"Yes."

His friend's broad face lost some color, became haunted, then turned away. He could hear a convulsive breath drawn through the clenched teeth.

"How damn stupid." The mutter was hardly audible. It was difficult to recognize the Highlander's voice, so low and contorted it was.

"There was nothing we could do," said Coyotl helplessly. "There was no way to prevent that."

"Maybe there was."

"No, there was not. And anyway, why do you care?" The dark gaze leaped at him, in control once again. "I don't."

"You liked her, didn't you?"

A shrug.

"Neither of us could do anything."

"No, I suppose not."

"Actually, she did ask me to tell you something."

A flicker of fear passed through the large eyes, this time unmistakable. "What?"

"Well, it's something strange that didn't make any sense. Something about market intervals."

Kuini leaned forward so abruptly, Coyotl felt like backing away. "What? What did she say about the market interval?"

"Something silly. She asked me to tell you that a market interval is six days, not half a moon. She seemed upset with the fact that you didn't get it. She said you were learning other things fast, but not that one." He shrugged. "She was not really herself through the ceremony, so I suppose it's only natural that she didn't make much sense with this statement." He peered at his friend. "Don't you know what market interval means?"

"Yes, I do know that now," muttered Kuini, his voice strained, trembling a little.

Abruptly, he turned away, hugging his knees, peering at the lake. Coyotl watched the Tepanecs too, but the air seemed suddenly diluted, empty, lacking in its vital qualities.

He glanced at his friend, seeing the tight jaw, the clasped lips, the white knuckles of the clenched fists.

"I'm sorry," he said once again, his compassion welling. Whatever happened, the Highlander seemed to take it even worse than he took it himself. Was he in love with her? Probably. He could not blame his friend for feeling that way. Were she not his sister, he, Coyotl, would be in love with her too, he realized. But it was all for the best. There could be nothing between the exalted Acolhua princess and the commoner boy from the Highlands. She might have been nice to him, but she would never allow him as much as to touch the rim of her gown. He shrugged. His friend was better off without such infatuation.

"I suppose we should start moving back to the camp," he said, getting to his feet. "So, let us rehearse our story. You are the young warrior from the provinces I picked on my way. Say from Acolman. Or Coatlinchan. Which one?"

"Coatlinchan. Definitely Coatlinchan." Kuini's voice was still empty, lacking its usual mischievous ring. "I've been there briefly, so can try to get away with a general description, if challenged."

"Oh well, Coatlinchan it is. And of course, the Tepanec version that worked the previous time would do. Mother or father?"

"What?"

"We'll say you are half a Tepanec. It won't be held against you. Half of our force has this or that amount of Tepanec blood. So which half? Who was the Tepanec? You mother or your father?"

"My mother," said Kuini, a little too hurriedly.

"Then let us go and dive into these particular waters. Keep close to me, at least in the beginning. I don't want you to get into any trouble this time." He smiled cheerfully, peering at his friend. "Come, stop looking so gloomy. We are about to fight together, at long last. Oh, it's going to be a great battle, and we will win. You'll see." He glanced at the darkening sky. "We will beat these Tepanecs. You just wait and see."

"I believe you. And you know what?" Kuini's smile was wide, even if not as carelessly cheerful as of old. "On second thought, I'll cross this lake with you, old friend. It will be interesting, and I have to see Azcapotzalco or whatever this Tepanec Capital is called. This *altepetl* made me curious."

Coyotl clasped his friend's arm. "Now you are talking!"

He pitted his face against the strengthening wind that blew as if trying to stop him. His skin prickled. The Tepanecs were the Masters of the Great Lake for many, many summers. But it was about to change. Or was it?

AUTHOR'S AFTERWORD

In the beginning of the 15th century, Texcoco, the capital of the Acolhua people located on the eastern shores of Lake Texcoco, was a fairly large influential *altepetl*, with some provinces and dependent entities, towns, and villages to rule. Their influence spread along the eastern shores of the Great Lake, allowing the Acolhua capital maintain their independence while paying tribute to the greater regional power of the Mexican Valley – the Tepanecs of Azcapotzalco.

At the times addressed in this novel, the Tepanecs ruled a considerable part of the Mexican Valley, with many important city-states paying them tribute and deterring to their will.

According to the 16th century Acolhua annalist Fernando Ixtlilxochitl, the Texcocan revolt against the might of Azcapotzalco began back in the very beginning of the 15th century, when the Texcoco ruler put aside his Tepanec chief wife in favor of his Mexica wife who happened to be Nezahualcoyotl's mother (the same Nezahualcoyotl who was to become one of the most famous rulers, poets and engineers in Mesoamerica). Other primary sources, Diego Duran and Domingo Chimalpahin among them, back the claim that the matters that started with switching chief wives in 1405 escalated over the next decade as Texcoco openly defied Azcapotzalco and thus, brought the Tepanec warriors to the eastern shores of Lake Texcoco in the dry months of 1415.

In the following first clash, Texcoco indeed managed to repulse the Tepanec invasion. Encouraged by his initial success, the Acolhua Emperor led his forces across the Great Lake, capturing and sacking some villages and a few towns on his way, and reportedly, even laying a brief siege on Azcapotzalco itself. Eventually, the Acolhua forces went back to their side of the Great Lake, to prepare for another Tepanec invasion. Tepanecs may have lost a battle, but they were not used to losing wars.

Through all this, the Mexica Aztecs of Tenochtitlan remained neutral, refusing to commit to either side. Their own relationship with the mighty Tepanecs was complex enough through the rule of their first emperor Acamapichtli, but at the time of the Texcocan revolt, Acamapichtli's son Huitzilihuitl was ruling Tenochtitlan, and his ties to the Tepanec royal house were stronger, his chief wife one of Tezozomoc's daughters, a dominant woman according to many primary sources. Treading on a fairly thin ice, Tenochtitlan managed to remain neutral for the time being. The future might of the famous island-capital and the most important city-state of Mesoamerica in its time was some decades from the Mexica people's reach.

What happened next can be read in the second book of The Rise of the Aztecs Series, **"Crossing Worlds"**.

ABOUT THE AUTHOR

Zoe Saadia is the author of several novels on pre-Columbian Americas. From the architects of the Aztec Empire to the founders of the Iroquois Great League, from the towering pyramids of Tenochtitlan to the longhouses of the Great Lakes, her novels bring long-forgotten history, cultures and people to life, tracing pivotal events that brought about the greatness of North and Mesoamerica.

To learn more about Zoe Saadia and her work, please visit www.zoesaadia.com

Made in the USA
Columbia, SC
06 May 2019